THIS UNLIKELY SOIL

02 03 04 05 06 27 26 25 24 23

Dagger Editions, an imprint of Caitlin Press Inc.
3375 Ponderosa Way
Qualicum Beach, BC V9K 2J8
www.caitlinpress.com

Text design by Sarah Corsie
Cover design by Edmund Arceo
Edited by Anne Fleming

Caitlin Press Inc. acknowledges financial support from the Government of Canada and the Canada Council for the Arts, and the Province of British Columbia through the British Columbia Arts Council and the Book Publisher's Tax Credit.

Library and Archives Canada Cataloguing in Publication

This unlikely soil / Andrea Routley.
Routley, Andrea, 1980- author.
Short stories.
Canadiana 20220215510 | ISBN 9781773860985 (softcover)
LCC PS8635.O874 T55 2022 | DDC C813/.6—dc23

This Unlikely Soil

stories
by Andrea Routley

Dagger Editions

Contents

Appropriate Behaviour

Freddie moved to the Coast not long after the Great Leap, as she called it. She'd jumped from her sixth-floor balcony and miraculously survived the fall with only rib fractures and a head injury, causing relatively minor cognitive impairments.

She'd hit a car first, which absorbed the deadly impact, and then bounced into a second five-foot fall from there. Ironically, it was this second fall to the pavement that caused the head injury. There was even an article in the paper—"Woman survives fall thanks to parked car." But she wasn't aiming for the car. "I guess I just have a magnetic personality," she joked with the psychiatrist later.

Time was weird for the next several weeks in the hospital. Everything took longer for Freddie now—her brain like an old lawnmower that just wouldn't start some days. Can you repeat the question? Was that a question? The people at the brain injury clinic said the fatigue would lessen but it takes a long time. Everyone talked about things taking time but without using actual time words, like six weeks or six months or six years. "It's different for everyone," they sometimes said.

Freddie thought about when she was a kid, how Papa Dave and Belinda would say "time flies" each time they saw her, but to Freddie, it was eons between visits. "Be. Here. Now," her mother, Morning Star, would say, tapping Freddie's forehead with each word, then gently petting the fine hairs of her cheek.

"I don't know what I was thinking," Freddie told the psychiatrist. She remembers the way the curtains caught the sunlight and framed the green tops of oaks in the park beyond. The school bell rang in the distance, calling the children back to their classrooms, and in that sudden afternoon silence, the wind billowed the curtains inward, as if reaching out to Freddie. No time like the present. She glanced at her watch. Its metal bracelet sometimes pinched her arm hair, but the watch had belonged to Papa Dave. Of course, she'd thought about this leap before. Even those evenings on the balcony spent chatting with the neighbour's cat, who perched on his own railing, she imagined how easy it would be to let go.

But she avoided windows now, as if they had a gravitational pull of their own and she did not want to be pulled over the edge again. "I guess I'm afraid of heights now, Doc. But I'm going to miss those conversations with the cat."

She said she had no intention of taking another "flight of fancy." Laughter is the best medicine, Freddie thought, but the doctor did not agree in this case. "I don't want to jump, I mean. I know it's not the answer." Her brain had changed. Must have. "I want to be alive," she said. "Present."

When the hospital was satisfied enough that she no longer posed an immediate risk to herself, Freddie returned to her apartment to discover her key did not fit. The building manager had moved her things into storage and told her she needed to pay for that—the storage fees, the month's rent, and the labour to move it, minus the damage deposit. Freddie supposed it was fair. He'd evicted the film student last year after she chucked a pumpkin off her balcony. Surely, she couldn't expect to stay after chucking herself!

"Good luck to you," the manager said.

ᔐ

That was two years ago—two years? Yes. Freddie now lives in one of a string of small towns along the coastline, which suits her much better than the city, a place where you could go an entire day without seeing anyone you know. Here, she's part of the community. She likes seeing people in more than one place—running into a neighbour at the mailboxes or an IGA cashier at the library or a librarian at the IGA. She grew up here for a while, on Arbutus Farm, an intentional community of back-to-the-landers, which is now a corporate retreat. Most of the people from the Farm moved away, and Papa Dave and Belinda, who retired here, are both dead now. But Freddie's mother, Morning Star, is back, and Freddie knows her neighbours, mostly. Like Willow, the basket maker. With her rustic leather fanny pack and feather earrings, Willow usually looks as though she's heading to a comi-con. An Artemisian babe, Freddie commented when she first met her. "Move over, Xena!"

"That is the nicest thing anyone has ever said to me," Willow joked.

This year, Willow is participating in the annual Art Hop, opening her home to strangers to come check out her pine-needle baskets and stiff satchels made of kelp. "You should come by," she tells Freddie. "Sign my guestbook." For two days, Willow discusses her techniques and offers anecdotes about harvesting materials and laughs at potential buyers' jokes about her name. No, she did not weave willow—"Was that ironic?" she asks Freddie later.

One of the jokers is Robert, the neighbour with the dog. Freddie has only met Robert twice, down at the mailboxes, but she's seen him around many more times—he drives a giant black truck that never has anything in the back. She's heard his kids playing on the trampoline and his wife calling after them, though she's never seen them. In the brief interactions with Robert, Freddie has managed to learn that his dog, a collie blend of some kind, is called Beethoven II, perhaps after the film *Beethoven's 2nd,* Freddie thought. But Willow explained that Robert and his family had another dog before Beethoven, who was also called Beethoven. The first dog was an unusual breed—stout and aggressive, bred as a sentry and typically adopted as a sort of trophy pet, in much the same way a python is acquired by a tattooed fan of heavy metal music. (Willow's ex-boyfriend was such a person.) The dog was way too much for them, lunging at passersby, and it nearly broke Robert's wrist, which he'd wrapped the leash around for a better grip. So Beethoven was returned to the breeder. No refund. No matter. They chose a new dog, "a rescue."

Freddie also made the joke about weaving willow. It seemed funnier when Freddie said it, Willow would tell her later, and not simply because Freddie had said it first—something about Robert makes Willow feel like he's making fun of her name.

Freddie is examining a kelp satchel as stiff as raw hide, wondering if a "purse dog" would enjoy gnawing on its salty flap, when Robert makes the joke. She nudges him with her elbow in a vaudevillian sort of way. "I, uh," she says, smoothing down an imaginary moustache, "like your style."

"What, my shirt?" Robert says, examining the part of him that her elbow had touched.

"No. Your, ah, *witticisms.*" She says this last word with a British accent.

Willow sums it up, placing the guestbook down. "She just made the same joke."

"Yeah, but it was funnier when I said it." Freddie mocks an aggressive stance, half pointing and half wagging a finger at Robert, who just raises his eyebrows and turns away.

Freddie shrugs, then mimes a cane hooking her neck to drag her off stage, but less boisterously than she might have done a moment before.

This was the first miscommunication with Robert, Freddie would think later, trying to make sense of how things degraded so swiftly.

❧

Freddie learned about her feelings from Betsy, her counsellor, with whom she is to meet weekly for up to twelve weeks. She learned, for one, that she has a lot of them, and if she has them so do other people, and two, that she needs to say what they are because Betsy is not a mind reader.

"That would be something like Braille—" Freddie reached forward to touch Betsy's head. Betsy leaned back, one hand out. "I get it, I get it," she said.

Freddie did not know what Robert was feeling at the time of this first miscommunication. She knew something had gone wrong there, but she was never one to make assumptions. She would have to ask for clarification.

After a counselling session with Betsy, Freddie decides to stop by the library for some new DVDs. No point in driving such a short distance, especially on a day like today, the uncommon sunshine reflecting off snowy peaks across the water. "Behold!" she says aloud. "I am Mountain!" Take it in, take it in. These glorious present moments, something to remember on the rough days, pain-brain and a blur of hours on the couch.

Cutting across the park, she discovers a Jack pine tree. At Art Hop, Willow explained how long the basket needles need to be, how she has a few secret spots, but the best kind of pines are not common around here, that they're not indigenous to the area. But tucked behind the library, these minty needles are nearly ten inches long. Freddie spends an hour carefully filling her grocery bag with fallen needles. What bounty!, she thinks, and heads back to her car to deposit them in the trunk. When she sees Willow, she could say, "I have a surprise for you in the trunk of my car—don't worry, it's not a body!" Or "My fair lady, how I've *pined* for you!" Then she'll show Willow the needles and Willow will laugh, say it's not too clever but it is cute. "Just like me," Freddie could reply, and maybe strike a Mae West come-up-and-see-me-sometime sort of pose, hand on the hip, shoulders going up and down, up down up down up down up down.

"Freddie!" someone calls. Morning Star trudges up the hill toward her, pushing on her thighs, arms like pistons. She's bigger than last time Freddie saw her, layers of flimsy skirts draped over wide hips. Today she wears a leather fanny pack, too. Maybe those are in style. "I thought that was you," Morning Star says, huffing.

Freddie has only seen her mother a few times since she visited Freddie in the hospital. When Freddie was a child, she'd rest her head in Morning Star's lap, and her mother would pet her, tucking her hair behind her ear, then smoothing it out and tickling her back, and Freddie would purr like a cat and paw at her thigh. "My little kitty!" Morning Star would say. But sometimes she didn't like her to be this way, like when Freddie meowed and pointed at her bowl, indicating she wanted more milk for her cereal, please. Freddie's playfulness and affection became simply a sign of dependency, and Morning Star would unhook her daughter's hand from hers, saying, "You're too old for this," but other times pull her onto the sofa. "I want my baby next to me." It's not that Morning Star didn't love her daughter, but the older Freddie got, the less she knew how. And Morning Star really did become like Venus, here then gone, here then gone, visible only briefly at twilight. "I'm here *now*," she would sometimes say, which perhaps was meant to reassure Freddie, but sounded more like an accusation.

"What were you doing with your shoulders?" Morning Star says as she reaches the car. "You look weird."

"Hey, hey," Freddie shakes her shoulders again. "Come up and see me some time."

"Oh." Morning Star catches her breath, visible in the cool air. "Is this yours? How do you even afford a car?"

Freddie follows her gaze to the driver's door, which is grey although the rest of the car is burgundy. "Printing press."

"Oh, yeah. You worked there a long time, right?"

"A long time," Freddie repeats. "Years?"

"Years in that place? No wonder you were depressed." Morning Star waves her hand, as if fending off a housefly. "I didn't just say that. Come here." She embraces Freddie, much longer than others normally did, Freddie had observed, but this is how Morning Star embraces everyone. It reminds Freddie of mating slugs or uploading something big. When Morning Star finishes hugging her, she looks teary. "My little kitty," she says, squeezing her hand, then walks around to the passenger door. "Can you give me a lift home?"

❧

The following day, Freddie decides to clear up the miscommunication with Robert. His property borders Freddie's, but their homes are separated by several apple trees and then a forested area, all dark and soaking wet with the swamp, ferns, fungi and other soggy life forms; it had been a wet winter. Rather than walking all the way up her long driveway and then all the way down his, Freddie cuts across, hopping from one decaying stump or lump of ferns to another, only muddying one boot along the way. She wonders where the frogs are hiding—in the evenings, they chirp noisily, perhaps because it's dark out and they must fumble blindly through the crowd of frogs, searching for their moms or friends or kids. It reminds her of the Perseid parties at Arbutus Farm. Or maybe it's all just an orgy of horny hoppers and the chirps mean, "Do me! Do me!" Horny as a toad? More like horny as a frog! Sometimes she'd open her own window and shush them. *Knock it off, you horn-dogs!* Of course, there is always more to life than the search for a warm body—or even a cold-blooded one. And she likes talking to animals. They make more sense than people, even with the language barrier.

She can hear the kids playing with the dog in the backyard, its panicked yelping in time with the trampoline springs. "Beethoven, shut up!" one of them scolds. Freddie knocks on the front door and whistles the opening to Beethoven's Fifth.

Robert opens the door. "Hello, neighbour!" Freddie says.

"Hello." He holds a cordless phone in one hand and keeps his other on the doorknob. "What is it," he says. Freddie called them a couple of times recently to ask them to bring the dog in, that it was barking, had been barking for more than twenty minutes. It was Robert's wife who'd answered. They hadn't heard it—the TV was on, she said. Then, Thanks for letting me know. But Robert was the kind of man who felt his large property entitled him to all the noise he cared to make. ("They're from Burnaby," Willow summed up, as if this explained everything.) It was a long way from the suburb where he was so close to the neighbours that he knew what they were cooking for dinner on any given night. Here, space. But sound does travel, although the frogs did their best to muddy it for Freddie, offering a kind of white noise barrier. *Crek-ek, crek-ek.* Freddie wasn't angry about the dog; she just couldn't listen to its yelp any longer—she could not do anything else with her brain while it was happening. That was one of the cognitive impairments, an auditory processing impairment that made it nearly impossible to filter out background noise. Still, she shouldn't have to endure the barking—it was on her property without her consent. She was just giving them useful information.

"Are you on the phone?" Freddie makes a phone with her hand. "Hello, hello? Can we put you on hold, please?"

"No. What is it? The dog's inside now."

"Oh, well I wanted to drop by and say hello. Willow—we were at Willow's, and I thought perhaps we had a miscommunication? When I said the joke was funnier when I said it, I was just kidding, but sometimes I think people might take me too seriously."

"People don't take you seriously," Robert says.

Freddie holds her hands to her heart, as if trying to pull an arrow out. "You spurn me, my lord!"

"Is that it?"

She straightens up. "Why, yes, it is." Freddie hears the soft clicking of dog claws on linoleum, and then Beethoven II stands beside Robert, white crescents appearing below his eyes, so that he looks like a dopey cartoon puppy. "Well, hello there." Freddie extends her hand for Beethoven to sniff, but he doesn't move. "I'm a big fan of your music." Still nothing.

"I got to get back to it," Robert says. "And I'd appreciate it if you wouldn't cut across the property."

Freddie glances down at her one muddy boot. "The driveways are so long and life's so short, you know?"

"I don't want people wandering around the property."

Freddie recalls the deer trails of her free-range childhood, running through salal until she's spit out at another beach or a road. "Just be back before dark," Morning Star told her.

"I won't be wandering—I can see your house from my Toyota! Land ho!"

"It's my property."

Freddie nods, not because she understands, but to encourage him to continue with his explanation. She has never owned anything more valuable than her fifteen-year-old Toyota, but she had called him "my lord" earlier, and she wonders if this has gone to his head. "I don't really think you're my lord."

"Just use the driveway." He points.

Freddie wants to say something else. "This is a…" She can't think of the word. It isn't even on the tip of her tongue, but buried in the brains, letters jumbling around. (Aphasia, another cognitive impairment.) She's waiting for them to arrive and spell themselves out, like lotto number balls sucked up to reveal the winning combination. Instead, she turns to head up the driveway, her muddy boot squishing.

But before Robert can close the door, Beethoven II lunges, biting her on her right buttock. She smacks the dog away reflexively, and he releases her bruised cheek only to snap onto her hand. Robert shouts, "Leave it!" Am I "it"? Freddie wonders. Then Robert yanks at Beethoven's collar. The dog releases his grip, and Freddie clutches her hand. No skin is broken.

"For godssake!" Robert says, and Freddie isn't sure if this is directed to the dog or to her.

꙳

Freddie determines later that she felt scared when the dog bit her, not the first time because she didn't see him coming, but the second time, her stomach flip-flopping like from a sudden drop. At her next session, she explains to Betsy that she felt bruised. "Emotionally, you mean?" Betsy asks.

"No, my hand."

But this is not the kind of feeling Betsy wants to hear about. Betsy wants to help Freddie get in touch with her emotional feelings. She asks Freddie to tell her about a time she felt angry. Why did this matter? But Betsy persists. She tries other ones, a time you felt scared, a time you felt annoyed, a time you felt excited. Eventually, Freddie can pair these emotions with experiences, and Betsy seems so pleased that Freddie asks if she gets any stickers for this.

Angry: On hold with the Internet company for almost an hour and then they say that her email program isn't working because of her computer, but the computer people said it was because of the Internet provider.

Scared: A big black dog on a trail came out of nowhere and Freddie thought it was a black bear and her heart pretty much jumped out of her chest. Then the dog growled a bit and the owner said, "Don't worry!

He's friendly!" Come to think of it, this one fits under anger, too.

Good! Betsy says.

Annoyed: The computer/Internet thing. Also the dog or maybe the owner.

Happy: This one is more challenging. She supposes she felt happy when the lift home for Morning Star led to the "shell house," where Papa Dave and Belinda used to live. "You know, the one past the general store with the shell mosaic on the side?"

When Freddie was a kid, an assortment of meadow flowers grew up along the little gate and the blues and purples of mussel shells swirled toward the front door like a wave or a galaxy. But when Freddie dropped Morning Star off, she discovered blackberry had overtaken the yard and the shell mosaic was missing many of its pieces. It now looks like a forgotten project or something a child made after discovering Krazy Glue.

"You live here?" Freddie asked as Morning Star got out of the car.

"Where else?" Morning Star thanked her for the ride and walked through the gate and up the path. She opened the door and Freddie waited for her to turn and wave again.

Where else, Freddie rarely knew—sometimes years passed without hearing from her. When Papa Dave and Belinda retired here, Freddie occasionally sent things to the shell house for them to forward to Morning Star. She used those cards with the wildlife photos on them, an eagle or a black bear, and added a speech-bubble sticker. To the bear, she captioned, "Has anyone seen my keys?" For the eagle's wide-eyed paranoia, "Something fishy here..."

Freddie waits for Betsy to laugh. "They're fish eagles. Get it?" She asked Belinda the same thing over the phone. Then, "Can you forward this to Morning Star." And Belinda would say I'll send it general delivery, but she may not reply—she does move around a lot, okay, Freddie? But we love seeing these cards. You've always had such a great sense of humour.

But Freddie feels sick thinking of this now with Betsy, the way she does when she eats too much cheese. "I used to be able to eat a whole lasagna! Now a cheesy omelet makes me want to puke." Then she recalls another encounter with a dog, whining and whimpering as if in pain. "He's just excited," the owner said. So maybe this is excitement she feels or maybe pain or indigestion? Are those different?

Betsy wants to know about Papa Dave and Belinda. Grandparents?

Not biologically. "My grandma, my mother, my grandma, my mother!" Freddie jokes, pretending to slap herself, like the scene in *Chinatown* when incest is revealed. "You know that movie?"

Yes, Betsy says.

"Well, not like that. I don't know how Morning Star knew them. But I got to visit them sometimes at the shell house."

One day Papa Dave and Belinda even came to the Farm to visit—they didn't take off their shoes, and Belinda tidied up the living room while they were there, folding blankets and taking coffee mugs and dirty plates to the kitchen, then washing the dishes, being helpful except Morning Star told her to stop, and grabbed her arm and yanked it so Belinda dropped the dishcloth and raised her hands and said, Alright, alright. But they were there to invite Freddie and Morning Star to come back to town and live with them. Freddie sat at the top of the stairs watching and listening.

And Morning Star was like No, it's okay, it's good here, it's really good. We got a community. We look after each other. Papa Dave and Belinda said Okay, if you think it's good for you. But we're concerned about Freddie—she's a young woman now, but a girl. And we know she's met a lot of different kinds of people so she's worldly in some ways, but she's not in other ways. I think you know what we're talking about here, Papa Dave said.

"What are you saying?" Morning Star asked, except it didn't sound like a question because she kept speaking. "Did you come here just to judge?"

Of course not, we love you. We don't want to judge. We're just worried about Freddie, that's all, and we wanted to talk to you, to see if we can help.

"And there is that young girl..." Belinda began. "We saw her with that man—at the wall tent. How old is he?"

"There's nothing wrong here."

"He could be her father."

"No one is breaking any law."

"And she can't be much older than Freddie."

Freddie understood they were talking about Colin, who everybody called Einstein ("I'm an expert on bodies that are out-of-this-world"), and Monica, the other kid there at the time, so she called down the stairs, "She's fourteen!" Maybe they would want her to come live with them, too.

But Morning Star shouted at Freddie to mind her own business, which was confusing because they were talking about Freddie. "We're not going anywhere, and definitely not going to live in the fucking suburbs," she said. But then she said sorry, and then plopped down on the orange couch and she cried and Papa Dave and Belinda sat on either side of her and Morning Star put her head in Belinda's lap and Belinda moved Morning Star's hair off her neck and rubbed her arm. Maybe they thought this all meant something because Papa Dave said they can help her pack up today, that they got a room at the inn so they can wait until tomorrow if she preferred, and Morning Star got up and said, "You don't get it. You'll never understand!" And it looked like she was about to say more, but then she said, "Just go. Please?"

On her way upstairs to her and Freddie's room, she said, "I can't do this anymore, baby."

A week later, Morning Star told Freddie it was time to go. But instead of going to Papa Dave and Belinda's, they moved to a Gulf Island and lived in a cabin that had started out as a chicken coop.

Then the time soon came when Freddie really was a grownup. "I was a mother when I was sixteen, so I think you can handle a job," Morning Star said. The bakery is hiring and Morning Star wanted to take off, she had to get out of here, Kitten. I gotta go.

Freddie never understood what was so much better about Arbutus Farm or the chicken-coop or somewhere general delivery than the shell-house. She wonders if, perhaps now, Morning Star doesn't either...

"Can you repeat the question?" Freddie asks Betsy, because she's lost track and isn't sure if this is a result of the brain injury.

We're talking about feelings, Betsy clarifies.

Freddie looks down at her hands as if they'll know what to do next. She has a new analog watch, the other one being broken in the fall. Instead of numbers, each hour is labelled *Now*. She got it online. "Ask me what time it is."

⌐

Betsy tells her to get a journal. Write down all your thoughts and your feelings. Freddie has done this before, except she recorded food and pain levels, to Nancy-Drew the cause of a gastrointestinal issue.

But she would keep up this practice. Due diligence. Yes, sir-I-mean-ma'am! The incident with Beethoven: Surprised, then scared, then bruised and throbbing, then confused. She notes the date and time. "Miscommunication?" Freddie writes, and she draws an arrow pointing at the word confused. Then she draws a dog, music notes, gives the dog angry eyebrows and wild hair like Ludwig himself.

⌐

A warm front rolls in, pouring rain all over the coast, so the dogs and children remain inside. The whole neighbourhood gets quiet, except for the frogs. Even the guy from across the street gives up sawing whatever he's been sawing—since he moved here a year ago, he's been in the middle of some construction project or other, yet he's still found time to accuse Freddie of uprooting his tomato plants—complaining to her landlord, Don, that he'd seen her on his property. "Maybe I look like a raccoon?" Freddie told Don and rubbed her hands together like she was up to something.

She never uprooted any tomato plants, but she had cut across the property to reach the trails behind. Out for a walk soon after that, the guy screeched past her in his blue SUV. She practically jumped off the road, skidding down toward the ditch. But that was okay because then she saw a mole. You don't see those above ground very often, and you definitely don't see them below ground!

Excited. *Now* is a gift—that's why it's called the present!

As she recalls the mole now, she wonders if that was the last time she went for a walk in her neighbourhood. She used to wander the trails that spiderwebbed between houses and up through the second-growth forests, just the squirrels and towhees to keep her company. Now she even drives to the mailboxes and her walks are confined to other neighbourhoods, with sidewalks and trails with names and parking lots and maps on posts at every fork. She used to avoid parks like that. "Those are for tourists," Morning Star would scoff. But now, the signage strangely reassuring. Reassuring? She wonders if she's afraid of her neighbour.

Freddie feels a migraine coming on and gets up to tack towels over the window. She notices the bruise on her hand has darkened, and now looks as though she's been writing inky letters. Any day, perhaps, Robert will walk down the driveway, then down the path to her cabin, and apologize for his dog. Or maybe he would call. That would mean she's hoping for two calls now, one from Robert and one from the vet, to tell her if she's won a gift basket. Freddie thought she might get a pet and if she won a gift basket this would help her make a decision—she'd entered to win both the cat and the dog basket—and also give her a start on supplies.

Maybe the rain is keeping Robert away.

She tries to watch *Shaun the Sheep* but finds herself squinting to dim the screen. She closes her eyes, but she can't follow the storyline with only the sound of cartoon sheep bleating their playful schemes. She lies down and listens to the rain on the shingled roof instead. It reminds her of her room in the Big House at Arbutus Farm. In the winters, when she was the only child, she had the attic to herself. Just one octagonal window looked out over the puddled property. It was easy to imagine she was living a fairy tale, a sort of tomboy princess locked up and forgotten in a tower, waiting for her rescuer, which she usually imagined was a horse. She pretended the horse knew Morse code, which she called Horse code, and used a towel to cover and uncover the window in short and long pauses, *SOS, Horse!*

Is Beethoven staring out at the rain right now, wishing he was outside barking at robins or wind? Or is his sadness not about a longing for sunshine and playtime but a release from his rainy-day confinement?

Freddie wishes she could ask him. What if the bites from Beethoven were an SOS—a "cry for help"? *Don't leave me!* A cry for help is when a person "acts out" with destructive behaviour or self-harm or too much sexiness, in order to get attention they need. Betsy explained this after Freddie said she never understood why so many people "attempt" suicide. Why is there such a high rate of suicide failure?

Freddie, on the other hand, had been intent on a permanent solution, hadn't she? Jumping off a building, that is serious. But there were ten floors in that building and a rooftop available for tenant barbecues, yet she jumped from her own balcony. Those four more stories might have made all the difference. "Don't give up," Morning Star said later at the hospital, squeezing Freddie's hand, her bruised face having faded to yellow at that point. She was surprised when Morning Star came to visit her. "How did you know I was here?"

"Because you're my baby," Morning Star replied. ESP?

But don't give up on what? Freddie wondered at the time, unsure if she meant she should try again.

The migraine is getting bad. She moves a pillow over her eyes to make it darker, but the pulsations continue, throbbing, somehow loud. SOS. *Ba-ba-ba! Baa-Baa-Baa! Ba-ba-ba!* She wants to cry but that will hurt more. Pain-brain will go away, she tells herself. It never lasts forever. Pain-brain will go away...

꩜

A day passes, and the migraine, mercifully, lifts, replaced by a cognitive fog that makes it hard to remember why she walked to the kitchen. A few days after that, Freddie feels ready to meet the world again. Even the clouds part, and the sun turns a dewy spiderweb into a glimmering constellation. Look at that. Will you just look at that! She retrieves her little spiral-bound notebook, and records the time: *Now*, but also 2:35 p.m. And the feeling: THANK YOU, Spider!! If she had a cellphone, she would send a picture to Willow. "Appreciating the work of your fellow weavers!" she might write.

Freddie takes the notebook everywhere so she can journal wherever and whenever she has a feeling. She keeps her notes tidy, except for the first page where a wild-haired Beethoven still floats among questions.

She calls Robert several times, but his wife, Olivia, tells her he's out of town, and then he's occupied in his workshop. "He's not available," she says finally, sounding a little sad. Freddie begins to think Olivia is home alone all the time. Alone with two young children and an unmanageable dog—or does Robert take the dog with him to all these places? Freddie wonders if asking her if she's lonely might be "inappropriate behaviour," something she sometimes did, according to her doctor. She liked to call him Doctor Poo-a-Little ever since he sent her home with a kit to do a guaiac-based fecal occult blood test. She was required to take "smears" of fecal matter—more than one for each bowel movement, and to include samples from three bowel movements. He explained she must "smear a thin film" on the test slides and suggested using plastic wrap over the toilet in order to catch her stool. "Catch my stool!" Freddie had repeated. "Is it going to run away?"

"You don't need a lot of it, Freddie, just a thin smear."

"Just a little."

"Yes."

"A little poo."

"Yes." He handed her the instructions print-out.

"Doctor Poo-a-little."

"No."

There was no blood in her stool, so crisis averted. The next time she saw him, she called him that, like it was a private joke they shared, like old college buddies reminiscing about dirty nicknames they'd had, but he flattened his hand like he was telling a dog to lie down and said, "That is not appropriate." Freddie dropped her arms—they'd been up to embrace him, a pat on the back. Inside his closet-sized doctor's office, he softened a bit, but reiterated his earlier comment, this time attributing her misjudgment to the brain injury.

Freddie knows she is different since the Great Leap. She was always funny—Morning Star told her once that she should write for *The Carol Burnett Show*—but since the brain injury, some of her previous hesitation has disappeared and she now blurts out whatever comes to mind. Which seems a good thing maybe—more spontaneity, creativity, opportunities for excellence in one-liners. But there's an accumulation of scenes like that with the doctor. Could she be losing her sense of humour? Still, there was never really evidence of "inappropriate behaviour," aside from that one comment from the doctor, and he was a bit of a stick-in-the-poo.

Freddie ensures she has room for a voicemail, in case she misses Robert's call—she got the cheapest package available, with room for only two messages. The vet had called during the brain fog and left one already: "Your lucky puppy has won the gift basket!" She hasn't got back to them because it doesn't make sense to claim the prize without the dog, but she isn't entirely sure yet she would not acquire one soon. A dog might be good company on those difficult days at home, a warm body and cuddles on the couch.

On her fourth attempt to reach Robert, the phone simply rings and rings and finally goes to voicemail after about five rings.

"Howdy neighbour! Yes, I wasn't expecting to leave a message, but here goes: Robert, it's Freddie, from next door. We had a disagreement, I think, when we saw each other last and then your dog attacked me. I'd like to speak with you in person, not in voicemail, but it seems you're not home very often, so. Anyway, I am here, you can call me back—" A beep cuts her off. She calls back to record the second half of the message. It doesn't ring but goes straight to voicemail. "Oh. That was weird—it didn't ring. Maybe you're home now?" She waits, as if someone might be rushing to pick up the way she used to do when she had an answering machine, skidding around corners in sock feet. People were hard to reach back then. But they're hard to reach now, always having problems with their email or cell service or being out of town or in a workshop or not hearing the phone or being "swamped," which has nothing to do with frogs, but something to do with being "up to my eyeballs."

"I guess you're not jumping out of the shower," Freddie says. She leaves her number and hangs up.

Perhaps she should have included his wife, Olivia, in that message? Whenever Freddie calls, she asks for Robert. When Olivia hears the message, she can't very well call Freddie back because the message isn't for her, but her husband. She might even think Freddie is trying to have an affair with him, with all those phone calls. If that were the case, it would make more sense for Freddie to call and then hang up when the wife picks up, which she doesn't do. But no one in their right mind would imagine Freddie is attracted to Robert! She's a loud and proud old lezzie, although it's been a while since she's used her between-the-leggal area for anything but peeing. She wonders if it still works. Willow might think that's funny. She could stand stiffly, like Tin Man, creak out "Oil can...Oil can..."

Freddie takes a box of maple leaf cookies from the cupboard and dumps them, along with a package of Breton crackers, into a Tupperware container.

"Afternoon tea!" Freddie says when Olivia opens the door. "Is Beethoven around? He has a few feelings about me."

"No, he's with Robert."

"Well then! Would you like some company on this fine, mix-of-sun-and-rain afternoon?"

Sometimes the answer to a question like that is simple, such as when the answer and the truth match up, as in, "Yes." Or "Yes, but I was just about to head out to run some errands. How about a rain check?" Freddie could look quizzically up at the sky—I've checked and there's no rain! But if the truth is No, I would not like company, this is more complicated. Is it No, I would not like company in general because I am not feeling well—stay back! It's contagious! Or is it No, I would not like *your* company. Almost no one answers a question with the truth if the truth is that latter example. Most people invent excuses, which are sometimes called "white lies," alluding to the idea of polar opposites, of black representing malevolence and white representing goodness. But people say there is never anything good about a lie, don't they? And Freddie doesn't find anything bad about the colour black: night sky, jungle panthers, new tires. Freddie is not a liar, so she can't really tell when others are lying, only that something doesn't match up, and follow-up questions are necessary.

"Oh," Olivia stalls. "I'm not really a tea drinker."

"That's okay!" Freddie takes the lid off the Tupperware. "Salty or sweet?"

"I actually just ate lunch."

"So, you want a cookie?"

Olivia places her hand on her stomach. A pink knit sweater reveals Disney princess-like proportions. It's hard to believe she's had two children. Spanx? "I'm not eating sugar right now," she says. "I'm on a cleanse."

Freddie understands. She puts the lid back on the Tupperware. She says something about not wanting to tempt her and then sings a little as if she were charming a cobra, moving the Tupperware container like the snake. Freddie doesn't know what to do after that, so she just smiles.

After a moment of silence, Olivia invites her in.

᷌

It turns out Beethoven's nails had not been clicking on linoleum that day, but hardwood floors. Wood is everywhere: knotty pine panelling and log beams. "Robert did the breakfast nook himself." Even the coffee-table glass rests atop a gnarled old-growth stump. Windows along the rear wall frame the trampoline and apple trees and forest and mossy treehouse outside. The house might have looked quaint except for all the track lighting and the kitchen where the sink has its own gleaming white island, reminding Freddie of a home living magazine or an ad for life insurance. "We realized we just needed to be close to nature," Olivia says.

She hands Freddie a cup of mint tea and sits down with a glass of water for herself. She makes chit-chat, asking Freddie how long she's lived next door (two years), and where she's from originally (Africa, Freddie jokes, intending to reference the origin of *Homo sapiens*. "Really?" Olivia asks. "You don't have an accent." A curious statement. "Neither do you," Freddie says. Olivia moves on.) Freddie does not say "What a beautiful home you have," or "Can you believe this rain?" So Olivia offers something instead. "I can't believe we've been here almost a year. Doesn't time just fly by?"

"Time flies," Freddie repeats, considering other things that fly, like fish, flights of stairs. Olivia asks Freddie what she does for a living.

This question comes up regularly and usually Freddie says it's a full-time job looking after herself, which she means quite literally, but which elicits laughter, "Tell me about it!" and comments about "Where do we find the time?" From there the conversations go to the price of produce and how many minutes on hold with Telus.

"Mostly I look after a bad brain," Freddie says.

Olivia looks confused. "Are you a therapist of some kind?"

"Ha! I like that!" Imagine she is Betsy, or the doc from the Psych Unit with the cool purple glasses, except she wouldn't know what to say next. "No, I have a brain injury."

"I'm so sorry," Olivia says, not expecting to really learn anything of substance from these questions. "You seem fine."

Freddie adjusts an imaginary coiffure. "Why thank you."

By this time, Freddie has eaten all the maple cookies. She asks Olivia about her own family, and learns she grew up in the Fraser Valley, that her mother is from Hong Kong, that her parents are divorced so Olivia takes the kids to Christmas at her dad's and every other holiday at her mom's, because her mom likes having the kids around more than her dad and his wife, Barb, who has some kind of degenerative thing that makes her uncomfortable with noise.

"But I think she just doesn't like kids," Olivia says. "She's always been a miserable woman." It's then that Olivia notices Freddie's hand. "What happened there? That's quite the bruise."

"Didn't Robert tell you?"

"Excuse me?"

"Beethoven II bit me—you should see my butt! Got me there, too."

Freddie stands up and turns, but Olivia stops her. "That's okay," Olivia says, holding up one hand. "Please, sit." Freddie sits.

"Robert told me, I just didn't realize it had left a bruise. He said Beethoven only nipped you. He gets excited—he's playful."

"He bit me."

"Okay, well he is a guard dog—there are bears and coyotes around here and we've got two kids, so you can understand why it's not a good idea to cut through the property."

"I was talking to Robert. I was leaving and then the dog just came out of the house and bit my butt and then bit my hand."

"That's not the whole story though. You slapped the dog, didn't you?"

"I slapped him *away*, after he bit my butt."

"Okay, let's just calm down." She holds her hands out like Doctor Poo-a-Little, as if telling her to lie down.

"I am calm," Freddie says standing.

"I don't think we should talk about this." Olivia takes the teacup and her empty glass and heads toward the kitchen island.

"When *are* we going to talk about it?"

Olivia places the cups in the sink, then quickly wipes down the pristine counter. "I've got to get back to work now. It was nice of you to bring the cookies. Normally I'm really busy, so it's better not to drop by. You just caught me on a break, but I've really got to get back to work now."

Olivia crosses her arms, and then shrugs, as if to say, "Oh well," which Freddie doesn't understand.

"Oh well," Freddie shrugs. "Oh well," she shrugs again. She wants to see what that feels like. Maybe this would explain something.

"You should go now," Olivia says.

"Please tell Robert to call me."

"I passed along your messages and he'll call you when he can."

This is also confusing. It's been over a week, hasn't it? What prevents an able-bodied man from using the phone? "I don't think he listens to you," Freddie offers.

Olivia walks past her and holds the door open, looking down at her feet as Freddie exits with the remaining Breton crackers.

꙳

Just a hair past *Now*: 4:05 p.m. Now feels something like a wool car-blanket, like the one that was too small to cover her feet, and scratched her legs, an inside kind of itch that made her want to scream except then Morning Star might take the blanket away and she'd be cold. Thank the sheep. Thank the weaver. The Universe provides. "Miscommunication," Freddie writes.

꙳

The notebook is filling up with dates and times and point-form lists of possible feeling words. Look how many pages! Freddie has been having a lot of feelings. At her next appointment, she shows Betsy, who nods with approval or maybe just acknowledgment, but after scanning several pages of these lists, asks Freddie, "Why do you think we journal our feelings?"

"It was your idea."

When Freddie journalled about what she ate and her bowel movements for the gastrointestinal issues, Doctor Poo-a-Little said it was good and very thorough. She'd made a connection between dairy and hurried visits to the toilet, and subsequently eliminated dairy. Freddie hasn't yet noticed a pattern with feelings because they seem to occur at almost any time, even when nothing is happening, just sitting on the couch or walking at the beach, and then, just as she notices them, they pass.

"We want to understand the causes of these feelings, too," Betsy finally says.

Betsy explained at the beginning of their relationship that they had up to twelve sessions together and that the focus was on the Great Leap, although she didn't call it that. She called it "your attempt." It seemed like she wanted to know how Freddie arrived at this place. Freddie worked backwards, like a detective reconstructing the scene of a crime and tracing the killer's steps back, out the door, to the knife store, to work, to home, to waking up and thinking about the knife store. The days before the Great Leap were all the same, as Freddie recalls. Just home, to work, to the grocery store, to home, and then repeat.

Freddie had been at the printing press for years by then, something like a factory job. It paid pretty well, but she missed having people to talk to. She'd make chit-chat on the commute, but most people would simply smile and then maintain a gaze straight ahead, like they were in an elevator instead of a fantastic train flying through the sky. She moved to the city for the same reason most people did—more to see, people to meet. Plus, she'd known she loved girls since Monica lived at the Farm, and the city was surely the best place for Freddie to find others like herself. But there seemed an inevitability to this migration, too, like the pull of gravity is simply greater with all those heavy concrete towers and bodies to fill them. And although she learned the names of many people, they might as well have lived on Venus, as far as friends go. "If men are from Mars, where are women from?" she asked Morning Star on a postcard. She had a punchline for when she writes back ("Vancouver"). But Belinda never forwarded that question because she got pneumonia and died, and six months later Papa Dave's heart stopped. When Freddie took the SkyTrain, she sometimes pretended to be invisible, a time-travelling anthropologist making observations about popular fabrics, paying special attention to who gives their seat to old people.

"But how old is old?" she asks Betsy, who says it's a good question. One day, a girl with green fingernails and a geometric doodle in black pen on her arm offered Freddie her seat, and Freddie did feel tired—it was the end of her shift and she hadn't been sleeping well, up until two or three in the morning trying to bore herself to sleep with some British crime drama with too much talking, then in a daze all day. How did this girl know? So Freddie sat down. Touched her greying hair. Said that is awfully sweet of you—or, not awfully, goodly sweet. And for a moment she felt the opposite of invisible. Visible? But that doesn't seem strong enough. Something brighter than that.

"Seen?" Betsy offers.

Thank you, Freddie said to the girl. And the girl smiled, in a way, but then she got off the train at the next stop, only seconds later.

Freddie sits quietly for a moment, then asks, "Should I write down feelings that I remember that are in the past or just the ones that happen in the present? If I feel, I don't know, sad thinking about leaving this girl, am I sad now or is that just a memory?"

"Leaving her?" Betsy says. Freddie imagines these questions as probes, tinfoil contraptions blinking along a dim horizon, that dreamy place between sleep and wakefulness, then evaporating in the white light of day.

꙳

The vet calls to remind Freddie that the gift basket is ready for her to pick up any time. Doggy treats, a bag of dog food, a doggy bed, a doggy brush and a gift certificate for one doggy "spa treatment" from Dog Star

Pet Services, which means nail trim, wash and brush.

"That's a lucky puppy," the receptionist says as Freddie takes the basket, even though the food is for an adult dog.

"It's for me actually. Yeah, I've been looking for a new bed for a while."

Back at home, Freddie tries the bed in various locations—by the sliding door, on the floor beside her own bed, but with a dog sprawled out there, she might trip over him or her in the night on the way to the bathroom. By the bathroom. Same problem. But she doesn't even know what size the dog would be. She could simply choose a dog that fit the bed, but something about that seems inhumane.

It also occurs to Freddie that she knows very little about dogs. How much do you feed a dog? How many times a day do you need to walk one? For how long? All these things. And then there's sitting, staying, rolling over. "No jumping!" How do you get a dog to listen? And "Come." That's important, but it seems the most challenging for dogs to learn or for people to teach them. "Leave it." Does Beethoven know these things? If Freddie gets a dog, will it bite her too?

She goes to the library to use the Internet and to take a book out. She can't read like she used to—she's good for about half an hour before her brain just sort of shuts down, so she needs lots of breaks. She logs into the library computer, looks up *SPCA* and browses the gallery of orphan dogs. Just one dog available. A miniature schnauzer named Molly, her picture displayed in the top left corner of an otherwise empty webpage. In the picture, Molly looks up at the camera, her eyes obscured by tufts of chocolate fur, mouth open in a smile, or what looks like a smile. She clicks for the next image: Molly by a rhododendron, mouth closed now and ears back, less sure of herself. In the final photo, Molly sits in an office chair, a computer behind. Did Molly jump up on her own or did the previous owner pose her for a photo? "It's time to do your taxes," would be a good caption. And now Molly is here, on the SPCA website, these moments between Molly and her owner (Master? Parent?) on display, to convince a perfect stranger to take her home. Who could leave Molly here? How, after eight years of being alive, did Molly end up abandoned in this place? Freddie takes out her spiral notebook and records the time, 3:14 p.m., and the feeling, "Sad."

Molly looks as though she'd fit rather well in the dog bed. Freddie could trim the fur around her eyes so she can see better, and scrub between those scrappy toes. Filing nails?

The library dedicates two shelves to dog training and cognition. *How to Think Like a Dog*; *The Other End of the Leash*; *Inside of a Dog*; *The Social Dog*; *The Genius of Dogs* and on and on. Does Robert know about this? She borrows two. She has a lot to learn, so she will cancel her next session with Betsy. She needs the time. She needs to learn more about dogs, what they need, how they communicate, how to make them stay, how to make them leave it.

$$\text{\textit{}}$$

Willow examined Freddie's hand once, before Beethoven bit it. The square palm and long fingers indicated "air" hands. Willow scrolled her phone screen. "It means you're curious and good at communication." She paused to read. "Or maybe they're water hands."

Freddie opens and closes her fist, stiff. Her knuckles are as gnarly as the old-growth coffee table and the skin is too many colours, the rosy joints contrasting with a tributary of blue veins. She could never catch a frog now, she thinks. Once at the shell house, she'd followed a low chortle to where a red-legged frog hid between a fern and the cabin's foundation. "Drop it—it could be poisonous," Belinda said. "Just look at the legs!" The red limbs evidence of toxicity. But the frog wasn't poisonous. Later Freddie would learn that her own hands posed the greatest danger, that in addition to its lungs, the frog breathes through its skin, inhaling the oils and salt of Freddie's warm-blooded flesh. The salt burns like acid, threatening to suck the water right out, which is death to a frog. She thinks of the slugs she salted, maybe that same day, for Belinda, whose lettuce was under attack. The way they curled into themselves, screaming. But that can't be right, can it? Were the slugs screaming? "They're just slugs," Morning Star told her later when Freddie cried. "They don't feel pain."

When Freddie thinks of them now, she remembers the way they looked dried up in the sun like goose shit. "I did that," she says, gently touching her hand. The bruise has subsided, so it looks like nothing has happened at all, that it's just a stiff old multi-coloured toxic hand. But it still feels weird. Nerve damage? Sometimes a fender-bender puts someone out of work for years, but Freddie survived a six-storey fall, so you never know. Stranger things have happened. The brains are mysterious cells, a prison full of cells, each one containing a dog, like in a pound, a brain full of rescue dogs crying for help.

She would have liked to keep the red-legged frog. She couldn't understand the impulse at the time, but it was something to do with love.

❧

Freddie calls twice more, this time leaving a message for both Robert and Olivia, explaining that they seemed to get off on the wrong feet, which was really a clumsy thing since you can't take a step with two feet at once, especially not two wrong feet. "What else, what else. The bruise is gone, but my hand feels weird, like numb and sometimes really sensitive. It also occurred to me that maybe Beethoven II didn't hear you call him off—maybe he's hard of hearing, like the master!"

By this she is referring to Beethoven the master of music, who went deaf later in life, first becoming notoriously bad-tempered. People were less sensitive to special needs back then. One of the dog books talked about identifying the causes of biting like fear or territoriality. Freddie wrote "protective?" in her notebook under the drawing of Beethoven. Is that a feeling? But pain can also cause aggression. Was Beethoven the dog suffering?

One day, while Freddie is at the grocery store, Robert comes over, not to Freddie's cabin, but to the house where the landlord, Don, lives. Robert installed a breakfast nook in Don's house the year before, so they can talk, friendly.

Freddie returns from the grocery store, a bag of videos in one hand and a bag of groceries in the other. She whistles "Somewhere Over the Rainbow" as she heads down the path to her cabin. Somewhere behind the dark blue clouds, the sun pokes through, making a rainbow that terminates at her cabin, the pot of gold. She stops to take it in. Sometimes the place is so picture-perfect she can only shake her head, like it's just too much, it's overkill. Who would believe this is where I live? Before she reaches the cabin, Don comes up the other path.

"Look! It's Don!" she says. "Hello Don! Back just in time to see this rainbow!"

He waves only briefly, then places the same hand on his knee as he climbs up the gentle slope. He stops to catch his breath, his giant forehead sweaty and the grey hair along his head curled in the humidity.

"I see you put the curlers in," Freddie says, pretending to fluff up her own hair.

"Huh? Oh yeah."

Don wasn't about to reprimand her. She's the best tenant he's ever had: she gives him a year's worth of post-dated checks every January. The first year, she offered to mow the lawn while he was away, but she enjoyed it so much she just kept doing it. "Makes me feel studly," she said, flexing her biceps. "Give the robins a show."

"I need to talk to you about something." He explains how Robert told him that Freddie had been leaving a lot of messages. He doesn't say "harassing his wife," as Robert did. That they got your messages and just want to be left alone now. He's summarizing. Robert told him she'd trespassed, been nipped by his guard dog, and had since been harassing them with unannounced visits and phone calls and leaving insulting messages and we just want this to stop, that's all, we don't want to have to report her, and we know she's already been reported for vandalism, that she ripped up Trevor's tomato plants, so this could be big trouble for her if she doesn't back off. So what are we gonna do about this one?

"They just want to be left in peace," Don says.

"I want peace, too." A woodpecker hammers nearby. Freddie doesn't say anything about that.

"Okay, yes. Just—take my advice, would you? Just leave it alone. Just..." He pretends to wipe his hand. "Clean slate. Okay?"

Freddie thinks of a chalkboard slate, working out a problem on it and then erasing it all—making it a clean slate. But there is still this problem to work out. "I'm confused."

"Just—clean slate, okay?"

Don looks like he's waiting for her to say something, but Freddie doesn't know what to say, so she just repeats him. "Clean slate, okay." He nods once and holds up a thumb. "Okay." He pats her on one shoulder. Turns. "That is some rainbow." Walks back down the slope.

᷌

Once she'd found a meal that struck that balance between "comfort food" and "gastrointestinal comfort food," she stuck with it. For Freddie, this means a lot of turkey meatloaf with cucumbers. But she browses the aisles at the grocery store as if she is contemplating new possibilities. She especially enjoys examining the discount shelf by the staff door, with its great deals on dented canned food or seasonal candy. A heart-shaped box of chocolates at half price. This could complete her joke about pining for Willow. She could conceal the box under her zip-up hoodie, make it thump like a cartoon heart, "My fair lady!" Thump, thump, thump... ta-da! "How I've pined for you." Pop the trunk. "Et voila!" The bag of Jack-pine needles. She tucks the box in her grocery basket.

As Freddie places her groceries on the conveyor belt at the till, someone lines up behind her and jabs one finger into her back. "Alright, hands up."

Freddie spins around, an apple in each hand. Willow raises her own hands in surrender, cheek dimpling with her sideways smile. Willow must be in her forties, too, but she has the kind of face that could belong to a teenager if you squint just enough to blur the deepening lines at her eyes. It's those big cheeks, perhaps. "How do you like *them*..." Freddie says, pretending to examine the Pink Ladies, but she can't think of the word.

"Apples?" Willow offers.

"Apples." She places them on the belt. "I lost the word. I was gonna say melon, but I knew that wasn't right." Cauliflower. Potato. Freddie is tired.

Willow glances at Freddie's items. "Chocolates—who's the lucky girl?" She leans over the counter to retrieve a divider, her long hair falling softly across her shoulder except for one dreadlock, decorated with a few wooden beads.

"My fair Rasta maiden," Freddie begins. She holds up the box to do the thumping, but something stops her, like this thumping heart might be too much. Of what, she's not sure, but her doctor comes to mind then, the papered bed in the tiny office, and she puts the heart down again. "They're for you, but I had another present to go with them." She pats the box, as if thanking it for a job well done. "I was going to surprise you, but I guess it's still a surprise because you weren't expecting it in the grocery lineup either!"

Willow smiles, not at Freddie but at her groceries, and begins unloading her basket, placing one tiny purple potato after the other on the belt. "What's the occasion?"

"Occasion?" The purple potatoes look almost like ginger roots, their knobbly exteriors, but the wrong colour, and Freddie wonders if they are potatoes at all. Is there a word she's forgetting? Another one, more pink than purple, and round. "I pined for you," Freddie says. "I meant to tell you at my car—the chocolates are just part of it." Several yellow ones come next, which look like ginger root, dry with bits of gingery whiskers. Or perhaps those really are ginger.

The cashier keys in the chocolates. "You want these on top?"

"Yes, please and thank you!" Freddie says.

Willow stacks her basket and turns toward the magazine covers. "I don't even know who all these people are," she says. "I think that means I'm getting old." She takes a magazine, flipping to the middle.

"You'll always be younger than me." Freddie hunches over Quasimodo style as she searches for exact change in her wallet, but Willow doesn't seem to notice, engrossed now in some article.

Freddie waits for her to finish her purchase. "I've got a surprise for you in my trunk," she says as they exit the store.

"Okay."

When Freddie pops the trunk, she repeats her joke: "I've pined for you!" Takes the heart-shaped box and thumps it on her chest, a cartoon heart bursting.

Willow laughs, tucking her dreadlock behind one ear. "That's awesome. Thank you." She takes the bag of needles out of the trunk. "I thought you were going to ask me out or something."

"Oh," Freddie says. She hadn't thought of that before.

Willow unwraps the box, tucking the cellophane wrapper in with the needles, picks out a square-shaped chocolate and pops it in her mouth.

"What would you have said?" Freddie asks.

"Oh, that's cheeky!" She covers her mouth, full of something chewy. "I'm not even gonna go there. I value our friendship too much." She holds the box out for Freddie to take a chocolate.

"I can't eat that," Freddie says. "But you *did* go there, didn't you? You just brought it up. You just said you thought I was going to ask you out, but then when I ask what you would've said, you say I can't talk about that. But you already talked about it. I don't understand why the rules are different. How do you know when you can say something and when you can't?"

Willow chews more slowly, looking at the chocolates as if for an answer to this question. "I guess I just blurted it out. But upon reflection, yeah, I shouldn't have, because I value our friendship and I don't want to do anything that would jeopardize that."

"We're friends?"

"I think so, don't you?"

"Don't friends hang out with each other? You never phone me or come over."

Willow tosses the heart box in her grocery bag. "No, I've never come over—you've never invited me."

"Am I allowed?"

"What is going on with you today?"

"I asked if I'm allowed. Am I allowed to ask if I'm allowed? Because you didn't answer my question. Was it cheeky?"

"Freddie," Willow speaks quietly now. "I think Mercury must be in retrograde because we are seriously having major communication challenges right now. So, I tell you what, I sincerely thank you for this." She places her hand on her chest, tarnished silver rings decorating each finger. "This was such a sweet and thoughtful gift, okay? But I think our energy is just off today. Maybe I can check our horoscopes, but I think I'm just gonna go home now." She maneuvers the bag of pine needles over her shoulder and picks up the others with her free hands. "So I'll talk to you later?"

When Freddie doesn't respond, she puts the bags down again. "You're not okay today," she says, and gives Freddie a long, long hug.

Something uploading.

﹀

Dogs read with their noses. Their urine is a message on a community bulletin board. The position of a tail means dominant, submissive, happy, afraid, wary... Barks mean bored, lonely, excited, fearful. It seems dog feelings are as diverse as human ones, but Betsy never mentioned any book like this for understanding people. Freddie must learn to decode the body language. "Dogs are honest," one book says, to encourage dog owners that although training can be challenging, you can at least rely on your dog to tell you the truth with his body. There is no deception. This, supposedly, is different from other animals.

The treats in the gift basket will come in handy—rewarding a dog with food is a necessary component of a training regimen. Freddie wonders what the hand signal for "Sit" would be. Pointing at the ground? Molly may already know that one. She'll have to try out some options to see. But in the meantime, Freddie needs to get a handle on reading doggie feelings. After all, she can't ask a dog for clarification. She hasn't had much luck asking people, either.

There is no dog park on the coast, but there are off-leash trails more frequented by dogs. At Tower Point, for example, she's been startled by dogs exploding out of the salal or careening around shrouded corners of the trail. Most of the time they ignore her. The trail ends at a beach looking out across the strait and most people stop there for a while, finding a dry seat on driftwood while their dogs play with each other in the intertidal zone.

At low tide, the beach is the size of a soccer field, but one marred with puddles and littered with the ocean's rejects: Dungeness crabs hiding in the sand until the water comes back, clumps of bladderwrack and uprooted bullwhip kelp. Two children kick some ball around, playing what looks like a game of "Piggy in the Middle" with their dog, who attempts to intercept the ball. Just before each kick, the dog yelps, a high-pitched scraping sound, one that has an effect like nails on a clean slate for Freddie. Her body seizes with each yelp, then shakes. It won't be long before she's exhausted by adrenaline. Perhaps this is an excited bark, unless it's distress. The way the children out-maneuver the dog might frustrate it. Does it feel inadequate? After reading an entire book about dog cognition, Freddie suspects she knows more than the average Joe, and certainly the average Joe Junior. If the children knew they were causing distress for the dog, they would probably stop. Maybe they would just throw the ball for the dog to grab in its teeth and then return to them—fetch. This is a game Freddie hoped to play with Molly.

She keeps her fingers in her ears as she approaches the children and their dog. She's surprised how long it takes her to recognize them. Perhaps because she's never actually seen the children and she has such a strong image of Beethoven inside, staring balefully or menacingly or longingly out the window, that it isn't until she's a few metres away that she recognizes the motley crew in front of her. Beethoven pauses in his play, stands still, eyes fixed and tail wagging. Freddie has learned that a wagging tail does not necessarily mean a happy or friendly dog, but, in combination with this stare and stillness, could mean the dog is undecided about what to do, whether she is friend or foe, and how he will behave in response.

The boy holds the sandy ball in his hands now and looks to his sister, who is as tall as a grownup but flat-chested and with features like a mouse, almost indiscernible pink lips and eyes like tiny beads beneath her bovine eyelashes. She must take after Robert, while the boy has his mother's handsome face and wide smile that means nothing. Freddie takes her fingers out of her ears. She steps back and holds her hands up. "Don't shoot," she says to the dog without making eye contact.

"He's not gonna shoot you, he's a dog," the boy says. But Beethoven doesn't look so sure, all the parts of his body conflicting—a happy tail, an aggressive stance, a wary closed mouth.

"Could you please take the rein of Master Beethoven?" Freddie says with a British accent.

"You know his name!" the boy says. The sister steps toward the dog, stretches her hand out to his collar, but Beethoven slips away, repositions, barks. She doesn't look more than a hundred pounds and Beethoven is at least fifty.

"Beethoven, shut up!" the sister calls. The boy tosses the ball toward the dog, who glances momentarily, then ignores it. The boy steps forward and slaps Beethoven gently on the snout. "Careful—" Freddie says. The sister hooks Beethoven's collar and yanks him toward her. "Sit!" She tries again, Beethoven still fixed on Freddie. "Sit!"

Freddie steps back, continuing to avert her gaze. She speaks slowly, in a calm, low voice, her hands still raised in surrender. "I came over to tell you that your dog might be in distress. Nobody likes being in the middle the whole time."

"*He* does," the boy says.

The girl pushes on Beethoven's rump to make him sit, but it bounces right back up, like a balloon in water. Beethoven resumes barking.

"He's not a happy dog," Freddie points out. "I've been reading about dogs and he's showing clear signs of aggression." Out of territoriality or fear or protectiveness? "He's already bit me twice—you need to be careful not to aggravate him I think." Although Freddie has done nothing to provoke Beethoven, aside from simply being there. She needs to be brave, though. This is valuable information she's giving them.

"My dog is friendly," the sister says, turning her eyes into accusatory slits. She yanks Beethoven closer and pats him reassuringly on his side, a reward for bad behaviour. "It's because you're acting afraid of him."

But Freddie is not acting afraid—she *is* afraid. But she is also angry, not at Beethoven, but at this girl, Robert's proxy, for assigning the blame for this moment. Freddie is also sad. Why did sadness so often follow anger? There is disappointment mixed in, too. That may be mixed in a lot with sadness. She thinks of Molly, then. Sees Molly in Beethoven's wild eyes, the sclera visible like crescent moons. Does Beethoven even understand what is happening? The whites of a dog's eyes aren't usually visible, one of the dog books pointed out. It makes it more difficult to determine in which direction they are looking. Unlike humans, with the sclera always visible. We need to know where we're looking—we're visual creatures and this body language is vital in our communication. The girl looks to her brother, then to Freddie, only momentarily, then past Freddie. To the driftwood? The boy too. Freddie does feel an urge to turn and look at the object of their gaze, just as the dog book said a human would. But another part of her wants to do the opposite of what is expected.

"Beethoven probably was friendly at one point, but not anymore. Bad dog owners make bad dogs. Look at what you're doing, rewarding him for barking at a harmless woman on the beach. Affection is a reward, don't you know that? I'm sure you learned this from your parents." Neither the boy nor the girl are looking at Freddie now. "You kids are probably both ruined already, too." She looks at the girl. "You're not so friendly." Then to the boy, "You might be, except the way you tossed the ball in Beethoven's face. Yeah, I think you got a mean streak too, but it's not your fault. You've got bad parents, that's what's going on."

"What the hell do you think you're doing?" Olivia steps between Freddie and her children. "Go back to the blanket," she says to them, and the kids walk dutifully away, yanking Beethoven as they go.

"What the hell do you think you're doing talking to my kids like that." She begins with "what," but it doesn't sound like a question. "Who do you think you are?"

"Your dog is dangerous."

Olivia nods quickly and many times, but Freddie has learned something about nodding, that it doesn't always indicate agreement. "You know what?" she says. "I think *you're* dangerous. Don't ever talk to us again."

As Olivia turns to leave, Freddie realizes she still has her hands up in surrender. She drops them to her sides. She has an urge to pick up the clump of bladderwrack nearby and throw it at the back of Olivia's head. She decides to leave it.

❧

The frogs have been quiet and Freddie wonders if they're waiting something out under the mud, like the crabs, or if they just have nothing more to say.

The dog barks next door. As she sits on the couch, one hand on each knee, her whole body clenches with each explosive yelp, the back of her head tingling and the sensation crawling over her frontal lobes, too, until something goes on with her vision and she can almost see the bark, and it feels as though she might faint, as though the world is about to go dark, but then a bright light flips on and she feels the bark all over again, like *zap, zap, zap.* She puts in ear plugs, but Beethoven barks through the marshmallow. Closes her eyes. Nothing to do but wait. She wants to phone, to explain this effect—she realizes that in all her communication with them, she has never explained the distress the dog caused her, she never expressed her feelings, and they're not mind readers, either, right? But something stops her from doing this. "Trapped," she writes in her notebook. "Afraid?" Records the time. But now what? What is she supposed to do with these feelings?

"Acknowledge them," Betsy had said. She's missed two appointments already and can't remember if there were any instructions after that. The famous TV dog trainer Cesar Milan says to discover the causes of the feelings, except he doesn't say "feelings" but "behaviour." So if your dog is barking all day while you're out, you must first determine why. Bored? Then give him something to do—more walks when you're around, and a bone or something while you're away. Usually, problem solved. Maybe this was the biggest miscommunication of all, that Freddie had failed to share her feelings. Beethoven would continue in his life of distress and Freddie would, too. She considers writing a letter. Olivia said not to "talk" to them, but perhaps she can still write.

But none of it matters. A few days later, Beethoven is hit by a vehicle, which knocks his body to the side of the road, landing it at the top of the long driveway down to Robert and Olivia's but hidden in a cloud of periwinkle. The guy across the street, having completed work with the saw, soon after begins operating a squeaky excavator, so the noise of the hit-and-run is only the first of a routine cacophony, the sound of the excavator's pumps and chains, boom and bucket.

Freddie is at the SPCA at the time Beethoven is hit, where she discovers Molly is gone, and there instead is a collie puppy, jumping up and playfully nipping Freddie with its sharp white baby-teeth. The woman there tells her Molly has been adopted by an older man whose wife recently passed away. His wife's name was not Molly, no. She agrees that would have been a strange coincidence. Freddie asks for his phone number so she can give him the gift basket. She isn't going to use it now—it isn't puppy food and besides, Freddie definitely can't look after a puppy. "It's good to recognize that," the woman says, somewhat condescendingly although Freddie doesn't notice.

"Thank you."

The puppy will be gone by the end of the day, she adds, perhaps to reassure Freddie that it would not languish here long or to emphasize that Freddie need not play any part in its life. The woman can't give out the man's number, a privacy issue, although Freddie expects she'll run into him and Molly on a trail one day. But Freddie can donate the basket.

Six cats, however, languish in their cells. Freddie chooses Elle, one ear notched and sleep in her eyes. When Freddie pets her, a cloud of short black fur swirls away. A shedder. Elle is six. Freddie can guarantee she'll look after Elle until the end of her life. "Six is my lucky number," she says. But the woman requires a form from the landlord confirming that Freddie is permitted to have a cat. "Don said pets are okay," Freddie tells her, but this isn't enough.

"Unfortunately, we can't just take your word for it." And Freddie needs to get a crate.

She will come back. She won't just leave her there.

Soon after, posters go up pleading for Beethoven's safe return, and postings on Facebook in the FYI community group also display a photo of Beethoven by the trampoline, a wide stance and a happy, relaxed mouth, tongue hanging out and tail confident and alert. As Freddie no longer explores the neighbourhood on foot, she never sees any of these cries for help.

Escaping the noise of the excavator, she continues with her outings—a trip to the pool, more DVDs from the library, gathering Jack pine needles for Willow, whom she hasn't seen since the grocery store. Was that a long time ago? Willow said she'd talk to her later, which means anything after now. But this improvised schedule takes its toll. At the mailboxes, Freddie can't remember which one is hers, and she stands there with her key out, willing her brain to make a connection. When she returns home, she realizes she's missed another session with Betsy.

In the end, Robert finds Beethoven himself. He passes not one, but two dead deer on his drive back from the lumberyard and wonders if people are driving like idiots or if the deer are getting dumber. Without thinking, he begins scanning the shoulders and ditches for roadkill, when his eye catches the soiled white fur of Beethoven's belly in the periwinkle.

꙳

Freddie is watching *Shaun the Sheep* on mute, ear plugs muting almost everything else, when she notices the excavator has finally stopped. She takes out the ear plugs. No trampoline springs or woodpecker or barking dog. Only the distant whinny of a robin. Another day passes like this and she feels some relief, not just for her but for Beethoven, too. All that barking must have tired his voice out—he was running the risk of becoming hoarse, and a dog surely wouldn't want to be a horse. Freddie laughs. She wishes someone was around to hear that one. She wants to call Robert to tell him thank you for resolving this situation. She wants to give him positive reinforcement. You're welcome, he'd say. I'm sorry it took me a while to come around. I'm still learning how to be a good dog-owner. That's okay, Freddie would say. I'm just glad I don't have to learn how to be dog food. Robert laughs. You're such a kidder, Freddie.

Freddie picks up the phone but puts it down again. Picks it up. She hums in harmony with the dial tone. Puts it down. She's not supposed to phone. *Clean slate.* Maybe they should have this conversation in person, anyway, the next time they run into each other, which is bound to happen eventually.

One day as she is about to hop in her Toyota for the grocery store, Robert comes trudging across the property. He points at her. "I got something to say to you."

Freddie thinks of a swamp creature. Robert's dark clothes the colour of mud and moss, but he's not so amphibious, shaped like a man instead. "It's the frog prince!" He hasn't bothered with the driveways, so perhaps short-cuts are okay now, a gesture toward a new neighbourliness. "Hast thou been kissed?" she asks.

But as Robert gets closer, Freddie notices his lips, skinny and tense, and his hands that can't decide what to do, clenching and unclenching. "You think you're fooling anyone?" he says. He does not look like he is about to apologize.

Freddie considers the question, but before she can respond, he continues. "Cause you're not fooling me. You think you're cute?"

Freddie pinches her tie-dyed T-shirt, examining its galaxy of purples and blues. She made it for the doctor with the purple glasses, but he said it was too small, thank you.

"You hit my dog," Robert says, nodding and nodding. But Freddie has already explained this to Olivia. She hadn't hit Beethoven, she'd hit him *away*.

"He bit me first." Useful information.

This is not the response Robert wants. He strides toward Freddie and smacks the window of her car. The noise makes Freddie jump, but many noises have this effect. "You stay away from my family," Robert says, pointing at her again.

This must be how Beethoven learned his bad habits, Freddie thinks. Like those dogs on the trail that rush toward her with their accusing snouts. *He's just excited!* "They just want to be left alone," Don had said. Where is Robert's leash? Or maybe Freddie is just sensitive today. Poor sleep, too many errands, plus her stomach hurts even though she hasn't eaten any cheese. Still, there is so much unpredictable behaviour—short cuts, pointing, smacking cars, and now her right-hand begins to ache although Beethoven bit her weeks ago. Could that pain be a memory, too?

"You need to set a better example, Robert." Her knees become shaky. She looks down as she backs away. Avoid eye contact. One of her socks slouches at the top of her sandal while the other is pulled up tight, and it makes her stomach turn, the knit now like steel wool. She bends over to push the sock down. When she stands up, he's still there. An immoveable stance, fixed gaze, closed mouth, chest moving up and down. He looks like he wants something else, and she isn't sure if he needs more information. "I mean with Beethoven," she says helpfully. "I think he learned to bite from you."

Don't worry, he's friendly, that dog owner had said. Then called, "Come! Come! Come here!" smacking her thighs as she did so. In the end, she had to come to the dog, snap its leash on the collar, and Freddie stepped off the trail to let them pass.

"Go home," Freddie says to Robert.

At that moment, Robert pushes Freddie against her car, his forearm like a seatbelt over her chest. He leans into her, sharply, a kind of punctuation to his outrage. "You killed my fucking dog!" She looks every direction except to Robert's face, her eyes panicked and teary, her chin trembling, and he suddenly becomes conscious of himself as a man and Freddie as a woman. He steps back, raising his hands as if to indicate he's unarmed. "I'm not even gonna touch you," he says.

Freddie braces herself on her Toyota's sideview mirror, and Robert is afraid she might have a panic attack. He wonders if Don is home.

After a pause, Freddie asks softly, "Beethoven is dead?"

And then Robert doesn't know what to do. The truth is, the dog was for the kids, that after the first Beethoven nearly broke his wrist, he was done with dogs. "Get them a hamster," he told Olivia, but what was the point of all this acreage if the kids can't even have a dog, she protested. So along came Beethoven II, but he resented the dog, the way it barked unpredictably, the way it pulled the leash no matter how much Robert shouted at it to heel or yanked its collar to make it sit. The dog was easier to manage off a leash, on the property, until Freddie ruined that for him too. And now tears. "I told you we needed a fence," Olivia said as the children cried, cradling Beethoven's ragged chew toys like morbid relics. So, Robert's the monster again, is he?

"I never want to see your face again," Robert says.

Nausea swoops through Freddie's guts, and she gets cold inside like everything is shutting down, like there go the lights—towels up on the windows and not a horse in sight. She covers her ears, as if it's all just noise and she can block it out, but inside, the dogs in her brain cells barking, barking, barking. *Let us out!* And when she looks up again Robert has turned and is walking back toward his own property, not using the driveway like he said but cutting across. He doesn't even bother hopping from fern clump to clump, but stomps right through what remains of the mud and shallow puddles, and Freddie wonders if there are frogs hiding there, if Robert's boots are squishing their delicate bodies, if she'll find them later, dried up in the sun, their shrivelled remains like salted slugs and Freddie is angry and she is sad and she is protective and excited and territorial and fearful. She starts that roll in the back of the throat, like purring but with a voice this time, and it rises into a growl. She curls her lip into a sneer and fixes her gaze on Robert's back, willing him to turn, turn around, Robert, turn around, and he does. He turns. He looks as though he is about to speak, but Freddie beats him to it.

"Woof! Woof! Woof!" She stands, makes herself bigger, smacks the vehicle again and again. "Woof! Woof! Woof!" She barks for Beethoven, too, because even though he's no longer trapped behind that window or a piggy in the middle or tethered to a man like Robert, she knows he's not free. He's not free of suffering, he's only gone, like the master himself who went deaf, and maybe it wasn't the deafness that caused the suffering but the way people looked without sound or the sound in his own brain, too much now, *Duh-duh-duh Duuuuhhhh.* "Woof! Woof! Woof!" She should bite him, she wants to bite him, she wants to bite his hand, but he might hit her away. So she barks as authoritatively as she can, points up the driveway and then looks at it. Robert should follow her gaze. He should understand.

But he looks up at the sky, then back to Freddie. "You're fucking crazy," he says quietly and goes home.

Before the Great Leap, Freddie imagined flying. A leap from the sixth storey, how she could do it on a sunny day and it would all be wind and weightlessness and yellow light and then dark. But she wouldn't be conscious for the dark, only the light. But it wasn't like that. She climbed onto the outside of the balcony. Instead of letting go, backwards, like people do when they sky dive, she jumped, as if from a wharf, feet first. Her stomach turned as she did so, and in the same instant, profound regret. "Control-Z! Control-Z!" Freddie mimed madly tapping a keyboard when she related this to Betsy. It was a blur. Not yellow, but a chaos of light and shadow. Loud. There was nothing weightless about it at all. In fact, Freddie had never been so aware of gravity in her life.

In those moments before she jumped, though, the breeze in the leaves and the empty school field beyond, she felt relief, didn't she? She had the sense of an inevitability to this, too. Of floating along the river of time, that all the struggle up to that moment was resistance, and this leap—not a leap, but a letting go—was out of her hands. What was left to hold onto?

So that's despair, she thinks now.

When she asks Don if he'll sign her permission form for the SPCA, he says, "A cat? I think that's a fine idea. Just fine."

On the drive home from the SPCA, Elle mews from the crate, timidly at first, like a kitten, but the closer they get to Freddie's home, the louder Elle becomes until she is yowling like how Freddie imagines a cat might sound when giving birth. Elle doesn't come out of the crate on her own, even when Freddie tips it a bit, as if to pour her out. This only makes Elle edge to the back of the crate and Freddie does not want to frighten her.

"It's okay, kitty, there's no hurry," Freddie says. She puts food and water in her bedroom and leaves the open crate in there. When Freddie goes in to check on Elle, the crate is empty. She finds her under the bed, ears back and anxious cat-eyes, as if Freddie has walked in on her changing. Elle remains scarce and the next day Freddie finds her hidden behind the laundry basket in the closet, the shadowy movement and shining eyes startling Freddie and overloading her system. She's had a run of bad days lately and doesn't even pick up the phone when she sees Willow's name on the call display.

But one unremarkable afternoon, a spring drizzle and only the sporadic croaks of a few hopeful frogs nearby, Elle emerges from the bedroom. She swaggers toward the couch like she's always lived here, a tail pointed straight up, which Freddie imagines could mean confidence, like a dog, but the kind that doesn't require positive reinforcement. She is a cat, after all.

Elle sits, raises her right paw and licks it, then places it down again. She looks suddenly out the sliding door, some subtle movement catching her eye in one moment, and in the next, complete disinterest. She continues to the couch, hops up. Her charcoal fur is dusted with dandruff, but her eyes appear clear and yellow now. She sits, alert, assessing this moment, then lies down, tucking her forepaws under her chest and leaning against Freddie's thigh.

Freddie pets her behind the ear, ventures a gentle neck rub. This warm body, this creature who today chose Freddie.

She glances at her watch.

Damage

My basement suite had flooded for the second time in a month.

I wondered if the landlady, Ursula, clearing away so many of the giant firs and cedars on the steep back property had been to blame or if it was the fall, unusually wet even for the coast, that had transformed the suite from a "cozy one-bedroom for single professional, no pets" to a suffocating nursery for mould and mildew.

It wouldn't be long before I could move back. In the meantime, Ursula offered me a furnished room upstairs, in her part of the house, complete with a double bed. "I've been meaning to make a proper guest room anyway," she said. But I couldn't live with my landlady.

"I'm too old for this," I told Naomi. My girlfriend, then.

My rules were, no sleeping on Therma-rests past age thirty, no couches past thirty-five. My baseline lifestyle requirements improved in five-year increments, although my economic status did not seem to alter much at all. For Naomi, things were different. Her father, having died a few years earlier, left enough assets for her to liquidate and reconstruct into a house of her own. "Move in with me," she said.

We'd been seeing each for four months by then. So it was fast, for me, anyway, but Naomi had her own rules. No games after forty. "What's the point?" she asked, then answered her own questions. "There is no point, Rita. We're compatible and I love you. Wouldn't it be nice to come home to each other?"

I'd lived with a girlfriend only once, and for four years, until the relationship dissolved. I'd admitted to a stupid crush on another woman. It was only a crush, but a convenient excuse for my ex, I thought. She must have wanted to end things even before that. But later, I did admit to myself (not my ex) that, if the woman had shown any interest in me, it would have been an affair. So I can be honest with myself, even when it feels awful. I'd ached for that woman, the way she tucked in her shirts, tightly, highlighting an ample midsection, unashamed. I saw something rebellious in that, something carefree, so unlike my self-conscious partner who spent twenty minutes arranging her hair to look like she'd just rolled out of bed. Now when I think of the other woman, I can't believe how singular my focus was, that I masturbated fantasizing about her—imagined her yanking the shirt from behind her cheap belt, then stripping it from her body, revealing her spare tire and large pendulous tits, and climbing on top of me with unhurried lust, an ox mounting its cow.

I cringe when I think of this now, because I got to know the ox better later, and she turned out to be a real asshole.

What might have happened if I'd told my ex I felt suffocated? That I couldn't take another drunken winter of her ukulele jam group and tin cans of drowned cigarette butts on the balcony. Other things. Would she have listened? Changed? Would we still be together?

I wondered about all that, where the communication had failed, what might be possible if I just say how I feel.

Naomi, unlike the ex or the ox, was stylish and zealously direct. Even flirtation was unnecessary. "Are you attracted to me?" she said after I asked if she swam competitively. Yes, I suppose I was finding some roundabout way to comment on her body, supple. "Yes, I am," I said. It felt good to simply answer the question. Naomi had that effect on me—extracting some piece of truth I wasn't always aware of myself. It was later that I'd realized how much could be implanted.

I wanted to be clear—honest: "Do you mean move in until my place is dry again? Or until I find a new place? Because I don't know how long that's going to take."

❧

It wasn't only this that captured me about Naomi. It was sex, too. At first, anyway. With my ex, a kiss on the couch that turns into something erotic is quickly interrupted, the boundaries between normal interaction and sexual interaction fixed. Is this an erotic kiss? Are we going to have sex? Then we stop—a kiss makes a decision. Then it's time to shower and go to the bedroom and start over with the kisses and have sex. I followed her lead—she was the one who needed to shower to be comfortable, but I came to need this too, wondering about nose-blindness or what my comfort with bodily filth says about me. With Naomi, all boundaries were porous. I stood at the counter chopping pineapple for a smoothie and she slipped her hand between my bare legs, squeezing my thighs, guiding them apart like I was a goat about to be milked, but then massaging my clitoris until I abandon the pineapple to the fruit flies. I go along with these things because the idea of it—that I'm so irresistible in this moment that she must touch me—overwhelmed me with gratitude. If she wants me, she can have me.

But this was a comfortable role too. And I wondered later if it's the role I really wanted or if I'd only learned this from my ex, relinquishing my body in this way so she can tolerate her own, practised and masculine now beside my soft uncertainty.

So that afternoon with Naomi, the first time she lay on the bed, waiting, even looking shy for a moment, then asking, almost timidly, "Are you planning to fuck me," a strange excitement passed through me.

"Is that what you want?" I asked. I needed to clarify. Of course, I had the sense this is exactly what she wanted, but I hadn't known Naomi long at that time. The girlish way she asked could indicate she's triggered—is it an inner-child question? But she'd said "fuck," so that probably wasn't right.

Naomi lifted her knees to her chest, "I'm ready for you." There was something uncomfortably heterosexual about this scenario for me—something pornographic in this dialogue and presentation. During my single months, I'd begun browsing a porn website, searching for videos to hurry along my arousal for quick masturbation. But there is so much detritus to sift through—so many sexual encounters between consenting adults looking more like those of coked-up barnyard animals—and I would usually give up and concoct some fantasy of my own.

Still, with Naomi, something shifted. Just small at first. This glimpse of control. What it feels like to have power. I slid my finger in—just one because I didn't want to surprise her, to risk her discomfort. "More," she said. Then she laid her legs down flat and stuffed her hands beneath her buttocks, straining as if her own body held her hostage there.

❧

Two weeks into our cohabitation, I'd moved the last of my things into Naomi's storage unit—there was no place for it at Naomi's and the basement suite was a funhouse of tarps and dehumidifiers. I suggested I swing by Ursula's to double check that I hadn't left anything—a ring on a windowsill, a book at the top of the closet. I wasn't asking Naomi's permission, but she said, "Yes, go ahead." Perhaps it had sounded like a question.

Inside the suite, dehumidifiers whirred and hummed, and the tarps waved gently in the gusts of air from the heaters. Normally, a place looks larger when empty of furniture, but my suite looked horribly small. It was a sad little den. Without flooring, the grey concrete with its swirls of old glue was the colour of smashed shells, like a mess left by high tide. Where the mermaid tapestry used to hang were tack holes, chips in the drywall and other scrapes from various moves in and moves out. When was the last time Ursula painted? But it was difficult to find a decent suite here, especially with my unpredictable income, and this one, with its private entrance, bathtub and double kitchen sink was the best place I'd lived since sharing the house in Tahsis the last time I tree-planted. At Ursula's, I was even permitted to use the hot tub.

"There you are," said Ursula. Her long grey hair and collection of colourful fringed scarves implied a hippie past, but there was always something too neat and clean about her that made me cautious. I felt like a teenager around Ursula, reminded of visits to friends' nicer homes, the way their fathers asked me what my father did, as if making conversation but really sussing out what level of trash I am. Once I got to know Ursula better—or got used to her, anyway—this eased. It's usually like that for me, I guess. This assumption that I'm not smart enough and I'll muck up some etiquette.

"Hi Ursula," I said. "Is it okay to be here?"

"Well, it's not unsafe or something." Ursula nodded her head as if working out some plan. "I tried to call you, but you don't pick up."

It's true I'd been dodging her calls. I was afraid she would ask me something that I'd have to answer, but the answer would disappoint her so I'd just tell her something else, and this would create a whole other problem.

"I've been having problems with my voicemail," I lied.

"You didn't leave a forwarding address," Ursula said. "You said you were living with your friend? Anyway, I tried to reach you because you just up and left, and it looked like you were all moved out, so I could only assume that was the case."

"No, I'm staying with a friend. It's not permanent."

Ursula touched an orange tarp as if assessing fabric for a dress. I had the feeling she was considering two problems now instead of one.

"Okay, well, I thought you'd moved out, Rita. You didn't really inform me of what was going on here."

I became conscious then of my runny nose. It was the time of year when my nose leaked and my feet, which always felt damp and cold, began to itch, a recurring fungal infection I periodically beat into submission with medicated cream or vinegar soaks. "Sorry," I said. "I didn't know that was necessary. I'm staying with a friend until the suite is dried out. I just didn't want to invade your space upstairs while all this is going on."

Ursula smiled. "This does complicate things a little."

"How?"

"I just thought you were going to be staying upstairs. I don't know if I would have bothered to get a guest bed right now if you weren't, what with the cost of repairs and everything."

I wasn't sure if she wanted an apology or a thank-you. Maybe both. Even then, I knew Ursula deserved neither—I was the one who'd been displaced and was, as far as Ursula knew, homeless. "How can I help?" was the only question she had any right to ask, Naomi affirmed later.

"You didn't have to do all that—thank you," I said. "Sorry I didn't tell you. I guess I thought I had, but I guess we had a miscommunication."

Ursula nodded, not so much in agreement as approval. "So you don't need the room."

"No."

"Okay, that's good to know. I won't rent out the suite, then, if you're planning to return."

I would like to have seen her try. Photos on Craigslist of a suite without carpet, linoleum yanked up, tarps where doors used to be. "Thanks," I said instead.

Ursula let go of the tarp, smiled. "Of course!" She ran her hands through her hair again and adjusted the scarf. "It's going to be a little lonely here at the cottage without you." That was how Ursula referred to her gigantic house. It was probably the proximity to water and the presence of Douglas firs on the property that made her characterize it this way. Only someone with money could call a place like this a cottage.

"Yeah, hopefully it stops raining so much or we'll need to build a moat!" I joked. Sort of.

Ursula walked up the steps, her laugh like a robin's trill, melodious and practised. "I'll consider it!"

❧

I like to smoke weed. Not every day—I'm not a stoner, although Naomi disapproved, claiming this habit inhibits my work life as a painter, rendering it a series of gigs, never a business. But weed was one thing I wouldn't give up, though I kept it discreet, limiting my blissful fuzzy hours to some afternoon alone. And I had a few of those—like on the rainy days, even days with just too much humidity, when I couldn't paint the exterior of a house. And this suited me. "I earn enough," I told Naomi once, but she pointed out that I don't, that I feel short-changed, because I often complain about people like Ursula, although this class antagonism only provided an excuse to avoid examining my own behaviour. I didn't like this comment, although I couldn't really articulate why at the time. I just said her dad was rich, so she couldn't understand. "You're right." She laughed. "Pot is good for your career."

I loved Naomi—I believed I loved her. More recently, I've wondered if I actually just admired her. She was better than me, but she wanted me, and this somehow made me better, too. But when she made those comments about the pot-smoking, I saw myself as something else, a summer fling with the help, like maybe I was painting her house and she was getting off on pineapple and pussy while we waited for a coat of paint to dry. But she said she loved me, and she wanted me to live with her, so I figured this was *my* hang-up. "Maybe you're right," I said about the pot. "Maybe I should quit."

On those rainy afternoons, when I'd partake in stoned masturbation, I'd watch porn, too. It's so accessible and I'd thought up some search terms that yielded more promising results. Something about anal sex became appealing, a brutish mounting, and I'd found a couple videos of not terribly grotesque or terribly modified bodies doing this work, and it did seem like work. Of course, the clips became familiar at some point, and I searched for some variation on this theme, the woman on something like a massage table, approached clinically instead. The woman roused from a nap and turned on by one squeeze of the breast, then entered. This disgusted me, too—she couldn't possibly be interested in this surprise in real life, but it was theatre. Still, I moved past that one because I was not a person who would find this alluring.

This is how Naomi walked in on me that afternoon: upstairs in bed, the sheets twisted up at one foot, nose at the screen, a little hypnotized by this grunting female. I nearly chucked the phone across the room when I finally noticed her. "How are you so quiet!" I said.

Naomi crawled onto the bed and nabbed the phone from me. "So that's what you're into."

"I wasn't into it," I said.

She scrolled through the phone and played another video, but she lay the phone on the night table, turning up the volume first. A woman grunts in time to some unseen thrusting, the pitch rising gradually in pleasure or pain. "I could hear it as soon as I came in." Naomi undid the buttons of her shirt and pulled her jeans down. "You're happy to see me, aren't you?"

"Of course," I said. "Just surprised."

She lay on her stomach beside me. Wagged her hips, playfully, some might say. "Come on," she said, an invitation though it felt like taunting at the time. The sound of spanking from the phone.

"Come on, what?" I pretended to be uninterested.

Naomi lifted her hips to tug her underwear down, lifted her butt and then clasped the sheets as if to brace herself. "Come on," she said again. "I know you want to fuck me."

˒

Naomi would say later that she was giving me what I wanted. That I couldn't ask for these things directly, so she took on the tedious work of extracting the truth from me, and that's why she grabbed the phone. She'd get to the core of me so I wouldn't have to ask. But even as I watched these videos and felt myself getting wet, I hated them, too. This private conflict, at least, affected only my relationship to this screen, to masturbation, and perhaps indirectly with this actress, and what kind of porn she might be asked to make by filmmakers, if they're called filmmakers? It was some complex thing I was playing a small part in but separate from my relationship to the woman I loved. Sex was entirely separate from porn for me at that time.

But with Naomi like that, this invitation or taunt, the fact that she'd created this situation against my will, my phone now providing ambient sounds of what I regarded as violence—and I was angry with her for that—all of this meant I had to fuck her. Because she wanted me to, because I wanted to, because I wanted to be on top of her, proving something.

At one point, she moved her hand to rub her clitoris, and I didn't like this, how I was suddenly not enough, only supplemental. With my free hand, I took her wrist and gently moved it away, as if making a minor adjustment, something she may not even notice. But she did notice, and she moaned as if this act alone could bring her to orgasm.

Yes, I felt good after. I wasn't stoned anymore, but still fuzzy, and I thought what I'd just done had demonstrated to Naomi that weed does not inhibit anything.

Although Naomi's hair was greying, it felt silky as I petted her, and I thought she might be falling asleep. But then she said, "So what do you plan to do about Ursula?"

I'd told Naomi earlier what Ursula had said about renting out the suite. "My plan?" I repeated.

"Why don't you just tell her you moved out and get your damage deposit back?" I thought we'd discussed the risks of cohabitation, the need for a lifeboat, but Naomi continued. "You said yourself the flood is her fault."

"I don't *know* if it's her fault. I just wonder if maybe it's because she took the trees out."

Naomi sat up, leaned over to retrieve her shirt from the floor. "Did it flood last year?"

"No."

"Then it's probably her fault. You should get compensation for being displaced."

She began to dress. I reached for the twisted sheet, something to cover my body, my growing gut evidence of too much snacking, the snacking evidence of a lack of self-control, symptoms or causes of failure. Maybe it's the pot. "It's fine." I tried to change the subject. "She's nice. Nothing is damaged that bad—I didn't have anything that valuable, as you know."

"What about the accordion?"

The ex had given me the accordion. I said I liked the movie *Amelie*, so she dragged home some accordion she found at a yard sale on Canada Day. I continued dragging it from place to place. I didn't want to hurt her feelings by getting rid of it, and I thought it might be a waste of money not to at least try a lesson. But I also thought it was a stupid gift, the last in a long line of stupid gifts including a "stay-cation" at a hotel only blocks from our place. "I want to pamper you," my ex had said. I argued about that, but I guess I was also arguing about the accordion, these things I'm pushed into being grateful for. "I appreciate the gesture, but it's a waste of money," I told her. She said it was her money to waste, but she'd begun getting payday loans and this was unbearable to witness. I was the one who was good with money then. We sold the package on Craigslist.

"I don't know if it's worth much," I told Naomi.

"Doesn't matter," she said. "You need to be compensated."

It might sound now like she was just looking out for me, maybe even trying to bolster my resolve. But I felt this comment was a directive, not for Ursula, but for me, to act. I looked up at the cedar-panelled ceiling, which continued down the walls, giving the room the look of a sauna. My feet became hot and I scratched one with the other, slowly so Naomi wouldn't notice—I didn't want her to know about my foot fungus.

I felt hot, so I pushed the window open. Outside, a tree frog joined another in its croaking, then another and another, suddenly a chorus of frogs, songs of intimidation and desire.

﹃

Behind Ursula's house, a forest climbed. In the winter, branches often broke from the trees, tearing through quiet nights like sharp whip-cracks. Ursula had a tree removed the year before, one that I suggested she have assessed—leathery conks grew all around the trunk and I knew that a fungus weakens a tree by ingesting its core. "It could have killed me in my sleep," Ursula said, marvelling at how fragile and vulnerable life is. Afterwards, she viewed the forest differently. It was no longer wild and charming, a habitat to indigenous species (she always specified "indigenous"). "There are so many house sparrows around," Ursula had said one day on the back deck, disapproving. "Those are European." Soon, even the deer were vermin. "We've extirpated all the natural predators," Ursula explained, although I hadn't asked. "There should be more cougars and wolves."

Earlier that year, after attending a workshop at the Community Hall on permaculture, Ursula decided to grow her own vegetables. With the help of her "man-friend," Don, she constructed four boxes, filled with alternating layers of grass clippings, horse manure from the farm up by the Tramway Trail, straw and kitchen scraps, and planted squash, kale, cauliflower, zucchini. But the deer made regular trips through the yard, nipping any new growth. Ursula made a fence with posts and twine, brightly coloured flags of ribbon tied along, snapping in the breeze, but this didn't stop the deer either. "I have to build a brick wall to keep them out!" she complained.

I've never been a gardener—I had a small collection of potted succulents once. If they can stay alive in the desert, I figured they could survive me, too. But I'd absorbed enough about the principles of permaculture by living on the Coast. I'd been to enough Seedy Saturdays and Slo-food festivals and Wildlife Society talks on installing bee houses and bird houses and bat houses and which flowers to plant to attract which birds and bugs, transforming any yard into a veritable Eden to know that the solution to deer in the garden was not a brick wall.

"I think there's deer fencing at Canadian Tire," I said.

"I'm not doing that. It'll look like I'm on the set of *M*A*S*H*. Who wants to be fenced in like that?"

Soon, Ursula complained of the shade on the property. The trees that had once cast a fairy-tale shadow, now only obscured her vision. The ferns, which she had considered prehistoric and mystical ("They're as old as the dinosaurs, you know"), now were out-of-control weeds, the only useless thing that can grow in this acidic soil. Ursula envisioned a vast lawn. "Have you ever been to Versailles? It's so open—you can breathe there. I just can't breathe here. I shouldn't have to feel like that, living so close to the ocean."

She had trees removed, weeks of chainsaw work that upset one of the neighbours, who was at home during the day, living on a disability pension. "She complains about everything." Ursula tossed the last sips from her coffee mug onto the lawn. "It's my property. Am I not allowed to renovate because she can't hear her soaps?"

I doubted this woman was bilking the government so she could watch soap operas, but I just shrugged, wondering myself how much longer the noise would continue. I started my "gig" at seven in the morning, so was usually home by three-thirty, early enough to hear the din of chainsaws for at least another hour and a half.

In the end, Ursula left enough trees to be useful—she strung a hammock between two large firs and suggested she could have a treehouse built in another one, for the grandkids "when they get out of diapers." At the back of the property was a wall of forest that rose farther up the mountain. In a way, it was nicer, more breathable. There was space and a horizon distant enough to see the mountain behind, whereas before, it had been concealed by the trees. The tree service company ground down the remaining stumps and the turf company followed, unrolling a green carpet over compacted soil.

Naomi seemed pleased when I talked about all this, using words like *hydrology* and *drainage*. "I'm not a total bumpkin," I said. I like to read. So I do take initiative sometimes.

~

Naomi told me to make an inventory of my belongings, their value, and a description of the damage and then find out what it would cost to fix or replace them. This would be the foundation of Ursula's bill.

I'd learned it was better not to counter a suggestion like this. Naomi would follow up, offer to help, so it was no use saying I would do it and then not do it. It was easier just to do what she suggested. Besides, part of me was grateful for the direction. No one ever walked over Naomi, I was sure, and I knew I should be more like that.

The accordion, stored in its case on the closet floor in an inch of water, was now spotted, a Dalmatian pattern of mould overtaking its pearl exterior. Several of its keys rested too far up in a buck-toothed smile, and I wasn't sure if that, too, was the result of water or if I'd caused the damage during one of its many moves, things piled upon things. I looked up similar accordions online, prices ranging from less than two hundred bucks to more than a thousand. But mine was in terrible shape.

I'd brought it into the house to have a look, to see if I could learn something new about its worth by awkwardly handling it. Naomi came home to find me testing notes, moving the bellows in and out. It was easy to move them, which I've learned indicates a leak.

Naomi did what she always does the minute she walks in the door— turns on the electric kettle, takes the tea tin out to select a flavour, the mug, then finally removes her shoes. I placed the accordion back in its water-stained case, and gently closed it, hoping to avoid a conversation about the instrument.

"Is that the accordion?" Naomi asked. "The case looks quite damaged."

"It looks better than the accordion." I immediately regretted this comment.

Naomi smiled. "Hm," she said, like I'd given her a clue to something. She turned and held the kettle's handle as she waited. When the switch flipped, she filled her mug. Somehow, she can drink the tea immediately after the water has boiled. She joined me by the accordion. "You should take that to someone for a repair quote." She squatted and opened the case. "Smells like mould. That's bad."

To be fair, Naomi might have been under the impression the accordion was a valued possession. I had told her so, early on, by accident. Naomi had been describing her grandfather, how he'd founded some cultural centre in the prairie town where he'd found himself after the war. She had faint memories of him, mostly about cigarettes and a beard, and the dingy case that housed his accordion. He sometimes played, clumsily, she said, recalling then with more detail his tobacco-stained fingers and shaky hands.

"I have an accordion," I'd said, wanting to share something with this fascinating woman. "But I don't play. It's on the bucket list, I guess."

"You guess?" Naomi always teased me about my uncertainties. I wonder now if that was a red flag. I think now I would see that as a red flag.

But I just laughed at that time. "I *want* to play. I have one, so that's half the battle." For a moment, this almost seemed true. "Timing is everything."

$$\text{\textcommabelow{}}$$

Hello Ursula,

How are things going with the suite? At least it hasn't rained this week! But I guess we can't really count on the dry weather for long, eh?

I'm sure you've got so much on your plate right now, but I wanted to send this along in case you need it for budgeting or insurance or something. Anyway, I have attached a list of damaged items from the flood and the cost of repairs. Fortunately (or kind of depressingly?) I don't have much of value, so the main thing is just the accordion. I took it to a guy in Vancouver when I was there and he said it would cost more to repair it than to *replace it and that I could get a similar one in Vancouver for around $500. He said they are cheap in Vancouver, and he seemed kind of miffed about that, but good news for us, right?*

Also, I'm sure you just forgot, but I paid rent for the full month of September, but had to move out before the last week, so that last week of rent is owing too. I did some research, and turns out this situation is called a "frustrated tenancy," so we can just cancel the tenancy, which maybe will take some stress off you, too? You don't need to worry about getting everything fixed super fast. Anyway, that being the case, you could also include my damage deposit with the cheque. It can be forwarded to my friend's place (address below) or I could come pick it up if you want.

Rita

By the time I pressed "Send," my hands were shaking. I re-read it, rather pointlessly, after sending, scanning for hostility or anything overly bossy. Nope, all good. I had Ursula's best interests in mind, mostly—the thing about taking her time for repairs. Should I have called it an invoice, though? I worried that was too formal and may get Ursula's back up. But it was an invoice, that's what it was.

I told Naomi I sent the email. "Good," she said. "*En garde.*"

Naomi had said this was just Ursula's duty as a landlord, that she was a businesswoman—maybe not now, but she'd run the Sun Coast Market for at least ten years, so this would just be another invoice to square up with. "You're the only one who thinks this is awkward," she'd told me. "You're just uncomfortable with money."

And now, *en garde.* "I was nice about it," I said. "It was a polite email."

"I hope you weren't too nice. You could have shown me the letter before you sent it." Naomi lay on the couch and stretched her legs out, placing her feet in my lap. This was another routine we'd developed, watching documentaries and me holding Naomi's feet. I usually didn't mind—her feet were pedicured, skin buffed, unlike mine, where dead skin flaked between my toes. But on that night, I didn't like the weight of them there. I wanted to feel I could get up at any moment, without disturbing anyone.

"I just wanted to get it over with." I lifted her feet and got up.

"Where are you going?"

"I just have to go to the bathroom."

Naomi followed me. We'd reached the point in our relationship when we could pee in front of each other. Naomi slid the pocket door aside. I was examining my face in the mirror. I had a young face and had been ID-ed into my thirties. That hadn't happened in a decade. The shift occurred suddenly, after a long season in the bush followed by a shorter haircut. I'd grown my hair out again, but it never gets very long. Too curly. My hair is as unpredictable as the weather, sometimes expanding into frizzy ringlets as the humidity rises, other days relaxing into something almost passably stylish, except for the hairs floating up with static electricity. I couldn't be bothered to use "product," as Naomi called it, and I could never shave my head like she did—I'd only look dumpier. So my solution was to subdue my hair. I yanked it into a tiny ponytail and restrained the wiry curls with pins and clips. I examined the wrinkles around my eyes, not from age but weather. And I was becoming jowly. I took the pins and the elastic out to let my hair rise like bread dough.

"You're upset," Naomi said.

I fluffed my hair. I didn't like it when Naomi looked in the mirror to talk to me. I didn't like seeing my face next to hers.

"This is hard for you. I'm just used to taking charge of things."

Was she expressing compassion? Contrition? I thought I heard a tone of pity, or even contempt. I wanted to snub her, now that I had something of an upper hand, possibly. She wanted me to respond, surely. So this is something I could withhold, but that would be poor communication. I wanted to be a good communicator. So I turned it into a joke. Maybe that was a mistake. Maybe that was a moment when I should've "spoken my truth" or "spoke truth to power," as I've since learned, assuming Naomi had the power. I think she did. It felt like it, but maybe if I'd just told her how I felt—that she was being bossy, that I wanted to handle Ursula my own way, which is to do nothing and so what. I did make it to forty without Naomi, after all. If I'd told her that, everything would have shifted. Instead, I said, "You don't always take charge," alluding to sex, how I was basically the top, I guess. I don't use that term, but I suppose it's accurate. "Get upstairs," I ventured. It felt strange, giving an order, and I heard myself saying it like reading a line in a script, but Naomi didn't seem to notice.

"Whatever you say," she said, and walked slowly up the stairs, me following patiently behind.

❧

Dear Rita,

I do not believe you have met the time requirement to deem this a frustrated tenancy. I offered you a room in my home while repairs were undertaken, and those repairs are nearing completion. As far as your property is concerned, that is what tenant's insurance is for. It is not my responsibility to compensate you for flood damage. I do not control the rain.

You do not have to pay rent for the time the suite is not inhabitable, but you do need to give notice. The suite will be ready for you to move in again within the week. If you are giving one-month notice, you will have to pay rent for three weeks of the remaining month, less the week of rent still owed to you (that was correct and I am aware of that), which makes it two weeks' rent still owed to me. I can apply the security deposit to this amount and we can call it even, if you do not intend to move back in.

Ursula

Obviously, I didn't tell Naomi about Ursula's response. I wanted to drop it. Before Naomi, I would have. The damage deposit was a sunk cost. It wasn't an amount I missed—I didn't need a deposit at Naomi's—but that was a childish way to think about money. Something that perpetuates my class antagonism, I guess.

❧

In the two weeks that followed, the maples became bare and the trails to the creek were soggy with decaying leaves. Mushrooms and fungi spotted the forest floor, fluorescent orange sponges popping out of rotting stumps and deadfall, conks the colour of Jupiter's storms docked to other trees, which appear to go on living, but are, in fact, dead.

I could see my breath when I exhaled and I had the feeling of being immersed in water, of swimming through the woods. My toes were always cold, despite the wool socks, yet somehow also sweaty, making the socks damp. I never dressed for the weather, according to Naomi, who wore gloves and a base layer merino wool shirt even on milder days. I crossed my arms and hurried faster up the slope toward the old tramway.

"Want my scarf?" Naomi called up to me.

"I'm fine. It's good for the metabolism, I think." I jogged cartoonishly in one place, as Naomi caught up to me and kissed me. This was a habit of hers, to kiss me whenever we paused on a trail. I thought it was romantic. I took it as affection. I don't see what else it could be, so that was one of her sweet habits.

I took Naomi's hand, but her leather glove felt too cold, so I stuffed my hands in my own pockets, along with the balled-up Kleenex.

As we approached what remained of the steam donkey, a rusting vessel with moss and fern growing up all around it, two hikers headed toward us, returning from one of the upper viewpoints. They laughed as the first one stopped to unsnag her delicate orange scarf from the tip of a low-hanging branch, then tucked it safely into her sweater, a pattern of alpaca silhouettes knitted into it: Ursula.

I thought I recognized the other woman from a realty billboard. Her wide-set eyes and patronizing smile reminded me of Oprah, but her greying hair was cut into a distinctly unglamorous bowl. She jabbed her telescopic hiking poles into the ground like they were her emergency brake. "Hello," the woman nodded, standing to one mossy side of the trail for Naomi and me to pass, but Naomi wanted to examine the steam donkey first.

"It's amazing they got this up here," Naomi said.

Ursula smiled politely. "Yes." A waft of patchouli.

Rain began to make its way down through the forest, pattering on the few leaves that remained and tinkling softly from the boughs. Out of the trees, it would no doubt be much wetter.

"It's starting to rain," I said.

Ursula stepped past me to where Bowl-Cut was waiting, and I realized she intended to continue her walk without acknowledging me at all. I wouldn't let her.

"Naomi, this is Ursula," I said.

Ursula turned, touched her wrist as if adjusting a watch and nodded to Naomi. "Nice to meet you." Then, to me, "Is this the friend you're staying with?"

"I am she," Naomi said. I loved how she said that, how formal she sounded and how gorgeous she looked, her skin dewy and shining, even in this dim setting.

Bowl-Cut was now staring down at the dirt, leaning over her poles, as if examining some patch of lichen. I knew then that Ursula had talked about me to this woman.

"That I'm *living* with, yes, my girlfriend."

"That you're living with," Ursula repeated. "That's nice." She nodded, as if there was something satisfying about this remark, but I knew she didn't feel as smug as she appeared. "Feel free to make that official any time you like." She looked to Naomi. "Nice meeting you. The waterfall is quite something today if you're heading up farther, but it does get a bit muddy."

She glanced at my feet, my thrift-shop triumph, a pair of Doc Martens with purple laces, scuffed and worn. I don't need four-hundred-dollar boots just to go for a walk.

"It may be a bit wet," she added.

"That's okay," I said. "I'm used to it."

Ursula laughed but did not have a response. She turned to hike down the trail and I felt an urge to push her, or grab the ends of her scarf and pull, tighten it around her neck until Ursula fell backward. "Watch your step!" I called after them.

"What's that?" Ursula said.

"Just watch your step. It's slippery and you don't have poles. I don't want you to break a hip."

I regretted the comment. Ageist. And I wasn't so far behind—maybe fifteen years? I knew I came out sounding like a spiteful teenager.

A woodpecker pummelled a tree nearby. The bird hopped upward and tried again, searching for larvae, ants or a home to nest, a soft spot to tunnel into the rotted core. Ursula glanced in its direction. Then, without looking at me, she and her friend turned and continued down. I could feel Naomi's eyes on me. "What?" I said. "That was interesting." Naomi laughed. She held up one hand in a claw and hissed. "What can I say? She deserves it." I spotted the bird as it drilled one more time. "That's a hairy woodpecker. They're indigenous."

⟩

I don't want to just blame everything on Naomi or Ursula. *I am an adult and empowered to make my own choices.* That's something I've started saying to myself every day. It's awkward, though why should it be? I *am* an adult—I'm forty-one. That's middle-aged, even. So I do make my own choices, obviously. Still, it doesn't sound right, and there is some voice inside me, maybe whiny, that says it's not that simple. Something about money, about privilege, about a power dynamic I couldn't define because I couldn't see it and Naomi was paying for groceries. *...an excuse to avoid examining your own behaviour.* But is it better to listen to Naomi's voice dismissing my childish protests?

⟩

After the day at the steam donkey, it rained and rained. Rain had never been so satisfying. It slammed down washing over roads and rivering along sidewalks. The grassy path from the backyard soaked in rain, and reminded me of tree-planting, when I was tasked with filling a beetle-killed pine forest with new seedlings, jamming the delicate plugs into sphagnum moss, a forest floor like wet sponges.

With the window open, the *thwump-thwump-thwump* of rain on the summer umbrella filled the room. Frogs croaked their appreciation and Naomi and I lay in bed, quiet. I wondered about calling Ursula's bluff, saying, "Okay, you're right, it's not a frustrated tenancy. I'm going to move my stuff back in." Naomi tickled my arm and drew circles with her finger on my stomach and around my breasts, her eyes closed, and she smiled softly. Sometimes it was like that. Quiet. In the quiet, I could be honest. I think I feel that way still. No words to obscure the body. She sat up on her elbow and moved her hand down my legs.

It took so little to provoke my arousal. All Naomi had to do was open her mouth, a sideways smile that looked like she was about to ask a question. The answer was always yes. I wouldn't mind being taken over by her. I wanted to weakly clasp her arms as she fingered me, like oh yes, whatever you want from me, take it, but this was never what Naomi wanted.

She lay back and stuffed her hands under her pillow. I held her arms and pushed my tongue into her mouth. Naomi tried to lift her arms, as if she wanted to get up, but I'd learned that she only does this to amplify the restraint, so I kept kissing. This was easier by then, because I was sure this was what she wanted, that although I may be the one on top, the one holding her down, Naomi was in control—it was consensual, safe. Perhaps even something like a trust exercise, a therapeutic activity to promote intimacy.

"I can't get up," Naomi said.

I kissed her neck and she twisted her face away from me. "Please stop," she whispered.

I stopped.

Everyone knows what a "safe word" is, some entirely unsexy word selected to break character from a sexual role-play, or to stop the encounter, I suppose. Same thing. Words like *avocado* or *capri pants*. After all, "stop," may be part of the role play. Since this word had, presumably, become part of Naomi's fantasy, I thought it would be responsible and good communication to decide on a safe word.

"A safe word?" Naomi laughed. "If I want you to stop, believe me, you'll know it."

"How will I know it?"

"You can't tell the difference between honesty and pretending?" Naomi petted my cheek. "Okay, just because I love you, let's go with... *fungus*. Then we'll immediately think of your feet and you'll get shy and go hide under the blanket. How about that?"

I might've had a look of horror at that point because I didn't realize she'd even noticed my feet. I never put my feet in her lap and I kept my cream in my own toiletries container. Maybe she knew I was embarrassed, and she thought acknowledging this would help de-stigmatize it.

I lay my face on the pillow beside her and laughed. "Please kill me now."

"Yeah? You want me to kill you?"

"No. I mean *fungus*."

But I felt reassured at least that there would be no ambiguity.

I was awkward at first when I said, "I'm going to fuck you," and Naomi noticed.

"Are you sure?" she teased, which was nice. Levity. This was supposed to be fun, after all. Sex is fun.

"I think so," I said. "I mean I washed my hands and everything."

Then Naomi brought us back. "What if I say no?"

I had never considered whether I actually wanted to fuck my girlfriend as she cried out, "Stop." It was just a fantasy. Naomi's fantasy. Though actually, I don't think she ever said stop again. Or no or let me go. These protests moved inward, mute, but I could still read them on her body, and the more we did this, the more the fantasies became mine, too.

Another time, she wanted me to fuck her from behind, and I believe that privately, she imagined she was sleeping. Another time, she wanted me to do this as she stood, pushing herself against the wall, and she widened her stance in a way that did not look comfortable. I don't know what she imagined then, but this is what sex became for me. And when Naomi wanted to make me orgasm, she asked me to sit and she kneeled and sucked or even straddled me as she pushed her fingers inside. So I got used to this and, like I said, I enjoyed this glimpse of what felt like control in some way, but not quite. Even my flabby gut bothered me less, as if the more masculine my role became, the less the shape of me mattered. My flesh was not meant for consumption; I was the fire. I would learn that over the coming months with Naomi, and sometimes this would feel like power.

But I remember that afternoon as the beginning.

So when she asked me, "What if I say no?" I thought, as long as she didn't say "fungus," it didn't matter. I answered by pushing two fingers inside. She caught her breath suddenly, and I worried I'd surprised her, for a moment I worried, that maybe I'd even caused a little pain. "Is that too much?" I nearly asked. But Naomi began pushing her hips down onto my hand. "Don't move," I said, knowing this is what she wanted, and Naomi stopped. She lay quietly, resting her hands at her sides. With her body limp like that, I felt as though I were molesting a scared teenager. Something inside me fell away. Inhibition, I thought at the time.

ᣂ

When I first learned about Naomi's business, I assumed the products were emblematic of her values—natural face masks and cleansers made locally, with local ingredients like locally harvested kelp, indicated a passion for sustainability and healthy living. But I later learned that promoting sustainability or health (or skincare) was not at all what drove Naomi. The reason for the product was twofold: First, "local" and "natural," in Naomi's opinion, were buzz words, a branding tool, and the reason her product found distribution in lodges and spas across most of the province, not to mention health food stores and a substantial amount of e-commerce. Second, she had access to the key ingredients that got her started—kelp, which she harvested herself and highlighted by providing GPS coordinates of the harvest location on each bottle, and marine clay, which she had access to after her father's death. He'd purchased acreage on the North Coast several years earlier with the idea of building a summer cabin, something which never was realized for some reason. Naomi had forgotten about this cabin-in-the-woods fantasy until she inherited that property. There, she had access to a substantial intertidal clay deposit and knew to test its efficacy for costly applications like spa mud and facial masks. Within a year, she had hired her first staff and since that time, the business has grown, but not so much that Naomi didn't oversee all aspects, from harvesting to package design.

"Obviously, I want the products to be sustainable," Naomi had said. "But that's not why I do it."

I certainly had never considered a mission or branding when it came to my painting business. I had my name and number on the rear window of my minivan and occasionally updated my posting on Craigslist, and this had always been enough. I thought about calling my business "Woman in Labour" once. I told Naomi because I thought it was funny and maybe clever. "But you just paint," she said. "*Labour* makes it sound like you're a handyman."

What got Naomi most excited when talking about her business was not the feedback on the products or new ideas like aromatherapy lines or, conversely, stripped-down recipes for those with greater sensitivity, but sales, particularly the kind of sales that displaced another product, something she asked for in exchange for a better wholesale price to a certain health-food store chain.

"*Terranium Clay is hand-harvested on British Columbia's rugged North Coast,*" Naomi read. She didn't want to tell me where, exactly, the property was. "Corporate secret," she said.

"What do you think your dad would say about all this?" I asked her once.

Naomi laughed. "Probably nothing. Maybe marvel at how much people will pay for mud."

So when it came to money, I did value Naomi's input. I never said I didn't want it.

> ⟩

Ursula,

I ran into Tim the other day, who obviously doesn't know that I am not living in your spare room like a teenager. He asked how we were getting along, adding something about "third time's a charm," and saying eventually summer will come and maybe by then the suite will be dry. This he found very funny.

So I guess I can assume the suite has flooded a third time. Why am I not surprised? You said you don't control the rain, but you did control the deforestation of the property. Ever heard of hydrology? Did you know that trees drink water? So actually, the flooding is your fault. Besides that, the whole process of logging the backyard caused the "loss of quiet enjoyment" for weeks and I have up to two years to make a claim for compensation. So I could ask for money for that, too, but in the spirit of neighbourliness, I won't. But if this continues, I will and I will take this to arbitration. I have obviously moved out now because the tenancy agreement is frustrated and I have Tim as a witness if I need, too.

You can forward the cheque to the address below.

Rita

❧

I don't believe I am exceptionally negligent when it comes to this foot fungus. Naomi, for example, has spent countless evenings at a public pool, walking around Croc-less, and has never had a fungal infection. I, on the other, am routinely re-infected. I believe I will never be rid of the fungus; it's about management.

At that time, I was using an over-the-counter cream but skipping the vinegar soaks because I didn't want Naomi to see me doing that. My feet itched more and more, especially after a shower. There were now streaks of dead skin on the soles, as well as the flaking bits between my toes and beneath that, they were red and raw. I wondered how it got out of control so quickly. I went to the walk-in clinic and got a prescription cream that I was expected to apply twice daily for two weeks. No matter how cold I was, my feet felt sweaty and damp in my boots. I started changing my socks several times a day to warm up. The laundry bin filled with blue wool socks.

"Have you heard back from Ursula yet?" Naomi asked me one evening. She'd paused the documentary on crocodiles to get a snack. The monochrome nighttime footage froze hundreds of crocodiles in their polite procession for a piece of dead hippo. I hadn't told Naomi about Ursula's last letter, or that I'd already replied.

Naomi smeared peanut butter onto toast with a steak knife, then cleaned the knife with her tongue, licking from its dull spine toward the serrated edge.

"Yes," I said. "And then I emailed her again. She's being a pain, predictably."

"What did you say?"

"I just pointed out that the flood was her fault. But I have no proof, so it's all just bluffing. If she doesn't send me anything, there's really nothing I can do about it."

Naomi was shaking her head.

"What?" I said.

"There's something else going on here."

"Can we watch the show now, please?"

Naomi put her plate of toast on the coffee table and sank back onto the couch without taking a bite. She pulled gently at the curls at the base of my neck, and I could feel her spiralling one around her finger. "You're so cute," she said. "You never get mad."

"Yes, I do."

"You don't express it very well then."

I picked up the remote. "Would it help if I threw this?"

The truth is that I wasn't expressing myself very well. I was already annoyed with Naomi. Earlier that day, a package had arrived in the mail, addressed to me. She'd purchased it for me online. "What is it?" I had asked.

"A gift." Naomi handed me a steak knife to open the box. Inside was a dildo, but not the kind I'd ever used before. It wasn't firm or erect on its base, but soft and fleshy, an imitation of a flaccid penis, with something like a scrotum where a simple geometric base for the harness would normally be. The copper colour swirled with threads of black so that is almost looked like wood grain, but the feel of it was all wrong. The texture reminded me of strange children's goo, the kind whipped at walls then laughed at as it slowly then suddenly plopped off.

"It's to wear," Naomi explained. "See how it feels to walk around with a full package. It changes how you walk—you'll see what I mean. It makes you feel powerful."

Sometimes Naomi said things strikingly unfeminist for a lesbian. A strange "forgive and forget" comment about a celebrity rapist, another comment about women aging badly compared to men. I almost didn't hear these things, an odd noise I couldn't place but rationalized into bird song or the overtones of a distant vehicle.

"Will you wear this for me?" she asked.

"I don't want to be a guy."

"That's not what it's for. You just have to try it—you'll see what I mean." She held the dildo against my groin then and kissed my neck. Despite my annoyance, I found myself getting turned on. I imagined Naomi on the floor in front of me, kneeling. Later, Naomi boiled it, "to disinfect it," and I had served it to her on a plate at dinner for a joke. It seemed like that might have been the end of it, an expensive joke, until the crocodiles began tearing into the hippo.

"Just try it." Naomi took the remote, my hand now an empty threat. "You'll see what I mean."

◥

I'd moved into Ursula's suite the previous spring. It was unusually dry that summer, so Ursula spent most afternoons on the back porch reading novels and drinking her homemade sugar-free iced teas. The door to my suite was beside the porch, so she was unavoidable. Ursula described her iced teas like they were medicines, citing the health benefits of various spices and leaves, outlined the plots of novels she was reading, always trying to summarize the moral of the story, to pin it down, even at the beginning, as if it was all just a riddle to solve. After a few of these interactions, she invited me to come up and use the porch whenever I wanted. There was also a hot tub in the yard, which Ursula had not "fired up" yet, but if I thought I might enjoy it, she would. "It's just such a waste of energy if it's only me." The hot tub was her ex-husband's idea, but then he'd hardly used it after the first couple of months.

I managed polite excuses to avoid sitting up there with Ursula. I thought this would imply a friendship and I wasn't sure yet if this was a good idea, if I'd feel obligated to visit even when I no longer wanted to, since Ursula was my landlord. As the weather grew hotter, Ursula wore less, opting for loose Mexican blouses over a bathing suit, her skin getting darker and always shiny with coconut oil tanning products, which I could sometimes smell even from my door. But Ursula kept up the chit-chat, peppered with allusions to the ex-husband, Rory, a painful divorce and casual complaints about men her age, that the "pickings are slim," and "you're lucky you're gay."

It was obvious to me that Ursula was lonely for company. Maybe more than company.

Eventually, I had to join her on the porch, and it didn't turn out to be so bad. Ursula once said I had a fascinating life, after I'd described some particularly horrible day of tree-planting, involving a windstorm, falling trees and a grizzly bear. I felt like I had too many of these stories—not stories, nothing so meaningful as stories—just anecdotes of petty hardships. But I've never experienced any great loss—I never had anything to risk, really. I said this once to Ursula for some reason.

"You'll meet someone," she reassured me, although that wasn't what I was getting at. "I already had my one-and-only, but that's over now. It's such a cliché story, that's almost the worst part. I never told you what happened with Rory, did I?"

I said no.

"He had an affair. A post-modern affair." I suppose I looked puzzled then. "Online," she clarified. "First, he became addicted to Internet porn, which, it turns out, is a real problem for a lot of people these days. Did you know that? Eight-year-olds are watching it. It's just everywhere." Ursula dog-eared a page in her paperback. "You probably think I'm just uptight, to be so offended by it, but you young people don't understand. When I was your age, we protested things like this. Not me, specifically, but many women I knew. Some women I knew. But it wasn't just the pornography." Ursula rolled the paperback into a tube. She usually had some giant hardcover in her lap, and I was curious about the ratty slim volume she had now.

Ursula explained how the computer (they had one desktop in the home office) started to get all these pop-up ads for pornography sites and she was worried about the computer having a virus, something she didn't understand. "But surely all those fake-breasted oily women must be a symptom of some kind of disease," she joked. Rory said it's nothing to worry about, but Ursula, being the one to do things like pay bills and call tradesmen, took care of it by contacting Mitchell, the computer guy who also sells spot prawns. Mitchell looked embarrassed when he came over to clean up her computer, evading her questions about the causes of the ads. "Look, Mitchell," she'd said, "I really want to know so I can deal with this if it happens again." He explained about cookies, targeted advertising, web viruses, asked if she'd downloaded any free software. Ursula didn't know, so Mitchell went through the browser history, revealing a long list of websites with names like "butt-fucked-teens" and "deep-anal." She didn't tell Rory. Ursula usually went to bed before him, and she'd never given that much thought, but after Mitchell's visit, she began to wonder if Rory was staying up only to look at "some old fart sticking his thing into an eighteen-year-old."

"It sickened me. I was going to confront him about it, but what do you even say? It's sick, isn't it?"

At that time, I hadn't really looked at porn much. I shrugged, because I knew a lot of people did, so it's common. And if it's common, I thought, it probably wasn't "sick."

"Well, I wasn't going to confront him," Ursula continued. "But then I found out about the online chatting. Do you know about that? Online video chatting. I found out about that in the history list, too. It was all there. Stupid man. He even saved his password on the website so I could login and see all the messages he'd ever sent her. I don't know who she is to be desperate enough to want to talk to Rory." Ursula laughed, but it was obvious she didn't think it was funny. She rolled her book the other way, flitting her thumb across the edge of the pages. She kept her eyes on the book when she spoke next. "I honestly think I'm just done with men." She looked up at me, smiled, as if she'd offered some happy conclusion to the story. "Ready for a new chapter." She held up the book. "No pun intended."

I could see the cover then. Ursula was reading *Ruby Fruit Jungle*, a book that came out before I was born, but being a lesbian classic, and the author also named Rita, I'd read it when I was nineteen. I stumbled across it at the library—the cover was turned face-out, as if by fate, and I knew instinctively that a book with such a title was somehow connected to being a woman who wants to have sex with other women. "Rita Mae Brown," I said to Ursula, pointing at the book.

"You know it?"

"Yeah, of course. It's in the syllabus."

"You're taking a course?"

I shook my head. "The lesbian syllabus. I'm just kidding."

Ursula laughed, too much. Offered me a drink.

"This isn't iced tea," I said.

"I'm mixing things up."

But Naomi didn't need to know about all that. That has nothing to do with the frustrated tenancy. Still, when Naomi said, "There's something else going on here," I thought of Ursula that day, her golden legs and hard lemonade.

᠀

Naomi had a meeting in the city with a spa on the west side, one with locations in the Interior and on Vancouver Island. Her usual T-shirt and jeans were replaced with crisp, black drainpipe pants and blazer, black shirt, deep-blue tie, shoes pointed and shiny. She added an ear clip, a silver ring that hugged the cartilage with a delicate chain hanging down just past her earlobe. She squeezed a dime-sized amount of Terranium skin oil onto her hands and smeared her face, giving it a slight sheen. Everything about her was streamlined.

"Wow," I said.

"I'm in the beauty business." Naomi struck a pose, offering her profile, one hand placed gently under chin, Nefertiti.

᠀

I've never thought of myself as beautiful. There is something disorganized about my appearance, too short, features too round. Cute, possibly, in a clumsy, childlike way. But my ex would compliment my "sweet smile and luscious ass," and I'd be happy about that version of myself, though I'd wonder how I ended up in such a costume. The role wasn't uncomfortable—who doesn't want to be desired? Or maybe it was just the appreciation, the way she smiled and nodded when she slid her fingers inside me, asked, "Is that alright? You okay?" like she wants to take care of me. "Uh-huh," I'd say, and maybe I was childlike then. Maybe I'd meant to be. I think she liked that, too. "That is some beautiful music," she said once when I moaned. I felt embarrassed by that, not just because it's corny as hell, but because I'd never thought of myself as beautiful. Perhaps there was something therapeutic in the way she changed that story. Still, a story requires actors.

With Naomi, I was not the beautiful one. Not by a thousand miles. *Corporate secret.* But it's good to "step outside your comfort zone," they say. I imagine this zone as a circle, that no matter which direction I step out from, I move to the same productive and uncomfortable place. This is where growth occurs. But I can't help thinking of phellinus, a tree fungus I was instructed to avoid when tree-planting. I plug the rugged terrain with seedlings, scanning for microsites within my own radius—two, maybe three metres, until I stumble upon an infected stump, the core like soggy paper: phellinus. And I must backtrack, pull up any pine seedlings—within an eight-metre radius was it?—and replace with fir. It's not that no tree will grow near such a stump, but others may rot inside.

Now I realize I was never comfortable with sex with Naomi. Partly because she intimidated me, not on purpose, but because she was better than me, though I liked it for that same reason. I doubt I wanted Naomi to slide her hands into me and smile with appreciation, say what beautiful music I make. I wouldn't have believed her, anyway. So I was also considering this new story Naomi told, that I am a person who takes what I want, and she is a person helpless to deny me. I hadn't forgotten my newest costume, the dildo, which Naomi had tucked along with her lube and harness and erect dildos, items we hadn't used. I had never been into "gear," as I called it then, and I asked Naomi about this etiquette, if it's appropriate to use the same dildo with a girlfriend that she'd used with an ex.

"It's mine," she said. "You're not the first mouth on my pussy, either. You okay with that?"

I opened the window and smoked a bit of weed first. The rain pelted the tin roof of the shed outside and a squirrel peeped that relentless, annoyed peep. Something cackled nearby. A robin or a flicker, maybe? I wondered if there was some larger animal sniffing around to provoke this irritation.

I inserted the dildo in a harness. It didn't fit perfectly, but the harness held it in place as I yanked my jeans up, buttoning them tight over the appendage, a new pressure on my groin. I lay back on the bed, stretching my arms above my head, lacing my fingers together, and closed my eyes. Splayed out unapologetically on the bed, I wondered if this is what it feels like to be a man. I got nothing I need to do—I'm home. Someone else is making dinner. I know that's sexist, but that's what I thought. I mean, that's the thought I had.

I imagined Naomi in her velvet blazer, but without a shirt, pants, tie, shoes. Just her bare skin, nipples peeking out. *I'm in the beauty business.* Oh yeah? What kind of services do you provide? Then Naomi kneeling on the bed beside me, rubbing the bulge in my jeans like she needs it, like I have what sustains her.

I guess it would be dishonest to claim I'd never imagined such things before Naomi. With my ex, I let her fuck me like I was just a woman, a receiver, but sometimes when she tongued my clitoris, I'd long for her to suck it, so I could have my own fantasy. She would have hated the position I imagined for her, so I never asked. Maybe I am supposed to ask for these things, and she can answer yes or no. Those are the options. But could there be damage simply in asking, too?

So maybe Naomi had asked for these things, and I had said yes. I had indicated yes. I had enacted yes. I hadn't said no.

I imagined this sensation of tightness and then release when Naomi unbuttons my fly and takes me into her mouth. I felt close to orgasm and I hadn't even touched myself. I loosened the harness and rubbed myself beneath the pressure of the dildo, imagined pushing into her mouth, and I came. That must be a world record, I thought. As if to applaud me, a woodpecker outside drummed on a tree.

It turned out Naomi was right. After a couple of hours in and out of this stoned masturbation and napping, I went downstairs, still wearing the dildo, and tried out everyday activity. I finished the dishes. I tightened screws on a cupboard door. I wandered through the house and noted how my walk changed when housing something between my legs. My stride slowed, my steps lengthened. My feet turned out slightly. If there was a metaphysical thread tugging me through space, it was attached to my groin now. Maybe it was the pressure, just the way a hand on the shoulder makes a person aware of their shoulder. Maybe this was why my ex did not want her breasts touched. Could it be that simple? But I stopped sometimes to push against a wall, feel my groin pushing up against the wall. I imagined how good Naomi would look against that wall, her back to me, how I would like to push into her that way, place my hands over hers, pin her there, how Naomi would like that, maybe even say, "Stop." She hadn't said that since the night we discussed *fungus*, and I felt now that I was missing it. With my eyes closed, I put these words into her mouth: *Stop, don't, you're so big, no.* And I didn't think about it—I had thoughts, but I washed them away. Don't interrupt. I'm fucking Naomi. But I felt weird after, something new in my body now—was this desire or some unknown thing growing inside?

❧

Rita,

I have a cheque for you to reimburse the last week of rent and the security deposit, but I am not paying for any of the damage on your invoice. You can't just blame something on someone and expect your accusation to be sufficient evidence to warrant monetary compensation. But I don't want to argue about this. I don't think you were ever planning to stay here and I think you just saw the flood as some opportunity to scuttle away to your new girlfriend's house. I assume she is a new girlfriend because you never even mentioned her and I had never seen her before that day on the trail. Since you've decided to be so adversarial about things, I'm not risking the cheque getting lost in the mail, but I'm around all weekend if you want to come and pick it up.

Ursula

❧

I don't pretend to be innocent of all responsibility, but I've learned it doesn't help to ignore the damage, either. Ursula's cheque was an admission. I knew she expected some thank-you to sound like an apology. As I lay back on the couch, feet up on the hassock and dildo cradled in my groin, I felt ready to deny her that satisfaction. I couldn't wait to deny her that satisfaction.

Naomi arrived home. I'd removed my shirt by then, and rested my arms up on the cushions, taking up as much room as I could. Naomi draped her jacket over the back of a chair and untucked her shirt without saying anything. She slumped onto the couch without putting the kettle on and rested her head awkwardly on my shoulder. She must have noticed the dildo by then. I petted her hair and kissed her forehead. "Good girl," I said.

After a moment, she sat up, resting her head on the cushion. "I had a shitty day."

I took her hand and placed it on my groin, but she pulled it away. She gave a tired laugh. "I'm glad you like your new toy, but I think I'm just going to go to bed." She kissed my forehead. "If you watch TV, please keep the volume down," she said, and headed upstairs.

I don't understand how words can change a body. This flower is a weed. This tree is dead. This songbird is invasive. Beautiful music. Barnyard animals. Fungus: Stop. This power is a new toy. How can I ever believe I am anything solid when my body is again poured into some new shape, beautiful or cute or cruel or dangerous. So I don't know what hot shame I felt then, for the lie Naomi told me or the lie I told myself. But if this happened now, I would react differently. I think I would—would I find my own words to speak my body back into something powerful? I've read a lot of articles trying to make sense of it. But at the time, I had only this feeling like a body coming apart. Whose arms are these? Whose legs? Whose breasts?

Whose cock?

I yanked the dildo out of its harness and threw it in Naomi's direction. It hit the staircase not far from her.

"What was that for?" Naomi shouted.

"I didn't mean to throw it so hard," I said.

"Why did you throw it at all?"

Words would not come.

Naomi waited. "I'm too tired to figure this out for you." She continued up the stairs. I followed. I hated to go to bed with this rotten feeling. I had some idea that I'd just apologize, say I don't know what I was thinking, and this was true. I could say I smoked pot today, I'm ovulating. I'm being a brat. I'm sorry. Could that be true, too?

Naomi undressed and got into bed, lay on her side and turned her bedside light off, leaving me in the dark. I turned the lamp on.

"I'm too tired to talk," she said without turning. "It's okay though, don't worry, I'm not mad."

"I'm not worried," I said.

Naomi did not respond. I pushed her hip and she jerked onto her back. "What's got into you?"

I lay beside her, one arm across her chest, and kissed her neck, her ear. Naomi relaxed slightly. Her body often changed under the crush of kisses in this place. But she gently nudged me away. "Baby, I really just want to sleep. You're too much right now. You're not yourself."

"I notice you didn't ask me how my day was."

Naomi looked to the ceiling, exhaled. "You didn't ask me, either."

"That's because you just told me."

Naomi rested one arm across her eyes, as if shielding herself from some migraine-bright light. "How was your day."

The more I tried to interact with Naomi, the more I hated the person I was becoming in this conversation. I imagined later what I might have said. "The dildo was your idea, you pushed me into this and now that I finally try it on you make me feel like an idiot, like I'm a stupid little kid playing with a new toy. But this was always for you. It was never for me." But I heard Naomi respond. *You are an adult, Rita. You make your own choices.*

I took her wrist—I wanted her to look at me. I straddled her, taking her other wrist and pinning her arms above her head. Naomi wrestled briefly, then went limp. As if she knew how much I wanted her eyes on me, she kept her gaze on the ceiling behind. "You won't look at me now?" I said. I licked her nipple. I thought something would change, perhaps, that we'd circled far enough away from that rotten place for some new feeling to grow instead, and as I licked and sucked, I waited for her body to shift, to give away its arousal. I sucked harder.

"Ouch," Naomi said. "Get off me now."

I sat up, leaned more of my weight onto her wrists. "Don't you want me to fuck you?"

"Why are you acting like this?"

"You wanted me to fuck you hard whether you want it or not. You want me to wear a cock and rape you with it, right?"

Naomi's nose reddened.

"Well, now I want that, too."

"Get off." She twisted her body to one side. My weight shifted. I simply followed the momentum off Naomi, onto the bed beside her.

I longed to hold her like a baby, then. But I crashed on the couch like an unwelcome guest.

§

Ursula answered the door in her bathrobe, although it was the middle of the afternoon. Her face looked puffy, as if she'd been crying and she offered only a distracted hello.

"Is this a bad time?" I might've asked once.

Ursula waved for me to come in.

"I can't stay," I said. "I'm just here to pick up the cheque."

"Oh, of course." She went into the house, leaving the door open, and returned with an envelope. She held it out for me and as I took it, Ursula began to cry. She covered her mouth with one hand and gulped.

"What happened?" I said, as if I did not expect this.

Ursula moored herself to the doorknob. "It's nothing." She waited.

I considered leaving then. Turning, saying nothing. Maybe even scoffing or rolling my eyes for effect. Instead, I opened the envelope to check the amount.

"What are you doing?" Ursula said.

"No point in making two trips." The amount was correct. Ursula had also enclosed a letter.

"Don't read that now!"

I turned my back to her, as if she might try to snatch it away, and walked a few steps. Light rain dotted the paper.

Dear Rita,

It saddens me that our friendship has become strained as a result of this misfortune.

"'As a result of this misfortune'?" I quoted. "A bit formal, don't you think?"

Ursula had put on her garden shoes and now grabbed the letter from me. "I'm not going to let you humiliate me for it."

"What did you think was going to happen? You think I was going to move in with you? Be your girlfriend? Wasn't that just handy, the dyke tenant, eh?"

"That wasn't it at all!" Ursula cried. "That wasn't it at all."

"Give me the letter then. I won't read it here."

Ursula made no move.

"I'm sorry," I added. I knew Ursula wanted me to have it. It was the last word.

She held out the letter. "I'm going in now. I hope you are happy with your new life." She walked back toward the door, the tie of her bathrobe dragging on the wet pavement.

᠈

Naomi had just left for the North Coast, gone for about a week. I was between gigs, one couple having cancelled the job because they'd decided to sell the house and it went quickly. I never got a deposit, but I didn't tell Naomi that. I began to clear the cedar boughs, cones and other debris the winter of rain and wind had loosened from the trees, and then got a start on the Himalayan blackberry, digging out the roots with a mattock. Those are invasive.

Naomi and I had talked about the night I said the thing about rape. I knew I'd crossed a line and I owed her an apology. "I don't want you to apologize," she'd said. "I want you to realize why you were wrong. I never said I wanted you to rape me—that's your fantasy. If I *wanted* you to rape me, then that wouldn't be rape. But if you want to rape me, then you should examine that, but not with me."

I felt sick hearing this, and I couldn't tell if the burning inside me was shame or anger. "I never wanted to have sex like that," I finally choked out, and began to cry.

"Then you should have said something." Naomi tucked some curl behind my ear. "You're allowed to have feelings, you know." She got up to open the window.

The breeze felt good. The air in the room changed, and it seemed the conversation had blown away, too. "Will you sit beside me again?" I said. I'd imagined something had dislodged and our relationship would now flow unimpeded. But there was something clipped in the way Naomi kissed me then, something that left me with little to grasp, and I found myself straining for her to rest her lips just a moment longer.

I tossed another mangled blackberry root into the wheelbarrow. It had begun to rain, and my feet were driving me nuts. After a shower, they'd burn hot and I'd have to scrape them against the sill of the sliding door for any relief, but even that wouldn't remedy the irritation for long. The medicated cream was slow to act and I had considered my own role in this, that I'd failed to follow instructions, often smearing it onto unwashed feet and certainly never soaking my feet first.

Naomi had stuffed several hundred dollars into the grocery-money tin. "You don't owe me for this," she said.

"I'm still flush."

"Well, just in case—I don't want you to worry." Love. "Besides, I really appreciate you looking after the house while I'm gone."

I yanked my rubber boots off at the door, leaving a clutter of caked mud on the floor, and peeled off sweaty socks. I sat on the toilet and examined my feet. The dead skin formed a pattern of pale-yellow streaks, reminding me of rings on a stump. It seemed for a moment that the itch was subsiding, that I'd removed my wet socks in time. But suddenly my feet became hot, the itch a throbbing pain. I scratched, trying not to tear too much of the skin, trying not to rip into the part of me still living. How could it get so out of control? I wanted to cry. I pressed my feet against the cool side of the tub for relief, but none came. I would have to do better, I thought. Take charge of the problem. For now, all I could do was wait—for my skin to dry out, for the itch to subside, for the oxygen to suffocate whatever was growing.

❧

Dear Rita,

It saddens me that our friendship has become strained as a result of this misfortune. You have meant so much to me. You were an unexpected light at a time in my life when I felt like things were only ending—you were a beginning. I can't tell you how much happiness it brought me to visit with you. You changed everything, big and small. Even the hot tub! It had just been a reminder of my failed marriage, of how little say I had in that marriage, something I didn't fully realize until it was over, but now I look at it and I think of you and our summer visits and that time we lit the tikki torches and ate pineapple in the hot tub!

I was so hurt when you sent that bill, sending me those letters like I was just the landlady. That you didn't even tell me about Naomi. That you left without saying anything. Why couldn't you be honest? Now I feel like you just led me on, and for what? So you could use more of the yard? I never brought up money with you. I didn't want to confuse things, but you did.

Now I feel like I truly have nothing but can only tell myself things will get better. That's what they say, isn't it? I don't regret our friendship. I still hope like a teenager that we can have that again. You are always welcome here. I want you to know that.

I love you,
Ursula

❧

It was my ex who sent me the article, "10 Signs You're in a Co-dependent Relationship." I'd taken the accordion to the dump—it was beyond repair and I didn't play anyway. My ex would never know, but I felt guilty, so I called her, not to tell her what I'd done, just to check in. But I ended up doing most of the talking, which felt strange. Somehow I had so much to say, and I told her about Naomi, how I adored her, how I felt like a husk.

I didn't agree that I was co-dependent. According to this list, I always give more to my partner than I get in return; I think I'm helping her, but I'm bailing her out for the "umpteenth time"; My partner's happiness is my top priority; I frequently make excuses or compensate for my partner's bad behaviour; I'm quick to say "yes" without pausing to consider how I feel. And on and on. But Naomi did not need me for happiness or rescue. And no matter how much blackberry I tore out, I could never return her generosity. In fact, the more I looked at this list, the more I saw myself as this parasitic drain. And the more I wondered why she kept me around at all.

I told my ex this. "You have low self-esteem," she said. "You gotta get out of there." She used the term "emotionally abusive." Sent me other articles. But this didn't fit, either, and thinking of Naomi this way felt like a betrayal at the time. But it was enough to help me see that this living arrangement was untenable. I lined up more work and arranged another place to stay. One evening, when Naomi returned, the words finally flowed. I'd spent that afternoon writing, trying to come up with words that would not change after I'd spoken them. I said I needed to leave the relationship, that I wasn't blaming anyone—I take full responsibility for my role, but I just needed to leave because I realized the dynamic wasn't healthy for me.

"I'm going to take my shoes off now," Naomi said. "Where will you go?" Naomi said.

She didn't even try to make me stay.

And now it's been six months and, despite my careful speech, there is still something left to say, to be said. I keep contacting her, texting her, inviting her to meet, like I'm waiting for the words to unlock something still. And I don't know if this is love I feel—if I'm still in love with Naomi—or if I forgot something there, some piece of me on the window sill, another in the wheelbarrow, puddled and soggy now. When I think of Naomi, I recall the tarps and humidifiers whirring in my flooded suite, an unfinished and damaged place.

But the suite has since been re-done. It has cork floors and butcher-block counters. A woman who is recently divorced moved in and is "over the moon" about having her own space. That's how Ursula put it, anyway.

I have to realize I may never get what I need from Naomi. I'm trying to realize that. I'm thinking of leaving the coast altogether. Finding a new place, somewhere far away to get back to myself. Somewhere dry—the Okanagan desert, maybe. That might be good for my feet.

For now, I'm staying in the guest room at Ursula's. She said I was always welcome, and she meant it. "Water under the bridge," she said. She's not even charging me rent.

Guided Walk

Miriam had been dreaming about bears for years before the Canyon City guided hike near Whitehorse. In the first dream, she sits watching some show on TV, then turns to discover a black bear cub on the couch beside her. The cub leans into her, reminding Miriam of when her daughter Keely was little. Miriam searches her dream dictionary for meaning, but a dream bear can mean almost anything. The dictionary asks, "Are you hunting the bear? Is the bear hunting you? Is it a circus bear? A mother bear? A quiet bear in the distance?" The particular events of a given dream indicate a particular insight into her waking life and journey. The best description of her dream, Miriam thinks, is "hugging a bear." According to the dictionary, this means she is friendly with others in an unpleasant situation. Miriam thinks of her husband, Murray, and her daughter, too. Maybe the bookkeeping job. Things are not going well with her friend Jodi at the time of this first dream, either, so this interpretation rings true. The dream cub is fluffy and pale-eyed just as Miriam remembers seeing when she was a tree planter, and they drove slowly past a baby bear as it clung, impressively, to a juvenile lodgepole pine. In the dream, Miriam does not feel gratitude for the weight of this trusting creature against her.

More dreams follow, each one a new scenario and a new interpretation and all these meanings seem to cancel each other out—how can Miriam be both independent and vulnerable? Brave and terrified? It didn't make sense, Miriam thought. (Miriam has never been particularly insightful.) Although numerous interpretations indicate self-reflection is required, this is the one thing she wishes to avoid.

This is a coming-out story.

Miriam has been staring at the TV-series shelf at the video store for what feels like an hour. The existence of Viv's Vids already feels anomalous, but Miriam clings to her video-store routine even as vintage turntables and other collectibles begin to displace the shelves of DVDs. Since her daughter moved out, it's become apparent how much of Miriam and Murray's attention orbited Keely's small dramas and life choices, so they are left with a glaring solitude. They've filled some of this silence by bickering about when to prune a tree, whether to pave the driveway or not, and what to do about a black bear with a yellow tag in one ear who has frequented the yard in recent years. When Murray sees the bear, he rushes outside to yell at it. The first time he did this, the bear ran away, but now, the bear only casually turns, unmoved by Murray's displays. "I'm putting in an electric fence," he'd said that morning. "That bear is not getting the plums again this year."

"I refuse to live in a prison," Miriam said. "What do you need the plums for, anyway? You planning to make preserves?" Murray told her she was being melodramatic. Later, he imagined making plum sauce when she was out, how she'd just come home and see it all neatly jarred and realize she'd underestimated him again. He googled a recipe but lost interest immediately.

So here is Miriam, staring at the TV-series shelf.

Miriam wants to jump into a series, a hundred episodes, a hundred times she won't have to make a decision about what to watch next, but she's overwhelmed by the decision of what to watch first.

"You look a little lost," someone says. Miriam turns, in an instant solving the clues of this woman's appearance: bristle-short hair and a rainbow tie-dye handkerchief round her neck, cargo shorts and three silver hoops in one ear. "Lesbian," Miriam thinks. Although Miriam doesn't know it, this lesbian—Shauna—is an old-school sort of dyke, the kind who volunteered to bartend at women's dances before they were organized by professional event planners. Who owns vulva fridge magnets. Who has been carting around a collection of lesbian literature given to her by an even older-school dyke after a stroke moved her into assisted living. (As the new manager, Shauna is the one who persuaded

Viv—who was about to abandon ship—that Shauna's large collection of vintage vinyl could ironically steer Viv's Vids into the 21st century.)

For Miriam, the transparency of Shauna's accessories alone feels generous—why couldn't it always be so obvious? So many times, Miriam found herself with a new close friend, like Lily at the Sunday hiking group or Jodi from Tuesday-night Stitch & Bitch, immersed in an intense two months of emotional processing, but each woman would eventually drift away, busy with her kids' fall schedules or family getaways, and Miriam would be sad—unreasonably sad, Murray thought. How to grieve the loss of unarticulated attachments? Had she dreamed up these connections? Jodi even spooned her once (summer pjs, thighs hot against thighs and Miriam dripping behind the knee), but Jodi was just a cuddly person and Miriam could contaminate their friendship if she ventured some erotic gesture—even thinking about it felt like a betrayal. But if someone like Shauna spooned her, she'd know what to do. She'd push her butt into Shauna's groin and pull her hand up to her breast. From there it would be easy.

"I *am* lost," Miriam says.

"Thank god I found you then," Shauna winks, turning Miriam soggy. "What are you into—mystery? Sci-fi?"

"I just want something to be *good*."

Shauna squats and retrieves a DVD from a lower shelf. Miriam notes the fine hair along her uneven neckline. "You can't go wrong with *Star Trek: Voyager*." On the DVD cover, Captain Kathryn Janeway stands proudly, arms crossed and planets floating behind. Shauna taps the case. "You look a lot like her, actually."

Nothing so remarkable in the actress's appearance—shoulder-length brown hair and a face that's pleasant in its well-proportioned and forgettable arrangement, not unlike Miriam's. But Janeway's subtle wry smile suggests an intelligence that Miriam has never felt she possessed.

"She's got those soulful eyes," Shauna adds.

Shortly after this encounter with Shauna, Miriam dreams of another bear, this one unseen but heard gnawing or clawing at the side of the house, a grinding sound like termites. Miriam tries to speak out in this dream, to rip herself from this place of inevitable discovery. "It's not termites!" she tries to call out until she finally does, waking herself. "It's just a dream," Murray says.

ꙅ

Miriam and Murray got together the first shift of tree planting, so a couple months into the season, she felt she could tell him anything— that she should tell him anything. She'd known for a while about her queer desire, however unrequited it may be, and she was trying to be more honest in her life.

She looked down at her arms, still stained with dirt above the glove line. No one had bothered to shower at camp. They'd decided to just get to Prince George as soon as possible for their night off, a cheap motel room and a hot bath, a case of beer and a bag of coke.

"I think I'm bisexual," she confessed to Murray in their motel room.

She wished he didn't have that moustache right now. All the guys on the crew grew one after some joke about the unusually large spruce-seedling plugs being "Magnums," leading to some *Magnum P.I.* references and from there to matching Tom-Selleck facial hair.

"That's okay," Murray began. When Miriam didn't say thank you, he added, "You're not breaking up with me, are you?"

"No," Miriam reassured him, although she did then wonder for a moment what the point of telling him was. "I just don't know what to do..." She felt her face grow as red as her ears, already swollen from recent black-fly bites, her upper arm stinging from the juices of cow parsnip. Miriam worked harder than anyone but earned the least money—she had yet to unlock the easy rhythm that comes with speed, one that required an unthinking physicality. Murray placed one hand on her stomach, kissed her mouth. His moustache tickled in an irritating way, but when he slid his hand up to her breast and gently pinched her nipple, something shifted anyway because she was young and horny and Murray was still new. "We could explore that together," he said. They had sex in the shower, Murray narrating a scene he imagined between Miriam and a hypothetical generic woman.

After several drinks at the Generator, one of the nightclubs in

Prince George, the whole crew out together, practically in costume—garish thrift-store finds like sequined sweaters—Miriam had eased into a good time, comforted by Murray's arm around her waist.

"What about Natalie?" He nodded toward the tree planter dressed in a star-patterned muumuu cinched with a shiny green belt, and plastic hoop earrings to match. Natalie switched from ironic can-can to ironic disco finger-pointing. She pointed at Murray then, who Miriam noticed was waving her over.

"I don't know how to dance," Natalie said. "I can't take it seriously."

Murray tipped his bottle for the last drops of ale and grabbed Miriam's hand. "Natalie's gonna teach us some moves."

The night progressed, and the drinking continued. At one point, Murray pulled Natalie close and gyrated between her and Miriam. "Enjoy a magnum sandwich, ladies!"

At the hotel, when Natalie kisses Miriam's neck, Miriam's limbs go weak and cold, like some animal bleeding out. Is she going to faint? She kisses Natalie back. Possession is how Miriam would later think of this. Her whole body beats, her hands pawing greedily for Natalie's breasts, back, stomach, hind, as if Miriam has no mind at all, only nerves and arteries and appetite. Strange, how awake her body feels, yet how like a dream this unthinking desire. When she opens her eyes, she sees Murray place Natalie's hand on his groin. Soon, they are all naked, and Miriam is really doing it, going down on a woman, tongue on vulva and she's never been more excited, deranged panting and tongue swirling. When she comes up for air, Murray leans over to kiss her, urgently. "You're so fucking hot," he says, and this seems to break the spell. Suddenly her wild need is displaced by a domesticated sexiness. Murray's searching hands prove something about her and she responds with pornographic grace, squeezing her own breasts as if that alone is enough to climax. In this moment, like so many moments in Miriam's life, she watches herself from some other point of view, first Murray's, then some undefined location, sees the three of them on the motel bed together, the stiff quilted bedcover in a pile on the floor. What might be said about this scene? How to get back to her body? How to get back to Natalie's?

When Natalie left, grey daylight fell into the room and they realized the curtains had not been closed all the way. "It doesn't matter," Murray said, smoothing his moustache.

Miriam and Murray check out of the motel to join other planters at a greasy spoon before doing laundry. Natalie had already come and gone from the laundromat and was apparently at the Chinese buffet, hanging out with her own crew.

"Had a good night, you two?" Paul said as Murray and Miriam joined the group at lunch. "Magnum plug for maximum growth!"

"Twice the plug, twice the growth," a guy named Brandon smirked, whom Miriam had never talked to before. She realized that everyone knew what they had done.

"Fuck off," Miriam said.

"Yeah, fuck off, you guys," Murray echoed weakly.

Miriam wanted to stay in camp the next day off, to save money, she said, but also to get a break from everyone. Sick of the magnum jokes. One guy had bought a tropical-print shirt, another homage to Magnum, at one of the mall stores, and the plan was for all the guys to get one. She wanted Murray to stay in camp with her. "It'll be good," she argued. "One of the foremen is here, too, and we can use the truck to drive to that lake we saw from the last block." But Murray wasn't interested. "It's summer, Miriam. We have maybe three more shifts, if that. This is our last chance to hang out with everyone."

"I guess everyone is more important than me."

"That's high-school bullshit."

"You know what's high-school bullshit? Fucking dick jokes. Why don't you grow up."

"I'm out of here."

Miriam almost changed her mind—the truck idled, and Beastie Boys shouted from the stereo as Natalie rushed back to her tent to grab something. Natalie, her skin a galaxy of freckled constellations, Miriam thought. She should write that down. She should run over to the truck now, say I'm so sorry but I'm gonna come, too—I just have to grab my stuff. But there'd be a joke about coming, and Natalie would be there and they hadn't really acknowledged the threesome since it happened. They had to share a cache one day and Natalie just complained about how sick of planting she was and how it's gonna be such a cluster-fuck finishing off this contract.

And then the truck drove away and it was definitely too late.

The night in camp yawned ahead of her. She wrote down the line about freckled constellations and tried to expand it into a poem, but with the mention of a galaxy, Miriam already felt shackled to this metaphor, turning Murray into a spaceship and herself into Saturn's rings and soon it made no sense and Miriam gave up trying to express anything at all. She smoked a joint, reheated some chili for dinner, and passed out in her tent before sundown.

It shouldn't have surprised her when she learned that Murray and Natalie slept together while in town. "I don't know what your rules are," Natalie said in defence, as she smoked a cigarette at the cache.

"Then why are you telling me this?" Miriam said.

"I just wanted you to hear it from me, so it wouldn't be weird."

Murray pleaded his case later in their pup tent, the nylon walls providing an illusion of privacy. He nearly cried, blaming cocaine for the lapse in judgment. "I was too high, and it was confusing because of the threesome. I'm sorry," he said finally. "Can't we just get out of here?"

"I still need to make money." Miriam was entering her second and final year of a broadcasting program she would never benefit from. As a gesture of contrition, Murray managed to get them assigned to some day-rate "special missions," filling unplanted pockets left in cutblocks and walking through overgrown fill-plants. Miriam struggled through young alder on one of these blocks, afraid she might surprise a bear as she burst from the leafy thicket. On another block, every burned stump appeared like a bear in the distance, unmoving as it contemplated Miriam below. But at least the special missions kept them away from the crew and Natalie (except briefly at dinners), and the next season, they worked for a different company.

❧

The night Miriam spent in camp, a bear had appeared, not in dreams but waking-life. Miriam woke to the sound of the foreman's dog barking, something more pinched than its usual outbursts. A clatter of pots from the cook tent and the foreman's shouts followed. She was a black bear who'd wandered off course. Her usual route had been disturbed by a sudden interest from ATV enthusiasts, but Chili Night caught her attention, too, and she followed the beefy aroma for miles. She'd seen the chili in a dream, seen Miriam's tired hand spooning it onto a dinner roll.

Miriam sat upright in her pup tent. Was this her fault? She'd regretted not following Murray to town and wondered again why Natalie hadn't asked her to come, and, while lost in these thoughts, had forgotten to put the leftover chili back in the fridge.

The next night, Miriam slept close to Murray, nervous now of what might wake her in the night.

❧

Miriam now describes her attitude toward bears as "a practical fear." She will hike alone, for example, knowing she may encounter a bear, but she will call out "No bear!" to make her presence known, to avoid such a meeting. She rolls her eyes at bear bells. "Tourists," she calls those jingling hikers. "Dinner's ready!" she sometimes joked with Murray, who thought it was funny the first couple of times. She takes bear mace with her, if she remembers, in case she is unlucky enough to meet a predatory bear. They are out there. She's even read a couple books about bears, so, compared to everyone she knows, Miriam is an expert. This makes her feel competent.

❧

Over the years, Miriam's desire for women comes up periodically, usually prompted by a flood of feelings for someone new, feelings that at first energize her to return to pilates and re-start *The Artist's Way*, but soon just confuse and torment her. Murray rationalizes it (You're just lonely, you're just bored, fantasizing doesn't mean you're a lesbian—even straight women watch gay porn) and Miriam wants to be convinced, because at least she knows how to live the life she has already.

Then there are the distractions: Keely's babyhood, toddlerhood, childhood, adolescence. "Identity" seemed so selfish. Who has time for a "self"? "Anyone who cares so much about a pronoun obviously isn't a parent," she once commented. It didn't matter how wrong she was because this made her feel noble. She had sacrificed so much for her family, hadn't she? And this noble sacrifice provided a sense of purpose until the next woman came along to turn her into a watery mess.

But there is something earthier in her desire for Shauna, a desperate unfurling, mycelium vessels in search of nutrients, water, a doubling down. If not Shauna, who? When? She dreams of a den beneath a tree, roots above like stalactites, and the soily ceiling threaded with cottony fungi. In this dream, cool water puddles at her paws, the drip of spring rain outside, and the sound of her growling hunger.

Weekly, Miriam journeys to the video store to retrieve more DVDs of *Star Trek: Voyager*. She consumes the show daily. "You've got those soulful eyes," Shauna had said, and Miriam replays this line again and again, hoping each time she sees Shauna that this would grow into something more. And for a while, it seems to... the softball game, that special moment at the grocery store, then, last week, Miriam ventured some new gesture. "I bet the falls at Cedar Creek are pretty amazing right now, with all this rain we've been having."

"I haven't been there in ages," Shauna said. "You planning to go?"

Just like that, an invitation formed.

❧

The rain feels romantic in the trees, which are shaggy with moss and lichen like unmoving beasts. The whole forest breathes—Shauna's words visible as damp clouds that Miriam longs to inhale. Cool but muggy, Miriam sweats in her jacket and V-neck tee. "You've got a nice heart," Shauna said, glancing at Miriam's chest, but she meant the pendant that Murray had given her years ago. Miriam will later place the heart in a Ziploc, unsure what it means anymore.

Conversation meanders from *X-Files* to what to rename Viv's Vids (Say It Again Collectibles? Off the Record?) to past relationships, and all Miriam contributes are vague complaints about Murray, how her marriage was "never truly honest." She wants to say it's over. Instead, she says, "I guess I'm waiting for the right opportunity to change my life." She laughs, as if this were some adorably humble admission.

"I don't think I could go through all that waiting again," Shauna says.

"What have you been waiting for?"

Shauna laughs. "A woman who knows who she is and what she wants."

Shauna notices Miriam didn't ask for more details. She probably thinks Shauna is talking about her, and she is, in a way. But she's talking about many women all at once, because Shauna has often found herself in this role, an experienced guide for women always on the verge of transformation—divorce, going back to school, taking a job on the other side of the province without even discussing it with Shauna first, as if Shauna has just beamed down into their lives to fulfill some spiritual or sexual or psychological need to help them on their way. "Why do they always seem to find me," she's wondered. But lately, she has also considered the term "self-sabotage." Because she tells herself she wants a woman who knows who she is and what she wants, but instead finds them lost in the woods. And once she shows them the path to town, they never stick around.

Miriam wants to say it then, say, "I want you," but the words get stuck in her throat, then drip down into her stomach, making her sick.

"New bridge," Shauna says, changing the subject, and Miriam's opportunity to say who she is and what she wants drifts past.

The footbridge was rebuilt after a fir crashed into the previous one a couple winters ago. "I miss the old bridge," Miriam says. She thinks of the movie *The Bridges of Madison County,* of Meryl Streep's intense extra-marital affair with a photographer. "It looked so beautiful in photos," Miriam adds, wondering if Shauna might think of this movie, too.

Looking upstream from the bridge, the falls pound into Cedar Creek. In the summer, the flow of water was reduced to a trickle—most of the year, it was generous to call this a waterfall at all, yet the locals do. But on this day, with all the rain they've been having, the water gushes over slippery downed trees, gushes over their chaotic limbs reaching this way and that, gushes over rocks smooth and round. And although the waterfall is just what Miriam hoped it would be, instead of inspiring a revelatory romantic moment, it seems to laugh at Miriam, its passion in stark contrast to what suddenly feels like Shauna's trickling attraction.

Back at the parking lot, Shauna agrees to go for coffee later in the week, but she doesn't hug Miriam goodbye. And the next day, Shauna emails Miriam to cancel, suddenly remembering a trip to the city. *See you at the video store,* she writes in closing.

A day passes, then another, then another, until one day, the bear with the yellow tag returns for the remaining salmonberries in the backyard. Murray doesn't yell at it—he sits scrolling online, saying something about their ship coming in, but Miriam isn't listening. Outside, the salmonberry bushes shake as the bear tugs gently at the tiny fruits. If only Shauna were that bear, how Miriam longed to be that berry. Or is it the other way around?

In this needful state, Miriam returns to rent the final two discs of *Star Trek: Voyager.* "Prepare to be disappointed," Shauna says at the till.

"You promised it would be good." Miriam intends to hint at her playful mischief with this comment, something adorable to inspire Shauna's attention again. Because something has changed—Shauna no longer winks at her and Miriam is afraid to ask why. Had she done something wrong?

"It *is* good," Shauna says matter-of-factly. "It just doesn't end well."

"Oh," Miriam says. "Then I'm sad it's already almost over."

"Well, there's more *Star Trek* where that came from," Shauna says.

Are they still talking about *Star Trek?* "Not with Captain Janeway, though," Miriam says, "and those soulful eyes." She thinks Shauna might look into her eyes now, be captured there, but Shauna gestures to a man behind with a stack of vinyl, and Miriam scooches over to make room, waiting for a moment by the jar of chocolate mints, but then moves to the other side of the security alarm and gets in the way of a woman with a walker trying to come in through the narrow entrance. "Well, see you later," Miriam says.

"Enjoy!" Shauna says. "Enjoy," she says again to the man as he leaves, too.

Miriam replays this interaction on the walk home, considering Shauna's body language when she said, "It *is* good," when she said, "It just doesn't end well." Was there a pleading in her eyes? Is she waiting for Miriam to know who she is and what she wants? She wishes Shauna would get angry, grab Miriam and squeeze her, say, "I could fall in love with you, dammit!" Was that from a movie or just a familiar mix of sadness and lust? "You're right—I can't wait anymore." She would say it then, "I am a lesbian and I want you," but it's difficult for Miriam even to imagine choking these words out. She feels them like a plum pit in her stomach. That's going to hurt coming out. How she longs for rescue or capture... And now Miriam's body is on autopilot, walking as she dreams of the hike that might've been if only she'd known who she is and what she wants—misty rain, wet mouths, hurrying to Shauna's truck, the windows steamed with hot breath like in the movie *Titanic*. She stops walking, her body immobilized by this knee-buckling lust. With her eyes closed, Shauna is almost real, but Miriam's body remains untouched.

When she finally arrives home, a taupe motorhome sits in the driveway, the *For Sale* sign still resting on the dashboard. Twenty-eight thousand dollars.

Murray has been talking about a road trip to California for years. But each year, as the summer nears, Murray suggests staying put: "People are trying to come *here* for a holiday, why would we leave?" Miriam doesn't argue. She enjoys seeing the money accumulate in the "adventure" account and Murray's idea of fun, for Miriam, just sounds like being a passenger.

But today, Murray runs out with a bottle of Prosecco. "Check it out, baby! Our ship has come in!"

The vehicle has six tires. The "home" part extends above the cab and Miriam wonders if that's where the bed is. A "loft," perhaps, a stuffy coffin to share with Murray, morning farts to sock her in like bad weather. She will no doubt have to take the inside spot, because Murray is taller and needs the extra room for his arm to hang off the bed, or in case he has to get up quickly—like if wild animals start poking around the hibachi where they've eaten hotdogs every night for the last five nights at some state park filled with other couples—men and women taking holidays from their 55+ condos by parking in some other 55+ park with electricity and water and maybe a heated outdoor pool. Miriam is not even fifty yet, but she imagines being in this park, some American woman with a practical haircut inviting all the trailer-park folks to her shindig—it's my sixtieth! And then Miriam is sixty, then sixty-five, then seventy and Miriam is in the passenger seat while Murray winds up the jacks on the motorhome, ready to hit the open road again and again, every year because he's spent twenty-eight thousand dollars of "adventure" on it. "We need to get our money's worth," he might say when even *his* enthusiasm wanes.

"What do you think?" he says.

Miriam sits on the porch step, *Star Trek: Voyager* in hand. The plum tree's little white flowers have been replaced by the compact start of tiny fruit. How sweet must they be before the bears take an interest? One year, she watched from inside as the large male stood upright to pull the tender branches toward him, breaking several, yet plucking the plums delicately with his teeth. It must have been a hot day, as Miriam recalls the wag and droop of his scrotum.

"What year is it?" Miriam says quietly.

"It's an '88. But really low mileage."

"Not the motorhome." Miriam squeezes the DVD cases. "What year do you think it is right now."

Murray recognizes her tone, the way she asks leading questions he must answer, forcing him to incriminate himself. This again. "We've been talking about doing some road trips for years," he says, ignoring her question. "What do you think we've been saving for?"

"*We* is the operative word there, Murray."

"Well..." he says, and Miriam knows what he's thinking, that he's earned more than her for years, worked more, inherited more.

"Don't ruin this for me," Murray says. He looks like his father now. He looks like Miriam's father now. He looks like every man in the 55+ trailer park.

Miriam places the DVDs on the step. She takes the bottle of Prosecco, which Murray has already opened, tips it for a swig and it sparkles down her throat. Then she hurls it at the motorhome, hitting the passenger window, the view that was meant to be hers.

"I'm gonna tell you something, Miriam," he says quietly. "I'm just about done here."

One of the reasons Murray is just about done here is he's realized that while he seems to be married to a miserable middle-aged woman, he still makes sense in an ironic trucker hat and a pair of Vans. One of his former high-school students actually hit on him when he ran into her on a whale-watching trip with the international students. She was operating the small vessel. "I always thought you were the best-looking teacher," she said. She said that! They got a drink later and nothing happened, but only because she got so drunk she seemed like a teenager again and this was a turn-off for Murray, which made him feel proud. He even paid for her cab home. "I'm a good guy," he thought, and wondered about growing a moustache again.

"You're just about done," Miriam repeats. "*You* are." If only she had another bottle of Prosecco to throw. Murray turns to head back to the house. She could pick up driveway gravel to machine-gun the motorhome's hull. Murray might spin around then, but he'd grab her by the arms, demand to know, "What's got into you?" like he did with Keely when she senselessly dragged a Sharpie along the hallway wall. "What are you gonna do, Murray, hit me?" Miriam could say, but she imagines his satisfied smile, "So that's what you think of me?" How he'd take the upper hand as righteous victim once again. This is the role they both want so badly. But now Miriam feels tired thinking of this. She wants something new to happen. "Murray—" she starts.

He turns toward her.

"I'm not happy." She cries.

"What else is new."

❧

After the RV fight, Miriam walks to her cousin Carol's house. She doesn't pack a bag first, but simply wanders back up the driveway, DVDs in hand, down the road to the network of trails that meet up with the logging road off the end of Carol's street. She hopes this disappearance will demonstrate to Murray the intense state she's in, but she also doesn't care. Occasionally, she calls out, "No bear!" She's seen bears on cutblocks, in her yard and in her dreams, but with "No bear!" she's managed to avoid ever encountering a bear on a trail. A spotted towhee scratches around the salal before perching on a branch above, accusing Miriam with its red eye and soft shriek, presumably to alert others that she is moping through the forest, this miserable woman. *What else is new.* Has she always been this way?

Carol will look after her. Carol has a giant couch with huge throw pillows and a full cupboard of cocktail supplies. Carol is always available.

2

Miriam and Carol were not so much friends in high school as colleagues in puberty. But during the summer months, when Miriam found herself particularly alone as that year's romantic friendship inevitably came to a dramatic end, there was always Cousin Carol, tagging along on her family's annual beach camping trip. As the only girls on the trip, they enacted a close friendship. "Bosom buddies," Miriam's brother teased after Carol's chest ballooned.

Into adulthood, Miriam repeated this pattern: abandoned by a Lily or Jodi, she calls up Carol and moans to her about Murray, as if he were the cause of her perpetual state of disappointment. "I don't know how much longer I can put up with him," she always says. "You always say that," Carol sometimes points out. "But you love him too much." Miriam takes this as a compliment, a testament to her loyalty, a quality she imagines indicates strength, not paralyzing fear. So when Carol shares news about a new relationship ("flings," Miriam and Murray call them behind her back), which also inevitably washes away, Miriam takes comfort knowing at least she is better off than Carol.

Now, she's not so sure. As Carol purees fruit for another round of margaritas, Miriam notes something buoyant about her, some levity despite her ever-increasing weight. Carol is a woman who buys pineapple on a regular basis, who goes to Burning Man for the first time in her forties, who gets a pink streak in her hair just to mix it up. Miriam used to think this made her ridiculous, but seeing her now, the master of her own kitchen, a bookshelf of *Lonely Planet* guides, not even a cat to tie her down, Miriam thinks maybe single life isn't so terrible after all. Maybe this is the beginning of a new adventure, a change to put the wind in her sail or the hot air in her balloon. She may not have Shauna, but she'll always have Carol. They could go to Burning Man together. "I think I'm really done this time," Miriam says.

Carol delivers her margarita, this one red. "Strawberry!" she sings.

"For real this time."

"Why is now any different?" Carol says.

Shauna, Miriam thinks, but doesn't say so. If Shauna can't save me, no one can. "Because of this." Miriam holds up *Star Trek: Voyager*. "Captain Kathryn Janeway got thrown to the other side of the fucking galaxy and did she think, Gee, I wish I still had Murray? Oh, please Murray, can you pick me up in your used motorhome?"

"Hell, no!"

"Hell, no! She had a fucking adventure."

They polish off the final episodes of *Voyager* over several more margaritas. "Prepare to be disappointed," Shauna had said, and she was right. The crew makes it back to Earth, of course they make it back. But a time-travelling Janeway travels back to rescue *herself*—there is no love for Janeway in the end. No Shauna.

"Lame," Miriam says, slumps so far down the couch only her head rests on the back cushions, her latest margarita balanced on her stomach.

"Come on," Carol raises her glass. "Here's to life after Murray!"

"If the captain was a man, they'd probably still be lost in space, wandering around trying not to look stupid for each other."

Carol laughs. "Good thing you're not heading south with Captain Murray."

Who needed that heat, anyway? It's been intolerable ever since she got sunstroke tree planting. If Murray knew her at all, he'd have suggested somewhere cold. Maybe Burning Man is a bad idea.

One hand loosely grips her margarita, a yellow one now. "You gave me pineapple," she says quietly to the glass. "Pineapple!" She points at the TV. "You know what? Let's you and me have our *own* adventure."

"You mean a trip?"

"Let's you and me go north—the Great White North! The Mighty Yukon! And we'll fly—like Captain Kathryn Janeway!" More excited and slurry talk about when, about immediately, about let's do this!

Still, Miriam is surprised when Carol calls her two days later to say she's booked the flights.

❧

When Miriam returns home the following day, Murray has moved into the motorhome. He's taken one of the Adirondack chairs from the back porch and the barbecue, too, unrolled the motorhome's awning, and sits out there in boxers and a ball cap. An upturned bucket serves as a table, where the giant green bong he won in a 4-20 draw years ago asserts his reclaimed independence. He still comes in to use the bathroom, but it surprises Miriam how natural the arrangement feels only days later.

It takes Murray about a week to smoke the weed from the freezer. He tries to smoke it daily, because life's too short and he's here for a good time, not a long time. He wants to hear that song and he finds it on YouTube and plays it on his phone every time he takes a few hits from his bong. Miriam looked out from the house once, and Murray hoped she'd see in this contrast how she's been holding him back all this time. She used to be fun, he thinks. He's pretty sure.

But Miriam is not thinking about Murray. She has the bedroom to herself and she lies there, disabled by longing for Shauna. Even her breasts seem to groan for touch and sucking and she imagines Shauna shouldering onto her. How her lips would feel. The meat of her shoulders. The yielding muscularity of her haunches. But then Miriam thinks only of Shauna's smile, that lazy laugh caught low in the throat, and she replays this again and again until she falls asleep. Midafternoon she falls asleep and into a dream, and then she is following a line of blue flagging tape across a cutblock to the trees. Her bear paws punch at blowdown, knocking fat beetles and pill bugs loose from their lazy hiding spots. It feels like a muggy June, no-see-ums and black flies if she stops too long, but then they are gone and she feels the heaving lust of another bear and responds with her own aching satisfaction. Not a bittersweet parting, but a blinking gratitude and a belly-warm desire for something more to eat. She does not consult the dream dictionary for "sex with a bear."

❧

The first evening in Whitehorse, Klondike burgers and Yukon Gold beer, the sun sparkling through pint glasses on a boisterous patio outside, Miriam almost feels young again. Carol's unrestrained enthusiasm sets a new standard of goofiness. Miriam even makes a joke to the wildlife-sanctuary guide about how hot the musk oxen must be ("If they had my doctor, he'd tell them they were just perimenopausal"). When Carol stops to document a viewpoint or parking-lot raven with her smart phone, Miriam sometimes photobombs the shot with a starjump or 1980s-style aerobics dance move. She joins Carol in a selfie of mock fear at the stuffed polar bear, except they squeeze together between the bear's outstretched arms, so the bear looks more like their fierce protective mother than a danger. They laugh about this, and when they next go to the pub for beers, Carol refers to them as "a couple of cubs on the prowl." Miriam imagines the good times of the future, trips with Carol and scrapbooking the trips with Carol. These good-time present moments are sometimes interrupted by text messages from Carol's work, and Miriam's thoughts often drift to Shauna. But for the most part, Miriam is here, present, with Carol, having an adventure and everything is fine again, will be fine. Life is good. Everything is good.

Today is their last full day in Whitehorse and Carol has suggested the afternoon guided walk to Canyon City. They are about to head out, to grab coffees first, when Carol's phone vibrates again. Miriam left her own phone at home. Who does she need to call, anyway? No one who can't wait a week. But Carol was as bad as her daughter, placing it like cutlery beside her dinner plate or keeping it beside her pillow like a teddy bear.

"Is it work?" Miriam asks.

"Huh?" Carol taps in a response and the phone vibrates again. "Oh, yeah, sorry. Just a thing," she says absently. Miriam waits at the door for a moment, then sits at the end of her bed.

"Sorry," Carol says. "I'll just be a minute."

"Why don't you just phone them? I can get us coffees and come back."

"Really? That would be great!"

Miriam goes to the door but hesitates. "This will be our first time apart in almost a week. I feel like we should document it."

Carol holds up her phone. "One small step for a woman..." she narrates.

Miriam opens the door, her foot poised for a clownish step over the threshold.

"...one giant leap for a headcase like Miriam."

Miriam chuckles at her own physical comedy on the way to the elevator. She has a sense of herself emerging from some long sleep. "Are you going to get a divorce?" Carol asked when Miriam told her she'd got used to having the bed to herself, and Miriam laughed at that. But that is a logical outcome, isn't it? Still, divorce seemed so formal. So *adult.* "I'm not ready to think about that," Miriam replied. Because Miriam, burning with lust for Shauna, feels like a teenager. It's not too late for them—Miriam will have fresh stories of adventure and Shauna will see that Miriam is a woman who just goes for it.

Maybe she will go for it, too. After all, she can never go back to being Murray's wife. Something has changed, though perhaps Carol and Murray can't see it yet. She imagines Shauna walking with her, what it might feel like to take her hand or hook her arm. Miriam wouldn't like the prying eyes of pedestrians, and Shauna would sense that. "Come with me," she might say, and guide Miriam away from all these souvenir bear and moose pajamas and gold-rush era facades to some secret place in the woods. When she returned the last of the *Voyager* DVDs, Shauna was there. She smiled and said, "So, what did you think?" She smiled. Maybe something had shifted?

Lost in these thoughts, Miriam wanders past the Starbucks and finds herself at the railroad station, an unremarkable two-storey building painted the colour of Murray's motorhome. If this were *Star Trek,* she'd wonder about tears in the time-space continuum. How could she travel thousands of kilometres only to end up at the motorhome again? "You were right," Miriam told Shauna when she returned the last of the *Voyager* DVDs. "It doesn't end well... but it was still worth the trip." "Ha! Atta girl," Shauna replied. Miriam nearly died from pleasure.

≶

When Miriam arrives back at the hotel, Carol is studying the *Lonely Planet.* She's dog-eared several pages, noting the dates for significant events. She likes the sound of Frostbite Music Festival, some midwinter getaway with northern lights and cozying up to keep warm, marshmallows in hot cocoa.

"Why are you looking at that?—it's our last day," Miriam hands a Mocha Frappuccino to Carol and sits on her own bed, sipping her latte.

"I have to talk to you about something." Carol puts the Frappuccino on the night table. Miriam expects bad news, perhaps, like a change in flight plans. But Carol keeps her eyes on the book. "I've met someone, but I don't know how you're going to feel about it," she says.

When Carol dated the twenty-four-year-old Peruvian guy, Miriam said something along the lines of you go, girl. Go wild? But with Murray, she laughed at what she perceived as Carol's accidental foray into sex tourism. She assumed the guy wanted to immigrate and that he saw Carol as a ticket to Canada. She never imagined that Ademir might enjoy operating the boat-tour place and getting to meet lots of people from different countries. No, no, Canada is a promised land. How else could she explain someone young being interested in Carol? "I don't know," Murray shrugged. "She's a fun gal and, shall we say, well-endowed?"

"Is that who you've been texting?" Miriam says. "How old is he this time?" Friendly ribbing next? The relationship with Ademir fizzled over email in the few weeks following Carol's departure from Peru. It surprised Miriam when Carol explained there just wasn't enough for her to do in Pisco, as if she'd considered a move there.

Carol pats the guidebook. "The same age as me..."

Miriam laughs. "Okay, spill it. Is he in prison or something?"

Carol continues to pat the book.

"Oh god, you're not one of those women who falls in love with an inmate, are you?"

"Same age as me and same sex as me..."

Carol has practised this speech many times before this moment. In these fantasies, Carol never just says it, but spoon-feeds it, as if trying to explain to a child. Once she imagined saying, "If I were a man, it would be easier to tell you about this person I met..." In another version, she tried a long-winded description of how attraction is about the soul—just think about it. We feel attracted to people before we see them naked and men and women actually don't look so different with clothes on, right? Think about a man and a woman in jeans and a T-shirt, same haircut, like a ponytail tied back, for example. And on and on. She wants Miriam to know this love is pure, beautiful and deep, not just some lesbian thing. She's worn herself out now with these speeches in her head, so when she finally tells Miriam in this moment, she arrives quickly at the quite simple fact that Carol has met someone new, so she's now in a romantic relationship with a woman.

"Her name is Janice. And I know what you're going to say, but I think you're gonna really like her and I just don't want everything to get weird. I'm still the same person, I just happen to be a woman who happens to be in a relationship with a woman."

Miriam is speechless.

"It's about the soul," Carol says, and tosses the guidebook onto her pillow.

Miriam stares at the discarded book, as if it were the conversation itself and Carol is done with it. She wants to grab it, but instead picks up the remote. Pause. No, rewind. Janice. "I didn't realize you were so experimental."

"I knew you were going to say that."

"So what does this mean? Does this mean you're gay?"

Carol shakes her head as though Miriam has just said something cruel. "Why do we need to label everything?"

But it's too easy, Miriam thinks. Where is the torment? Where is the crying and loneliness and fear of rejection? Where were the unrequited friendships and suppression of self? And if this is genuine, what took her so long? Carol didn't have a husband or the responsibility of motherhood to hold her back—what's her excuse?

"Just asking, Carol. It's a logical question." Miriam squeezes the remote. If this were Captain Janeway's tricorder, she would scan Carol for gayness. If she had a tricorder, she'd scan everyone.

"Don't you have any other questions? You can ask me whatever you want."

"Okay..." Miriam believes Carol is full of shit. "Are you happy, I guess?"

Carol nods. "Happy?" She leans forward as if whispering some hot gossip, reminding Miriam of high school, the way Carol would place her hands on her thighs and lean over to report on some sexual thing—always heterosexual, Miriam notes—forcing Miriam to lean in, too, else Carol's face be at breast level.

"I'm having the best orgasms of my life," Carol says.

3

Despite her perceived buoyancy, Carol had in fact been weighed down all week, not by the shame of her latest secret, but by the extravagant effort it required to suppress her excitement. Her hormones have gone wild and she's experienced the kind of deranged happiness that makes her feel twenty years old again, how urgently she used to love. She can't tell Miriam, because Miriam is done with Murray, for real this time, and that is surely a big deal, so instead she shares her happiness in the form of buying tickets to Whitehorse and encouraging Miriam's photo-bombing and goofiness. It's been so long since she's seen Miriam that way. Carol books the hotel and makes an itinerary so they can cram as much adventure into the week as possible. She even cancels a rendezvous with Janice to get this done, and although she can only think of Janice every minute of the day and is swimming in the euphoria of new love, she tries not to let on—she doesn't want to spoil Miriam's good time and frankly, Miriam will probably just roll her eyes at Carol. She'll think Carol is just trying to be kinky—like how she thought Ademir was some boy-toy "latin lover." "That's racist," she wanted to say, but never did because Miriam is small-minded and she didn't want to make her feel bad. But while Miriam is out confronting the motorhome omen at the railroad station, Carol is a lovesick teenager on the phone with Janice, and Janice is building her up to be honest with Miriam, because this seems to be what Carol wants. If you can't tell her the truth, Janice says, the implication is its shameful, and you got nothing to be ashamed about, baby. But Janice doesn't really mind if Carol doesn't tell Miriam, because Janice isn't sure yet if this is a one-month relationship or a six-month relationship. She thinks of it as an "in the present" relationship because she's not sure if Carol is just turned on by the *idea* of her, if she'll be able to sustain her interest when Janice is no longer new, less a "woman lover" and more a middle-aged dyke who sells garlic at farmer's markets. But for Janice, there is something about being someone's first that makes her feel powerful and special. And there is a practical element, too, because this is a small town and she pretty much knows all the lesbians already, some of them for over twenty years, and has slept with many of them over the years, and just doesn't want to date anyone anymore because it feels incestuous. Typically, her relationships with women like Carol don't pan out very well and Janice feels very much the opposite of special when the other woman loses interest and returns to her husband, which is why she tries to break up with them at the first shadow of apathy, but in this case, Carol doesn't have a husband, just a potentially disapproving cousin, and if the conversation goes badly, Carol will passionately prove to herself how passionate their lesbian affair is and that could be a lot of fun for Janice, who has lately been wondering what her life is all about because at some point she was an actor who went to hundreds of auditions and had some small parts in TV shows filmed in Vancouver, and now she sells garlic for peanuts and works at the post office, which she considers fantastically reliable though she feels like a shadow of her former irresistible self, the one who attended sex parties and hooked up every Pride without fail.

"If we're not honest," Janice says, "we can't be fully present." So on their last full day in Whitehorse, Carol tells Miriam about her woman lover. She tells her so she can be fully present in this friendship, and she's also excited to tell someone. "I'm having the best orgasms of my life."

♪

By the time they start the short drive to the guided walk to "Canyon City," Janice, whose name was first dropped a mere hour ago, is splattered throughout their conversation. "I'm sorry I can't stop talking about her," Carol says. "I've been wanting to tell someone for weeks. I guess the pressure kind of built up." She smiles bigger than she has all week as they wind down the road toward the trailhead parking lot. *Weeks*, Miriam thinks. *Poor you.* She's been agonizing over Shauna for months. She lowers the window for the breeze.

"Are you okay?" Carol asks when they arrive.

"Yeah, why?"

"You've been pretty quiet."

Okay, Carol. I have something to tell you, too. "A lesbian?" Carol might say. "I don't believe it." Or maybe she would hug her. Maybe she would make some joke. "So that's why you're done with Murray—welcome to the club!" But what next? Would she have to say this again and again, to co-workers, her brother, her daughter, or would it just spread on its own, like root rot. And she'd know because people would look at her differently, Murray's friends smiling smugly when she runs into them around town. The cashier examining her as she swipes her credit card. *Where else have those fingers been?* Her doctor, her mail carrier, her pilates instructor. She wants to crawl into a hole again.

"It's our last day here," Miriam says, as if she'd been contemplating the trip's conclusion. She makes herself smile. "To Canyon City!"

♪

Their guide is a young woman named Aurora, who looks like B'Elanna Torres, the half-Klingon engineer of *Voyager*: ready for a fight. Miriam and Carol are the only hikers this afternoon. The first stop is the willow tree on the other side of the pedestrian bridge over the Yukon River. There, Aurora reviews health and safety for the walk—reminders about water, about resting when you need to rest. "It's weirdly hot today, so we'll take more breaks than usual." Aurora has a first-aid kit, bear mace, a charged cellphone and water. "We definitely won't encounter a bear today, but if we do, we just give it space." She demonstrates backing up and saying "Woah, bear," in a low, sultry voice that reminds Miriam of Shauna. *Uh-huh, uh-huh.* That sun is hot.

Carol nods earnestly, as if this is important, and not something Miriam has told Carol a million times before on a walk, or at least one time, anyway.

"Actually, Aurora," Miriam says, "our response to the bear depends on the species and how it's behaving." Between tree-planting bear-aware videos, books and her ursine visitors at home, Miriam is certain she knows more than Aurora about bears.

"That's correct," Aurora says. "Typically, what I described is the right thing to do. We have grizzlies and black bears here obviously, but you can follow my lead—I mean, don't worry because I'll tell you what we need to do. I'm a third-year biology major specializing in behavioural science. But we won't see a bear anyway. That like never happens on this trail because there's too much traffic."

Brat.

Carol lifts one foot, displaying her Velcro sandal with poly-whatever sole. "Is this adequate footwear?"

"Yeah, it's an easy walk."

"That's a relief—eh, Miriam?" Carol pinches and flaps her T-shirt to dramatize the surprising heat.

"I thought this hike goes to a city," Miriam says.

"It's more like a pile of rusted cans, but the walk is nice."

"Sounds like we'll get our money's worth," Carol jokes, because the tour is free. She holds up her smart phone, pans around. "The journey begins," she says. "Miriam, got anything to add?" Earlier today, Miriam might have impersonated a *Voyager* crew member, scanning the willow on this M-class planet. "I'm detecting three life signs, Captain. Oh wait, that's just us," meaning Aurora, Carol and Miriam. But it turns out Janice has been on this trip the whole time, too. "The journey begins," Carol said, and Miriam was only asked to add something—comic relief for Carol's travelogue? *Here's my cousin Miriam, that headcase.* Or was this trip nothing more than reconnaissance for some future rendez-vous with Janice? Is that why Carol marked pages in the guidebook?

Miriam thinks of Captain Janeway recording her video diary, a record of her journey that would find its way back to Earth with her—or be discovered among *Voyager* wreckage long after she's gone. *Captain's log. Star date: who fucking cares. How many years have I been lost in space?* The final entries of a grey and jowly Janeway, soon to be usurped by a new captain, perhaps, from the generation of crew members conceived in space, who grew up knowing only this trip through the cosmos and who tire quickly of their parents' impractical longing.

Miriam glances down at her legs, puckered knees and mosquito-bite scabs. As a young woman, she hated the dimples on her buttocks—cellulite, she called it then, although she now recognizes it was something much more alluring at that time, young and pinchable. She has cellulite now, probably. What would Shauna call it?

"I don't want to be filmed anymore, Carol."

❧

They follow Aurora along the narrow path, Aurora stopping occasionally to offer some interpretation. She kicks the dusty trail to reveal white ash not far beneath, explaining this is the ash from a volcanic eruption seven hundred years ago, which prompted the Athabascan migration. She explains that soap berries can be used to make ice-cream. "Oh yes, Indian ice-cream!" Carol says. "Another guide told us that." Aurora crinkles her nose, Carol's use of *Indian* like a bad smell. Aurora continues—a stand of aspen is the same organism, that's why they change colour at the same time. Leaf miners eat trails through the leaves, turning them silver. This is Labrador tea. This is juniper. This is stonecrop.

Carol nods in appreciation, as if she will remember the names of these plants. "Why do we have to *label* everything," Miriam wants to say, a good-natured jibe at Carol or mean-spirited mockery. Miriam knows what LGBT stands for, but she discovered online there were other letters and even numbers, and it all makes her feel old and straight and hopeless. But Carol's love transcends these earthly definitions. *It's about the soul*, not like Miriam's sweaty, unrequited lust.

At a ridge, Aurora stops to explain about the rapids that the river had before the dam, that it doesn't look like much now, but they were kind of dangerous, so some people made money moving stuff by tramway from Canyon City to Whitehorse, and that's why it's called Whitehorse, because the rapids looked like horses. She takes a binder of laminated black-and-white photos out of her backpack and flips through them, a clumsy slideshow at this stop right under the blazing sun. Miriam takes a gulp of water. Carol puts her hand out. "Me too please and thank you." It's a wide-mouthed water bottle, but instead of sipping from it like a cup, Carol puts her whole mouth around it. "Did you just back-wash?" Miriam says.

Carol looks at the bottle for an answer. "I'm sure I didn't."

"And see that brown blob on the rocks over there?" Aurora points across the river. "That's a little brown bat."

"Ah yes, a carbon-based life form," Carol narrates, filming. She slides her fingers across the screen to zoom in. "And I thought bats lived in caves."

"You have a bat box," Miriam says.

"You know what I mean—when they're not living in a bat box, I thought they lived in caves. Dark places, anyway, not lying out on a rock. Maybe they live in caves in the winter."

"Yes, they do," Aurora says. "They hibernate. The winter roosts are called *hibernacula*."

This is news to Miriam, and she's even seen bats flying around her own property. But life experience is better than book knowledge.

Carols laughs. "How fun! Like Dracula—is that why?"

"It's plural for *hibernaculum*," Aurora says. Not much of an explanation, Miriam thinks. She probably doesn't know the answer.

Aurora turns to put the binder away. Her short black ponytail is threaded through the back of her baseball cap, reminding Miriam of the softball game she attended. She was on Season Two of *Voyager* when Shauna had mentioned an upcoming game in a league Miriam had never heard of. It wasn't clear to Miriam if she were inviting her to play or just watch—the team was called the Gay News Bears, Shauna said, which made Miriam dizzy with anticipation. (The team was originally called the Butch News Bears, but some complained of femme erasure. "Gay" was also problematic though it fit well on a T-shirt.) Miriam's sports involvement over the years was limited to volunteering at Keely's school for Sports Day. She was never interested in joining in, perhaps because she expected to be terrible or to look frumpy while running, shorts riding up her thighs and tits wagging under a sweaty T-shirt. She'd always been self-conscious of her breasts, which are not large, but the nipples point too much downward, troubling Miriam in how animal they appear, bulbous teats. She turned up at the park to watch the Gay News Bears. A tall spindly woman squatted behind home plate. At bat, short grey curls poked out of another woman's helmet. The sun made shadows beneath the muscles of the pitcher's brown arms. Another in the dugout had long hair of purple and teal and a rainbow wristband. Were all these women gay? Shauna thanked Miriam for coming, said, "Could always use a fan," and winked. A bolt passed through Miriam, and she felt simultaneously nauseated and aroused. She just watched shows on Netflix for a while after that. What if she'd gone to the next game, instead? Is that what Carol would do?

Sweat outlines the shape of Aurora's sports bra beneath her T-shirt. Probably her nipples point straight ahead. "Did you know bears are not *true* hibernators?" Miriam says to Carol. "Everybody thinks they hibernate, and they are in a deep sleep, but their body temperature actually stays high and they can wake up quickly if they need to." She dreamed of such a state once, a distant drip tick-tocking her into oblivion, until the mumble of male voices yanked her into consciousness. Hunters! But it was only Murray and that idiot P.E. teacher friend of his outside.

"Trivia face-off!" Carol says. "I can one-up you, Miriam. Did you know that there are homosexual bats?" Carol turns to the behavioural-science expert. "Did you know that, Aurora? You can add *that* to your tour!"

"There's homosexual everything," Aurora says.

Miriam thinks of the article she saw about lions a few years ago, that there are gay lions. Just imagine, the iconic king of the savannah canoodling with another bearded beast. With bats, who can even tell which one's male or female?

"Exactly," Carol adds. "See, Miriam?"

"Excuse me?"

"I just mean like Aurora says—it's everywhere."

"You're an expert on bats now? A minute ago you didn't even know they hibernate." Miriam laughs, pretending she only intended a friendly jab, and that she'd already known bats hibernate.

A red squirrel chitters in a tree nearby. "There's homosexuality among squirrels, too," Aurora says. "And they're super promiscuous."

"Really!" Carol pockets her phone. "Cute little innocent squirrels, eh?"

"Yeah, everyone tries to say that this mates for life or that mates for life. It's total crap."

"You're too young to be so cynical," Carol says. "Even I'm still hoping to mate for life—which is less of a commitment every year, mind you. Do you have a boyfriend?"

Aurora hooks her thumbs under the straps of her backpack and hops to shimmy it up her hips. She exhales, almost huffs, as if this maneuver has taxed her, but this huff reminds Miriam of Keely, how she'd demonstrate impatience with Miriam's simple questions about her plans for the evening or what she was planning to do with the rest of her life.

"I have a girlfriend," Aurora says.

Miriam has sometimes imagined "coming out." In one scenario, she falls in love with an elegant, urban lesbian, like one of the characters from the L-Word, the one with a career as a gallery curator or maybe the celebrity hairdresser. Their love is surprising and sudden, and she is provoked into coming out to Murray. "You're sure spending a lot of time with that dyke," he would say, although Murray probably wouldn't say that. Or maybe he would. From there, they'd argue about how Miriam's entitled to her own friendships, although Murray has never been an obstacle to her independence, and in fact, has encouraged her many times to go out and get a life. The result was Stitch & Bitch and yoga. "I'm entitled to more than friendship," Miriam dares in this fantasy. It's not really logical, this idea of being in a monogamous relationship with Murray yet being entitled to sex with the hairdresser, but something about it seems fair, too. Miriam has never imagined coming out to someone who is gay. They would just know, like how she knew about Shauna, but maybe Shauna never did know about Miriam. It was never spoken of, anyway, not in so many words. It's hard to tell. So when Aurora announces her girlfriend, Miriam laughs—scoffs. Because this is ridiculous. One day she is the only lesbian in the world except for Shauna, and today surrounded like it's no big deal? It feels like Aurora is doing this *to* her, in the same way Keely had responded sarcastically about life plans, "No, I think I'll just drop out of high school and become a stripper."

"I have a girlfriend, too!" Carol volunteers. "Janice."

"Me, too," Miriam wishes she could say. If she had a girlfriend, she wouldn't have to tell anyone what she is—a lesbian, only who she is with, "Shauna," and that she's having the best orgasms of her life. "Shauna" is much easier to say than "lesbian."

"I don't believe in monogamy, though," Aurora says, as if to distinguish herself from Carol, and Miriam finds this strangely reassuring. She takes the opportunity to helpfully steer the conversation away from Janice. "I read an article in the *Guardian* that there are gay lions," Miriam says. "And they don't believe in monogamy, either." She winks at Aurora, a conspiratorial peace offering, not creepy because who would imagine an interest in someone so young and self-righteous? But the article or the monogamy comment or the wink only makes Aurora angry.

"See what I mean? Why is that even news?" She tells them about a family of grizzlies with two moms, as it turns out, and their three cubs, who were spotted not far from town earlier this summer. "It was in the paper, but with the headline 'Berenstain Bears Visit Chadburn Lake.' They made it totally heteronormative," she declares, and resumes walking.

"That's terrible!" Carol says. As if she even knows what that means, Miriam thinks, following. Or did she just learn the term from Janice? But Miriam knows—she first came across the term "heteronormative" on some lesbian website several years ago, and concluded it basically meant the idea that boys should be boys and girls should be girls. She found the lesbian website after Googling "how to come out as a lesbian." Most of the search results were tip lists for teenagers, step-by-step instructions on talking to parents or accessing services, which made Miriam wonder if it was just too late for her now. But one archaic website with too much bolded text explained "how to come out later in life." That coming out "is a long process of integrating lesbianism into the rest of your life," and how this is more difficult to do later in life when you've already developed a heterosexual identity. She'd never thought of herself as someone with a "heterosexual identity," just as Miriam, but when she tried saying "I am a lesbian" to the mirror, it came out sounding like lines in a script, and badly acted. She needed a director, someone to stand behind her, lift up one arm, *like this, that's right*. A kiss on the neck? Is that what Carol's "soulmate" did for her? Miriam imagines a stout woman in a men's shirt wrapping an oversized arm around Carol's expanding midsection. Miriam can't imagine Carol with anyone who doesn't look like a man.

"Do you even know what that means, Carol?" Miriam says. But the conversation has moved on.

"Natural selection? Of course I do."

"Anyway," Aurora continues, "it's probably more like 'survival of the most cooperative.'" She then explains something about Sexual Conflict Theory, that avoiding sex can have just as much impact on evolution as seeking it out. At first, Miriam did like sex with Murray, the contact, sweating, the sense of fullness. What the erection meant about her, that she was desirable, a success! It felt like power—she controlled his body. But after a while, Murray became familiar and so did sex. They found what worked and the whole thing became efficient. They were each other's tool for masturbation. Is this just what happens to a couple after a while? Is this when people get into Japanese rope stuff? But then this became something worse than boring. It became sad— frightening even. Miriam couldn't understand why, so she couldn't talk about it. Instead, she became tired, went to bed at a different time than Murray. It wasn't difficult to avoid, really. In the end, which is probably the last ten years, they had sex about once every couple of months. She wonders now why he didn't leave her years ago and how he could have been content all this time. How has this impacted their evolution?

Pine cones pop in the heat—serotinous cones, Aurora explains to Carol. The river below is blue-green serene. Glacial silt. Second-longest river in Canada. Longest salmon migration. "And home to the longest fish ladder in the world," Carol says, quoting the rail-thin fish-ladder guide who'd boasted days earlier. Who cares? Miriam thought. It's some place a bunch of rotten-looking salmon pass through on their way to procreate, which just means dumping a bunch of sperm and dumping a bunch of eggs. Do some of them choose not to bother? Do some just live their whole lives all silvery and free in the ocean? Is that Sexual Conflict?

"What about fish?" Miriam says. "Can they be gay, too?"

Aurora doesn't know, but she answers the question anyway. "Yeah, definitely. I don't see why they'd be the exception."

❧

Not far up Miles Canyon, a black bear wanders toward Canyon City. The trail is frequented by humans, but they never seem to leave a trace—no forgotten hot dogs like at the campground that one time with slurps of ketchup left on picnic tables. Still, Bear has a few secret places along the way, and the human activity makes it unpopular for other bears, which suits her, because she's small. It's unusually hot and she ambles slowly, irritated also by a hemorrhoid. The issue has plagued her since she had cubs, and always seems to flare up around the hottest time of year. In the fall, the rosehips will bother her, too, the itch unbearable. And today it is hot. Even the birds are quiet. She pauses at a patch of bearberry, nibbles all the dry and mealy fruits then lies down, the ground shrubs like perfumed cushions. She rubs her face against the waxy leaves, reminding her of nuzzling with her mate last summer, as her mate's cubs tumbled around in the shade nearby. As the weather cooled, the need to eat overtook her and they parted ways, each seeking out their own favourite spots to fatten up. The breeze off the water is dreamy now on this hot day—she'll make her way to that spot where she can go in, to cool off and relieve the burning itch. But she needs a rest—she can feel the hemorrhoid as she walks now, a distracting pressure. This green and leafy moment offers respite from the irritation, and she floats into unconsciousness.

She dreams again of a woman. In these dreams, the woman appears first in her peripheral vision, and when Bear turns to look, she is gone. When Bear looks ahead to continue, a sour-smelling tree is in her path. Then the woman steps out from behind the tree, fleshy as river fish, with black-lichen hair draped from her head. It's impossible that the tree could have concealed her before—it is always some scraggly balsam or spruce, pokey low branches rendering them useless as backscratchers. So Bear must alter course until she glimpses the woman again, turns to look, looks ahead to continue, another tree in her path, and so on. This woman is always in the way.

❧

After the softball game, the next time Miriam saw Shauna was at the grocery store, which was next door to the Viv's Vids. Miriam smiled when she saw her thumbing tomatoes, and Shauna smiled back, then continued to the cucumbers. Miriam thought she must not recognize her—out of context. Could Miriam be so forgettable? Normally, she would just go up to the person, say, "Remember me? Video store—you turned me on to *Star Trek: Voyager*?" Followed by oh yeah, out of context, ha ha. But instead, she pushed her basket-cart to the avocadoes to find one ripe enough to stuff her face with guacamole for dinner. She almost wanted to cry and shook her head at the feeling—hormones. Are we ever free of them? Then Shauna was beside her, holding out some exotic fruit that looked like a blow fish: "To boldly eat what no one has eaten before!" Miriam was overcome with gratitude, laughed too long and too hard, so that Shauna asked her if she was okay. Then Miriam cried. If Miriam kept a log, a record of her possibly doomed journey through space, someone might later identify this as a transitional moment—*Captain! You're needed on the bridge!*—because Shauna touched Miriam's arm that day. Their relationship became tactile. Physical, Miriam thinks. And she believed then that this progression toward intimacy was an iterative process, though she wouldn't put it that way. Despite her aversion for sports, Miriam would be more likely to use baseball metaphors. Softball. After that day with the exotic fruit, Miriam accelerated her *Voyager* consumption, discussing highlights with Shauna every trip to the video store. Yet after a hundred episodes, she's arrived at this vague location, like somewhere in the Delta quadrant, while Carol had made one trip to Seedy Saturday.

❧

Carol's pink streak sticks to her sweaty cheek, ruddy now with exertion. Aurora is also sweating, but instead of worn out, she looks like she's just stepped out of a hot shower. They walk single file through this narrow part of the trail. No one talks as a breeze shuffles the trembling aspen leaves above. High-bush cranberry lines the lower side of the trail, which Aurora points out as they walk. "In another month maybe, you can eat the berries."

Miriam thinks of the black bear at home, the female with the yellow tag, the tops of salmonberry bushes rustling in the backyard. She stays inside to give the bear space—that is the correct thing to do, Murray, you idiot. But part of her wants to be outside, too. She wonders, "If I joined the bear there with an ice-cream bucket, picked the berries from the other side of the bushes, would she tolerate me?" Miriam has read of this kind of relationship with bears, though it seems reckless. Murray derived cruel satisfaction from the death of Timothy Treadwell, the man who spent thirteen summers living with Alaskan grizzlies until he was fatally mauled. Being close to animals is stupid. And Miriam is smarter than that—she knows that bears and humans should stay away from each other, that the bear's safety depends on repressing this curious need to get closer. But, she was beginning to wonder, can a practical fear squash this odd longing?

"The bears must find these berries quite attractive," Miriam says.

"They do, but like I said, this trail is too touristy."

"I just mean we don't have cranberries on the Coast. But they love the salmonberries in my yard."

"Actually, you *do* have high-bush cranberry on the Coast." Aurora laughs. "It's okay, though—a lot of people just don't pay attention to this stuff."

"Well, they love the salmonberries and blackberries at my place. I've basically relinquished the yard to them." Miriam's comment is like a joke she might make to a dog-walker at the end of a taut leash—"Who's walking *whom*?" Miriam expects a polite chuckle from Aurora—she is much older, after all.

But instead, Aurora launches. "That is actually really dangerous. I know that bears are cute, but they are wild animals, and if you don't have a fence, you're basically habituating the bear to humans. I know you don't mean any harm, but it is actually harmful." Boundaries are important, Aurora thinks.

Perhaps Aurora could join Murray in the shouting outside. "I know they're wild," Miriam says. "I don't sneak up on it for a photo op, Aurora. I just watch from inside—there isn't a human in sight. I think chasing them off is actually what habituates them."

"I didn't say to chase them off—"

"And bears have a right to forage. People plant things for deer and rabbits now. Isn't that the permaculture solution? So why can't I allow my berries to be a stop on the bear's route. It's the same bear, you know. We live in harmony."

"But not everyone will stay back—you're teaching the bear that backyards are safe and it's a short step for him to just go into someone's garage or even their house, and then he'll just be killed. That's what conservation officers do—they basically just kill bears."

This sounds like a childish exaggeration to Miriam. "First of all, I can't be responsible for every other person on the planet. And second of all, the bear is a she not a he. What am I going to do? Just cut off a predictable food supply this year, right when she needs the calories more than ever?" Where's the humaneness in that? And why is Aurora arguing at all? Miriam is the guest on this tour, and Aurora basically works for her—it's free, but someone is paying Aurora, and it's probably tax dollars, Miriam thinks. Although it is, in fact, a non-profit conservation society that foots the bill, and Aurora's job really is to educate the public about flora and fauna, to promote conservation and Leave No Trace wilderness ethics. But this is exactly what Miriam is tired of.

Why must she always just *imagine* contact with a hot, breathing body? She can't survive on a touch on the arm. The sound of lip-smacking grunts on the other side of the berries. Miriam is an animal, too, isn't she? What is so immoral about wanting to be closer to that? And Carol is no help, with this talk about the soul. Sure, she wants Shauna's soul. But she wants her body, too. *Uh-huh, uh-huh.* Why is it so hot? It's all too easy for Aurora to say—she has a girlfriend.

"Maybe we can just agree to disagree for now," Carol says. "It's too hot for this conversation."

After a pause, Miriam adds, "The bear is the only reason I haven't ripped those blackberries right out—they take over everything."

Carol turns to Miriam with a pleading expression. "Why?" she mouths. Then announces, "Let's have a water break."

❧

They sit near a patch of bearberry and no one notices the tuft of black fur snagged on a nearby balsam or that the bearberry patch has been picked clean or that the ground shrubs have been squashed in a bear-shaped depression. Aurora has spent much of her time at the trailhead studying the field guide and memorizing names and bits of trivia to make the names seem interesting. This has filled her with facts but has not helped her become an observant person. Aurora is downright unobservant, in fact, which is why the other trail guide is not here. There should be two of them—for safety. But they fought this morning when Aurora failed to acknowledge their drunken make-out session the previous night. The other guide brought it up, hopefully. "What do you think last night was about?" she said casually, although she picked nervously at her fingers as she asked and if Aurora had bothered to notice, she might have observed a healthy fear. Aurora shrugged. "Cider." Ha ha. She hoped that would make the problem go away.

"So where does a gal meet women up here?" Carol asks.

"I don't know. I live in Victoria—I met my girlfriend at school."

Did they sit together in class? Miriam wonders. Go for coffee some time or a hike in the woods, and then Aurora told this girl she liked her more than a friend? Then what? Miriam imagines this other girl—this other *queer*—stopping, shocked by Aurora's confession. Aurora becomes nervous, sick even, afraid she's just blown it, and at their next Sexual Conflict Theory class the girl avoids Aurora by sitting on the other side of the room, careful to look past her as she checks the clock on the wall, if classrooms still have clocks, and Aurora, in turn, avoids her too, avoids everyone in fact, unsure of who is looking at her because she looks worried and who is looking at her because she's that girl who told the other girl she was in love with her. She's that lesbian. Or perhaps they went camping and Aurora suggested they zip their sleeping bags together into one giant bag because it was cold, but the other girl sensed there was more to it than that, because it wasn't that cold at all and also Aurora was too excited about what a brilliant idea this was, until the girl said flatly, "I said no," and Aurora knew that was it, first camping trip together and the friendship was over. But that's not what happened because Aurora just said she had a girlfriend. Somehow, something else occurred.

"I met Janice at Seedy Saturday," Carol begins. The annual market for all things garden-related, with information booths on permaculture, mason bee houses and those bat boxes. "Janice was selling marinated garlic cloves that she makes herself—she's really multitalented." Then to Miriam, "You'll like her a lot." So that was the beginning, and somehow, in just a few short weeks, that led to the best orgasms of Carol's life. It was the part in the middle that eluded Miriam.

"So, you met her at school," Miriam says to Aurora.

"At a friend's."

"At a friend's," Miriam repeats. "Then what?"

"What do you mean?"

"I mean you met... and then what?"

"Miriam, for godssake," Carol says. "You know how it works. You met Murray and then what? It's the same thing for two women."

After sitting with her devastation for a few days, Miriam had swung to anger about Shauna's comment—"A woman who knows who she is and what she wants." Was that passive aggressive? She should've demanded, "And who are *you*, Shauna! What do *you* want?" Hoped the answer was Miriam. Or if not demanded, at least pressed her to elaborate, to keep the conversation flowing. What if Miriam had said, "A woman who knows what she wants? Career-wise, you mean?" Shauna would say no, no, I mean in love, a woman who knows what she wants in love. And what flowed from there would have been different. Miriam even feels nervous imagining how she might have shifted the course of this conversation, eddying her wildest hopes and dreams. Maybe that moment with Shauna was the "right opportunity to change my life." But instead of transforming everything, Miriam said she missed an old footbridge. Was it too late now?

See you at the video store.

See you at the video store. See you at the video store. See you at the video store.

What if Miriam had gone to Seedy Saturday with Carol and beat her to the jarred garlic, complimented Janice's labels? "Why do we have to label everything?" Carol might have said, placing her hands on her thighs and leaning in, pretending to examine the bounty. Would that be charming?

"It is not the same thing for two women," Miriam says.

"Oh, really, Miriam. And you're the expert?"

Aurora stands and dusts off her shorts. She's taken out her phone and glances at it as she says, "We're almost at Canyon City, so we could maybe just keep going." She thumbs some message, and Miriam assumes she's communicating with her girlfriend. Maybe texting, *Stuck at work with total cow*, meaning Miriam.

"Come on, Carol, for godssake. You know how easy it is to meet a man—it's like every man you meet there's some assessment, everyone knows that. Getting a man in bed is as easy as flashing your tits."

"I wouldn't agree with that at all," Carol says. "You make it sound so primitive, Miriam. Where's the romance? I'd say it's more like a sixth sense."

"Yes, and the penis is a compass needle."

"What about connection? You don't fall in love with someone's butt or biceps—it's in the eyes, or something small, like just how they smile. You *know* this, Miriam. So that's what I'm saying is the same—you feel that connection. It's not like Janice flashed her tits at me."

"That's my point—it's harder to meet women."

Carol laughs. "Is it? Because Aurora and I don't think so. Do we Aurora?"

Aurora looks up from her phone. "Sorry, what?"

"Do you think it's harder to meet women than men?" Carol waits for confirmation.

"I wouldn't know," Aurora says, then texts the other guide, the one who is not here: *I didn't mean I don't take YOU seriously.*

"Oh, yes, of course not." Carol shakes her head. "It's a different world for them, hey, Miriam?"

The other guide replies to Aurora: *Maybe you're non-monogamous, but I'm NOT. And you knew that. So I guess you're just that selfish???*

"How is your world any different from Aurora's?" Miriam says. She imagines everything is easy for Aurora, who can just come out to two strangers on a trail like it's nothing. And Carol can just stop by a Seedy Saturday one day and change her spots to stripes. How long could she possibly sustain this experimental fling? Miriam gives it another month.

Aurora: *And you knew I was NON-monogamous, so why am I the bad one?*

"It's completely different. You know how we grew up, Miriam. It wasn't accepted. Not like now—we even have that rainbow crosswalk!"

"So you've been a lesbian all this time, suffering in silence until a rainbow crosswalk appeared by the slipper store?"

Carol is silent. Serotinous cones continue to pop in the heat.

The other guide texts: *Why is everyone poly? Why can't I be enough?*

Aurora looks up from her phone at the scene. These two middle-aged white women, sweaty and miserable, sitting in the dirt arguing about how to meet men or women or something—she hasn't been paying much attention. They're quiet now, but unmoving like children with no one else to play with. How did the day become so weird?

"I think I just want to go back now," Carol says finally. Stands.

"Canyon City is really close," Aurora says, as if this is an important factor to consider. She thumbs into her phone: *No one is enough for anyone. And it's wrong to expect someone to be.*

"Are you coming, Miriam?"

But Miriam is not finished here. Even dammed, the river continues flowing out to the Pacific. This atmosphere barely breathable. "I'm not homophobic," Miriam says, which makes her sound homophobic.

"We'll talk about it later."

"You just sprung this on me out of nowhere, like it's nothing. You know I have my own shit to deal with right now." Miriam feels she might cry. She might rest her head on her knees. It could feel good to let it out and it might help shift things. She doesn't like who's she's become just now, the homophobe in the group, and she can feel their accusing stares, even disgust. If they could see how much she's suffering, it could soften things, although that doesn't work with Murray, either.

"Yes, I know, Miriam. How could anyone possibly forget?"

The tourists are fighting now, Aurora writes. A change in subject might be good.

"It's why we're on this trip," Carol continues, "but my life goes on whether it's all about you or not."

Miriam shakes her head. "You still don't get it." She is getting ready to spit it out. Say it, just out with it. It could be a great release—the best orgasm of her life, the right opportunity to change everything, to say who she is and what she wants. I am a lesbian! I want to have sex with Shauna! Other stuff, too, I think! If she can just choke it out—

"I'm hot," Carol says. "Let's go back."

"But Canyon City—"

"I don't care, Aurora. I never cared." Carol begins to walk back down the trail, unmoved by Miriam's state.

"Well, I do want to go to Canyon City." Miriam stands. "We've already come this far. I want to see these fucking cans." To Miriam, this means the tour will continue, because they must stay together. This trail requires a guide, a bear safety talk, a binder. And the goal is to reach this historical site, so named for a glorified transit station that existed for a couple years.

"I'm not walking back on my own," Carol says. "I don't have bear mace."

"There won't be a bear, right, Aurora?" Miriam enjoys this question because it's awkward for Aurora. If she says no, it means abandoning her client. If she says yes, it means contradicting her earlier smug confidence.

"I think I should accompany Carol back. It's hot so this could be a health and safety issue."

Touché.

"But I don't know how to get to Canyon City alone!" Miriam says.

Aurora steps past Miriam. Miriam's neck is sweaty and she smells like baby powder and skunk. "It's honestly really close—just right up the trail like less than ten minutes."

Carol has sat down again on the trail going the other way. She's taken out her phone and is thumbing the screen. Aurora's phone vibrates and she also turns to her screen. They all three are silent as Carol and Aurora converse with women they've had sex with, and Miriam waits for someone to notice her waiting.

Aurora: *Yes, I'm safe. It's just two old women.*

Carol: *I thought Miriam would understand.*

Aurora: *Don't feel guilty—I get why you left. It wasn't just cider.*

Janice: *Aw, babe, I'm sorry. They say misery loves company.*

Aurora: *I can't change who I am, though. I love my girlfriend and I don't believe in choosing between love but expanding to include more. Why can't we just have fun?*

Carol: *Yeah, that's Miriam. I thought maybe she'd changed.*

The other guide: *Because I'm in love with you.*

Miriam: "I'm going alone then. You two can just sit here on your phones." And she walks off, quickly at first, then slowing so it's easier for Carol to catch up with her, but she makes it all the way to the pile of rusted cans without hearing a peep.

❧

The pile of rusted cans. A mysterious metal ring around a tree. A tramway car on two silvered logs, and an interpretive sign to explain why it's sitting in this unexceptional dusty clearing, shaded by aspen behind, and cooled by a breezy river nearby. It's here Miriam learns how short-lived the tramway actually was. Why would they name this place after such a blip? And Miriam sees the guided walks and brochures and interpretive signs as objects circling this blip in time, like orbiting some mass, a tiny dark spot, a tear in the time-space continuum. What would Shauna think of that description? "That's very poetic," she might say. Miriam imagines travelling back in time, walking with Shauna again, the same quiet drizzling day, not so wet that they're uncomfortable, but enough to be dewy and beautiful. "Makes you think," Shauna says in this fantasy, then takes Miriam's hand. The falls gush supportively as Shauna turns toward her and moves a lock of wet hair from Miriam's forehead, leans in. They kiss. Oh god, such a kiss. How Miriam longs for this kiss! Those soft, warm lips and the cool rain dripping down their faces, mixing with their hot tongues.

Miriam, hands on the interpretive sign to ground her, is lost in these thoughts when a black bear shoulders out of the trees. The bear almost doesn't see Miriam at first because she is distracted by pain and irritation and Miriam stands so still there at the sign, but the smell of this woman arrives, something sour and salty. The woman's eyes are closed and dark hair hangs limply. Normally, the bear would continue unceremoniously, more inconvenienced than afraid, but today she is hungry and her anus hot and achy, something itchy, too, and she wants to scratch but knows that offers no relief. It's hot and this could be contributing to her mood. She wants to take a plunge in the river, but first this woman, like the woman in her dreams, the one that keeps getting in her way. Of all the places each of them could be. The bear leans left, leans right. She does this to feel the ground beneath her feet.

Miriam has begun to sense a lumbering presence, and assumes it is a mute and apologetic Carol. When she opens her eyes, she'll come out to Carol. She'll just say it, all hot and tired. Would you listen to those cones popping in this fucking heat? An unmotivated spawning. "See how they're just reacting to the environment?" she'd say. "That's what I've been doing, Carol. You see, I'm a lesbian, that's what I am." And this will explain everything and what happens after couldn't possibly be worse than what has happened before.

Miriam inhales and exhales. This is it. "Carol," she says, but Carol does not respond—she's behind her now, on the river side, Miriam senses.

It tumbles out, muttered, uneventful like pebbles tossed into the water. "Carol I think I'm gay, I mean I *am* gay, I know I am." Too quiet. Carol will ask, "What?" And she'll have to say it again. Her stomach flips. She might throw up. Carol says nothing. Miriam turns.

In waking life, Bear has allowed her dreams to guide her: with a persistent vision of a lake, she lingered longer, looping the shore twice and this is how she encountered her mate last summer. In another dream, the berries turned black, shrivelled and were carried off by jays who heckled one another with their throaty rasps and Bear knew the high-bush cranberry would ripen sooner that year. She followed a trail of jays like mountaintop sentries to a bountiful stand of ruby-red droplets. And then the dream woman, the one who is always in the way: Here she really is—what can be learned from her now?

The woman slams one hand to her chest. Her eyes are wide now, wide, wide, wide. Her mouth, too. What has just come out of it? Bear thinks of bats falling from a dead tree, dark and fluttering chaos. This horrible energy like too much noise, a sharp pulsing in time with this woman's unpredictable heartbeat. The woman holds her hands out, a soft moan coming from the open mouth. Bear sways her head from side to side, cheeks puckering, huff.

"Whoa, Bear," Miriam says calmly, though she is terrified. Had she surprised the bear? She wants to back up, but she is in front of the interpretive sign. She realizes that in all her nearness to bears, she has never had to speak to one. This bear is showing signs of stress, she tells herself. How to relieve a bear's stress? "Whoa, Bear," she says again, looking slowly down the trail to where Carol and Aurora are probably still ten minutes away thumbing their phones. She should not make eye contact, don't make eye contact because this is a challenge and she doesn't want to challenge the bear. "It's okay, Bear. We're on the same team, okay?" She takes a step aside.

Bear jerks forward, smacking the dust with front paws and the woman startles, almost hops back against the sign. More incoherent sounds, low and patronizing. Bear dreamed once of beating the ground until a forest disappeared.

Miriam wonders if she is going to die, although that is irrational.

Signs of stress. Bears bluff charge. Bluster. Remain calm. Do not puke right now. "Okay, bear," she says again and takes a step aside. Sweat drips down the back of her knee.

Bear lifts her snout, huge nostrils opening closing opening closing.

Miriam is beside the interpretive sign now. If she can take a couple more steps back, then she'll be behind it—a protective barrier. She has imagined mute understanding with a bear, but now feels clumsy fear. Does the bear hate her? The dream dictionary would probably tell her to be grateful for this magical encounter, that the animal has come to teach her something. "Yeah, that you shouldn't storm off alone in the woods." But Aurora said bears never come to this touristy trail—had Miriam dared the bear to show? Miriam steps behind the sign.

The woman is retreating. Bear should leave, she knows this is what she should do, but she hesitates. Something holds her there.

In Miriam's peripheral vision, she sees the bear turn its head one way, then the other, as if contemplating its next direction, though it could be a stressful rocking. And then she thinks of Captain Janeway, navigating hostile aliens in the Delta quadrant. *We mean you no harm. We're trying to find our way home—can you help us?*

She tries psychic messages instead, like she does at home when the bear is at the salmonberries.

Miriam: *I'm going to move back now, back down this same trail, down the river toward the fish ladder.*

Bear noses. On a breeze from the river, metallic scent of Arctic char. A sharp itch pulses on her anus.

Miriam pictures the route, in case the bear understands images, not words: The high-bush cranberries, the willow, the bridge, the hotel. The plane, the ferry, the blackberries and salmonberries, the yellow plums that'll drop soon. Bins of plums, juicy, neglected and fermenting in the heat. Something sticky. Shauna's hands. Black hair. Bear?

The bear yawns—bored or anxious?—and looks toward the river.

With the bear now turned away, Miriam looks directly at it. A few white tufts stick to its fur, dandelion gone to seed. On its haunches, a faint orange confetti of desiccated cones. And Miriam longs to touch this creature, not to feel the thick black coat, its dense underlayer and smooth outer layer oiled by hot skin and sweat, but to feel it breathe, its ribs expanding, contracting, hear the breath within that chamber. She feels her own breath calm and takes another step back. Those ears, those shaggy elbows. Another step, another. Is it a hot day for the bear, too? Miriam moves away yet feels in each step an agreement, a rare camaraderie, a mutual respect for space. With each step back, she feels a connection grow.

The woman moves away, pausing between each step as if testing this new position, straight as a tree. It's unnatural the way she moves, the way she contemplates each spot. She holds her hands up strangely, too, palms out, making fleshy leaves of them. The sour saltiness diminishes as she moves away, and Bear feels powerful again. She beat the ground and a forest disappeared. Dream life and waking life separated only by a blink, she lumbers into the blue-green water.

᠈

Miriam will find Carol and Aurora waiting for her farther down the trail, at a spot where they could dip their feet in the water. On the walk back, Miriam is pumping with adrenalin and excitement and gratitude, and also can't wait to tell Aurora what happened, because Aurora was wrong. So wrong. Not only has Miriam encountered a bear on this "touristy trail," but she's had the most intimate bear encounter of her life.

But when she finally reaches them, she hesitates. Suddenly, she's not ready to share.

Everyone is in a better mood. Carol seems to have assumed Miriam's solo trip has brought her back to Earth. "There she is!" Carol says.

Miriam is grateful for her short-term memory, but she apologizes anyway. "Can I blame the heat?"

"It probably *was* the heat," Carol says. "Put your feet in the water. You'll feel better."

The bear had continued in the other direction, upriver, but Miriam suggests they head back right away. She splashes her face and arms, which satisfies Carol. Miriam is filled with some new energy, Carol can tell. "What's got into you now?" she asks, smiling.

"I'll tell you later." Miriam winks, gesturing to Aurora.

They walk back to the trailhead mostly in silence. Carol asks Aurora if bats really are blind and Aurora says no. Some even see in the UV spectrum, a whole other range of light. Just imagine, Carol says, all the colours we can't see.

At the car, Miriam pretends to want a brochure after all, for a souvenir, and she trots back to the sandwich-board sign where Aurora gathers her things from a locked box. "I didn't want to frighten Carol," Miriam says, "but you should know I met a black bear at Canyon City."

"Really," Aurora says. "Are you sure it wasn't something else?"

Miriam laughs. "Hm. Black fur? Big? Yeah, you're right, maybe it was a squirrel."

Aurora slides on a pair of sunglasses. "Have a safe journey home."

§

Later, Miriam and Carol go to the hotel bar. Carol orders a pineapple margarita, which comes in a ridiculous bowl-sized stem glass, but Miriam wants something austere, like Captain Janeway. *Coffee. Black.* She orders a vodka tonic, a spirit on the rocks.

"It's not that you saw a bear that shocks me," Carol says. "It's that you waited until we got to the car to tell me about it!"

Miriam sips her drink proudly at first. This restraint has impressed Carol. Miriam explained in the car that she just didn't want to freak her out, which meant she's considerate, and this makes up for what Carol perceived as homophobic irritation earlier. But Miriam had kept the encounter private for other reasons, and after a few more minutes of basking in this sweet praise, this little deception sours. "There's actually something else I wanted to tell you," Miriam begins. She drinks more, stirs the cubes with the tiny straw. "I've wanted to tell someone a long time, but this is really hard—for me, it's hard. I don't know where to start."

"What happens in Whitehorse, stays in Whitehorse?" Carol holds her margarita bowl up in a toast.

"Ha." Miriam clinks her glass. "You're the first person I've told. Or *will* have told."

"You can tell me anything, Miriam. There's nothing you can't tell me—we're family. Spit it out." Carol's straw is bigger than Miriam's, as if the mouth of a margarita customer is powered by more suction. Miriam watches the yellow drink move down the glass.

"Can I have a sip?" Miriam says, and Carol slides her glass over. The pineapple is bright and shining, but Carol's recipe is better, Miriam thinks. Some magical ingredient she adds—mint, perhaps. *Zest for life! Live a little. Why not?* All these rules Carol lives by. Miriam slides the drink back.

"Here's the deal, Carol. I kind of think I'm gay. Like a lesbian."

Miriam splays her hands on the table, something solid to ground her, but her hands are sweaty and cold. If this were *Voyager,* she might wonder about a life-support system malfunction.

Carol's mouth drops, then closes. She stares at her drink, and for a moment, Miriam thinks she's contemplating Miriam's germs on the straw. But Carol is with Janice, and such disgust would not make sense. "That actually makes sense," Carol says finally. She looks at Miriam. "Oh my god, Miriam. That makes total sense." It annoys Miriam the way Carol confirms this, as if it's just some hypothesis Miriam's floated past her, as if to ask, "So whaddaya think?" But this thought thrills Miriam, too, because she has said it, said she's a lesbian, and what happens next is a familiar irritation with Carol that has nothing to do with anything.

"Does it, Carol?" Miriam asks sarcastically. "You approve of my theory?" They cackle like teenagers. Then Miriam cries. Carol hugs her. Miriam says don't hug me I'm fine. Then she says she feels weird. Then, no, I feel fucking great. "I'm giving you a bear hug now," Carol says, and squeezes Miriam so much Miriam becomes conscious of a sunburn on her right arm. She must have walked on the sunny side on the way upriver.

After a couple more drinks, Miriam adds, "I hate that word, though."

"The basil is not doing it for me." Carol pushes her drink toward Miriam.

"Don't you hate that word? *Lezzbian...* It's so tonguey."

"That's not a bad thing, Miriam." Carol winks, which of course does nothing for Miriam except make her think of Shauna. Shauna, who is probably sleeping right now, holding a pillow, but one day, hopefully, Miriam, the two of them moaning in the dark.

"What time is it?" Miriam says to her glass. Out or not, her body continues longing for a wilder satisfaction.

4

"Run for the hills," Shauna thought after her hike with Miriam. She'd felt that first swell of attraction when she handed Miriam the *Star Trek* DVD. Shauna winked and Miriam flushed, red splashing up her neck. *She wears her heart on her sleeve,* Shauna thought. She needed that. Miriam was married, but relationships were never simple. With her former partner, it was simple, but it still ended. Her partner was offered a job at a northern university and she couldn't pass that up, but it didn't seem like she'd even considered the option. "What about us?" Shauna had asked.

"Do you want to move with me?"

"You mean *will* I move with you?"

Now, Shauna wanted someone who'd love her forever, or at least aspire to. *Please come with me.* Why couldn't her ex have said that? But as she and Miriam paused at footbridges or stopped to admire the lichen draped from the branches of old cedars, Miriam talked too long about how she was trying to be honest. "I'm trying to be more honest in my life." "It was never really an honest relationship." "It's not always easy, being honest with myself." And Shauna couldn't risk closeness with a person who can't be honest. She's worked too long and too hard at love to put herself through that again.

"So you ghosted her?" a younger friend says.

Shauna asks what that means. But she doesn't fully agree. "I still see her at the store."

"But you weren't exactly honest, either."

No, she hasn't been. And then she thinks of how, when the sun streams across Miriam's face, her eyes, flecked with brown and green, remind Shauna of her childhood marbles.

Before the yellow plums drop from the tree, Miriam picks them, tossing each one carelessly into a Rubbermaid. The container is so heavy when she is finished that she must drag it to her car, leaving a long depression marking her route through the grass. She can't lift it into the car, though, so she must split the load across two containers instead, and her hands and forearms get sticky with juices as she scoops and grabs at the bruised plums.

Once loaded, she drives up the logging roads, past the place where people are camped out and the trail with the signs that someone nailed on the trees one year. She drives perhaps only five kilometres up the road, although it's farther than she's ever been. She stops at the remnant of a pull-out, clumps of grass growing somehow, although she does not associate grass with forest. It's all second-growth or third-growth forest around here. This lot, judging by the height of the trees, was probably planted in the 1990s, not long before Miriam strapped on her own planting bags.

Still, in the forest, she hears a wren ring out somewhere and the soft chitting of some dark-eyed juncos, perhaps. She drags both bins until she is just far enough from the road that it feels private, and she dumps the bins of bruised and weeping yellow plums onto the ground. "Satisfied?" Miriam says, thinking of Aurora. And Murray. "I have so many plums," she'd told Shauna at the DVD sale—the renamed store, "Turn Back Time," now packed with vintage turntables and smelling like lemon wood-oil—needed the space. Miriam had planned on asking her if she'd like some. "I think I might drag them into the woods for the bears," she said instead.

For their own protection, Miriam won't encourage the bears on her property, but she won't pretend they're not out there, either—foraging, seeking, thirsting, yawning, squinting, napping, running, climbing, fishing and caressing and fucking and playing and looking and experiencing the thrill of their own discoveries, a dry cedar den, a berried path between gravel roads or a mountain of juicy plums.

Midden

I've come to associate Rita with muffins, and I don't like this. I don't like the way she picks at them, extracting the bits of dark chocolate first, then the oven-dried cranberries that stick out the top. The muffin looks like gulls have pecked it before she even bothers to tear it in half—she never uses a knife—and attempts to smear a pad of butter that is still too cold.

She moved out six months ago. "I've given this a lot of thought," she said. "And I can't remain in this relationship any longer, it's not healthy for me, and I'm not blaming anyone, it's just not a healthy dynamic and this wasn't an easy decision and I don't want to hurt you, but I have to do what's right for me." She never looked at me, but at the wall opposite and it all felt scripted.

"I'm going to take my shoes off now," I said then, because I'd just walked in the door. I wondered how long she'd been planning this.

Of course, it dragged on longer than that. Rita continued to text or call, first about logistical things like a timid custody request for the sushi plate jointly purchased at Art Hop, other brief interactions. Then, recently, she suggested meeting for coffee.

"A post-mortem," I said.

"I just don't like how we left things."

I humoured her. I was curious and wanted Rita to acknowledge how much I'd done for her. We waded into these discussions with chit-chat about summer plans or questions about how things are going with my beauty-clay business. It's not until this third coffee date that she gets round to why I am to blame.

"You're twisting things," she tells me. "I'm telling you this because I care about you—I couldn't see this when I was in it, but you have some problematic tendencies." As she smears the butter, it only rolls into cylinders. She gives up and pushes the plate away as if she's just lost her appetite. "You were emotionally abusive."

I like the Americanos here, the way the coffee sticks to my tongue, roasted so dark it almost tastes burnt. I can't help thinking of all my post-mortems, the bitter women who've sifted through the ashes of our relationships to find in me the ignition point. I thought Rita was different. Sweeter. "I haven't heard that one before."

"Are you laughing at me now?" she says.

I put my mug down. "Rita," I say patiently, "just because you feel powerless, doesn't mean someone disempowered you. I just tried to help you stand up for yourself. Clearly, my efforts have backfired."

Her neck starts to go blotchy the way it always does before she cries.

"I'll talk to you later," she says, standing.

"If you think I abused you, why are you going to talk to me later? See what I mean?"

She wraps the muffin in a napkin, stuffs it into her jean-jacket pocket and leaves. Crumbs and a couple errant berries remain.

꙳

I install the dating app again. Dating is tedious now, more like online shopping. After a while, they are no longer shoes or lamps or women, but simply pictures of these things, and how can I be interested in a picture? The women are "active" and "like to stay healthy." Photos demonstrate their playfulness through comical poses, like pretending to swim madly away from a gawdy orca sculpture, known in their city as "art." Oddly, several profiles include photos taken at Machu Picchu. Several butch women pose at the gym, most of them flexing a bicep.

The profile descriptions are even worse. Of their lifetimes of experiences and thoughts and feelings they might include, the bios sound instead like a collection of words and phrases pulled from a hat, a mix-and-match of generic details.

I'm active, enjoy hiking, Netflix, and chillin'. Love to travel and have random adventures!

But meeting in person has proven just as painful. I sit across a table from a stranger, trapped there already by the premise of coffee, and the illusion that we know each other, that we've talked for hours, when in fact we've had what was probably fifteen minutes of banal exchanges spread out over several days by the communication triumph that is direct messaging. Rita was never great at text communication, either, but in the flesh, I liked her immediately, so I keep thinking I just have to meet these women to know—sense them, smell them, hold them in my hands.

I'm not picky—love is easy, though it still has to meet some basic chemical requirement. But for the few I've met, it's like pulling up a trap only to discover the crab is too small and I have to throw it back.

My most recent waste of time required a trip to the city. On the ferry, an announcement over the PA pointed out the pod of orcas off the port bow. The little round café tables emptied and humans gathered along the portside windows, so it looked as if the boat had tipped and rolled them there like marbles. Upright dorsal fins glided along the water then disappeared, appeared, disappeared. But I've seen orcas countless times, when I worked three summers as a "cultural liaison" for ESL students, chaperoning them on trips to museums and whale-watching, where orca sightings are practically guaranteed.

In her online profile, my date looked like a bit of fun, false eyelashes and a leather jacket, a refreshing shift from all the outdoorsy shots of women accessorizing with backpacks and wearing yoga pants instead of legitimate pants. Her interest in archery intrigued me, too, but I learned this was accompanied by a social life built around fantasy role play, the kind that involved bowls of M&Ms and potato chips, nothing erotic at all, as I had at first thought. "You should say that in your profile," I told her after my date explained what she really meant by "Dungeon Master."

I said I find fantasy boring, sci-fi, dystopias—all of that. "I don't have patience for imagined catastrophes."

"It's symbolic," my date said. I almost felt sorry for her.

But here I am, creating my online profile yet again.

For my picture this time, I select a photo of the pier, where the crab fishers toss hoop-traps. As a profile picture, the pier tells this database of body-seekers nothing except that I also live on the West Coast. I hate this app. I want this app. But composing another sales pitch for my would-be mate is a humiliation I can't endure right now. This way, I can browse anonymously, like a robot with a Go-Pro camera stalking the ocean floor.

Once at the pier, a fisher took the Dungeness crab from his hoop trap, snapped off the pointed tip of each leg and tossed the crab, disarmed, into the bucket. It made me laugh, the shock of it. Such an insignificant cruelty, but one I knew could inspire a letter to the paper. "Ouch." I said.

The man smiled. Looked to the bucket and back to me. "This?" he said. "No problem."

Maybe he's right, I thought. Maybe they don't feel pain. It's not like snapping the feet off a deer. As I teenager, I once removed two limbs from a daddy-long-legs, held them side by side, the limbs still kicking. "And one, and two, and one, and two," I said, inspiring a fit of stoned giggles from my friend Lauren, who my dad used to call the Pea Princess because she was "demanding," something she did not appreciate at all. Maybe the spider has brains in its legs, like an octopus, a reflex screaming, "Run!"

How many nights had Rita lain beside me contemplating this "unhealthy dynamic"? An impulse to get away from me, tempered by cowardice.

"Where will you go?" I asked her after the "I don't want to hurt you" speech. I asked out of concern because she didn't have a lot of money and her old suite at Ursula's house was long gone.

"I have a place," she stated.

"Where is it?"

"You think I have nowhere else to go?" she said. Sometimes it felt like I had a teenaged daughter instead of a partner.

"I'm simply asking a question," I replied.

꒖

I get a notification from the app. Someone has liked my Go-Pro robot profile.

Then a text from Rita: *I hate how you make me feel. Like I'm the irrational one.*

Then another: *I regret that text now. You'll just think it proves you right.*

The woman who likes me: Callie, forty-two, flaming-red hair halfway down her back.

Of all the fish the in the sea, an ex-girlfriend. I'd say, "What are the chances?" but the dating pool is small, so perhaps this has its own inevitability. Except for a narrower face, thicker shoulders, Callie looks the same as she did twenty years ago. To her, I am a pier named NM.

I like her back. On the app, a flame pops up: *It's a match!*

꒳

We're supposed to love more desperately when we're young, but this was never the case for me. I've learned how to commit myself to a person, although I seem to have no control over how that's interpreted by the object of my dedication. But Callie found me "pathologically ambivalent" to our relationship. She was in her second year as a psychology major and we both worked as cultural liaisons. I disliked her immediately, her enthusiasm for stilted conversations with students too much like a performance. But at the aquarium, she unbuttoned the top of her shirt in the Rainforest biosphere, and something about the way she scooped up her hair to cool her neck changed everything. Later that summer, I suggested a camping trip to the little gulf island where my dad used to take me as a kid. I've taken all my girlfriends there. When Rita learned this, she seemed to regard it as a kind of betrayal. "It's different every time," I reassured her. "Variety is the spice of life."

Callie and I slept in a tent in the woods above Duck Bay, swam in the ocean, ate oysters we illegally harvested from the beach, and macaroni and cheese. The shells collected in a pile in the woods, our modest midden. I'd learned on one of the ESL tours about middens, these treasured dumpsites, the guide had joked—calcium carbonate of centuries or even millennia of discarded shells that preserve waste and other artefacts of human life. The idea that even refuse told a story appealed to me. "Dumpsite" seemed reductive. Middens are, in fact, stories of what it means to be alive—accumulation, damage, permanence, impermanence, waste. "What do you think an archaeologist would make of our trash?" I asked Callie.

"Probably that our diet was not sufficiently varied," she said. Besides the oysters, our primary survival task involved hiking to the general store for fresh water and more macaroni and cheese. After nearly a week of this menu, Callie said she was desperate for a vegetable. "And they'd assume we died of scurvy."

Almost on cue, she broke a tooth that day. The horror on her face was immediate. Her mouth dropped open, revealing a half-chewed barbecued oyster obscured by her tongue as it searched for the broken tooth. She spat the mass out on her tin plate and something clinked. She sifted through the pulverized flesh with her fingers and located what looked like a tooth, but black at one end, a small twisted globule.

"It's a pearl!" I said, taking it from her to examine. What a hideous creation.

"Where is my tooth!" She continued searching, although I didn't see the point.

"Maybe you swallowed it. Open up." I held her cheeks and scanned her mouth to locate the injured tooth, but she kept tonguing her molars. "Move your tongue," I said. I could not see any chip, but noted she'd had numerous fillings, the white bond visible against yellowing teeth. "I don't see a chip anywhere. You just felt the pearl in your mouth."

This seemed to comfort Callie at first, but when she took a careful bite of another oyster, her face twisted in pain and her hand went to her cheek as she inhaled sharply. "Something is fucked," she said.

❧

Hello Callie, I write.

Hey!

What intrigued you so much about my void profile? I ask. Am I so desperate for communication?

The fact it is a void, I guess! What intrigued you so much to ask?

I'm not intrigued. It just sounds like a reasonable question to ask someone who believes me to be a stranger. But I'm not sure I want to surface just yet. *I guess I find redheads irresistible. You know, the Bodecean babe. :)*

I officially hate myself.

Typing...

> *Ha ha ha! I used to hate my hair when I was younger. And my freckles, blonde eyelashes. One of the advantages of getting older, I guess— growing out of this disdain for oneself.*

I wondered if she continued with psychology. She'd wanted to be a child psychologist back then, but probably only because it was intimidating for someone so young to imagine counselling adults.

I'm surprised you felt that way, I write. *I thought everyone wanted red hair after Titanic came out.*

Lol

> *Typing...*

> *I secretly love that movie*, she writes.

I think of the Heart of the Ocean, the precious gem the old woman chucks into the sea at the end for purely sentimental reasons. *Bloop*, into the drink.

Everyone secretly loves that movie, I reply. *It's like porn—it's not a multi-billion-dollar industry for nothing.*

You're funny.

᠅

Callie couldn't eat another oyster. Broccoli was definitely out of the question and drinking water was even worse. I gave her ibuprofen, but this didn't help. For food the next morning, she swallowed pieces of scrambled eggs without chewing. We learned later that she'd cracked a molar and the change in temperature or pressure stabbed at her nerves. But I wasn't the patient person I am now. Before the pearl incident, Callie was already beginning to get on my nerves. The broccoli purchase followed an argument about groceries. She wanted to share the cost down the middle, but she was eyeing the chorizo and gnocchi and jarred pesto and fresh tomatoes, which, pound for pound, probably cost the same as a steak on that island. I'd managed to squirrel away a surprising amount of coin from my trips to the aquarium and whale-watching, and I didn't want to spend it on food I could get for half the price in town, if I can only wait a week. "Buy what you want and I'll buy what I want," I'd said. But she complained she couldn't eat the whole package of chorizo and didn't want to weigh down her backpack with half-eaten jars of sundried tomatoes or asparagus. "Too bad," I said. "Get instant noodles if you want to eat something else." I relented on the broccoli. It looked wilted and the price reflected that.

So when she said we had to leave because she needed to see a dentist, I felt more fed up than I was entitled to. It's not that I wanted her to just suck it up and endure the pain, but I resented this expectation that I should accompany her. It was my vacation, too. She wouldn't get to a dentist any faster with me by her side.

I hitched a ride with her to the wharf and waved goodbye as she left on the water taxi. I'd planned to stay another week, but I left two days later when I finished my other book.

"I don't think you even know what love is," she told me later when I finally caught her on the phone. I was only two years older than her, but even to me there was something ridiculous about hearing that from someone so young.

"I'm sorry I didn't get you the pesto."

"Fuck you," she said predictably. "You just invited me so you had something to do."

I thought about what she'd said later and called her back. "I just want to clarify one thing," I said. I hate to think of this now.

꙼

How about you? Callie writes.
   Typing...
      What's your big secret?

꙼

"What do you want to *clarify*," Callie said. I could tell she was in the kitchen by the sound of the hood fan and some sizzling not far below the phone.

"What are you making?" I said.

"Something expensive."

I laughed. "You're the one who broke up with me and you're being such an ass."

"What do you want?"

"I just wanted to clarify that I never said I loved you. I mean, I didn't love you. So that's why it didn't feel like I did."

❧

I still have that pearl like a rotten tooth. It always seemed an appropriate souvenir.

I think I hate oysters, I finally write.

❧

When I was a kid, I thought pearls were eggs. My dad was a bit appalled when I'd inquired if that were true. "It's an irritation," he said. A pearl is what happens when a parasite penetrates the shell or when a crab or other predator damages mantle tissue. The mollusk forms a pearl sac around the torn flesh and secretes layers of mother-of-pearl—nacre— to surround that, and after a couple years it's a pearl, rarely round. Callie's pearl was not iridescent, but a dull eggshell-white, and blackened at one end, the pupil of its bruised, distorted eye. I've tried to discover why one end was black like that—*Why is a pearl black? Why does a pearl look like a rotten tooth? Why is an oyster pearl flat-white and black?* But all I can find online are images of tropical black pearls and stories of the broken teeth of unsuspecting diners. The words for my question elude me.

❧

I don't think Rita is *irrational*. The idea of saying that to a woman makes me think of my father. He was always dumbstruck by rejection. One summer on the island, he brought a "lady-friend" named Kathy. All I remember about Kathy is her banana clip and her one-piece like a narrow bandage. It barely covered her most certainly depilated vulva and made me feel at age twelve like I was a hairy beast. Growing up without a mother, I was unaware of bikini-waxing or any other of the feminine dark arts. I can just imagine if my father were alive to see me exhibiting at health and beauty trade shows. "Now there's irony," he might say, not because he considers me ugly but because I was an exception to his understanding of women.

One day, my dad hitched a ride up the island to visit his friend Mike for the afternoon. Kathy stayed behind with me at the rented cottage— we were going to the general store to pick up some things and she was going to make her "specialty." I can't remember what she made. My dad never made it back that night. Some of Mike's pals were visiting, too, and they flew in on a little Cessna, landing on the now deactivated sandy air strip. So they all went for a flight—how can you pass up a free air tour? "Do you know what that's worth?"—and when they got back, they cooked up a sockeye salmon the boys had flown in with them. Beer, campfire and what a feast!

Almost no one had a phone on the island. To my father, this explained everything.

Kathy left the next day. "Unbelievable," my dad said to me, taking the seafood lasagna out to reheat it. Seafood lasagna—that was her specialty. He shook his head for a while, then laughed. "Unbelievable," he said again. Shrimp and crab, creamy ricotta and mozzarella baked golden brown. "Where did you get this crab?" my dad said.

"They had some at the store."

He shook his head again. "We've got a trap—I could've got some if she'd just waited."

❧

I'm sorry you felt upset today, I texted Rita. Suddenly it didn't look right to me, the way I removed myself from this interaction. She probably calls this "gas-lighting" now, further proof of my "emotional abuse." But what would it mean if I wrote, "I'm sorry I upset you." Then it's true that I am the cause of this pain, not her lifetime of low expectations, like an undercurrent tugging at her feet. Occasionally she surfaces, inhales a breath of self-esteem, like today, I suppose. I suppose it took courage for her to tell me that.

What if I'd cried instead? "Emotionally abusive?" I might have begun, reddening. "Is that what you think of me? Is it abusive to want to help you, to support you and stick up for you?" I could have listed the things I'd done—if it weren't for me, she never would have got her damage deposit back from Ursula. I got her to say no to that painting job with the dangerously high dormers—she was not equipped to do that job alone—and supported her while she drummed up more work. I never held this over her or asked for grocery money. "So my love feels like abuse to you? Is my love so oppressive?" No matter what I said, as long as I cried then I could be the victim, too.

After that, Rita might apologize to me: "I'm sorry I upset you." But that doesn't sound right. Rita wouldn't be sorry that I reacted; she'd be sorry for what she'd done.

I haven't thought of Kathy in forever. Only now do I notice the embarrassing similarities to my trip with Callie. It's even more embarrassing it took me twenty years for such a trite revelation.

LOL ME TOO!!! Callie replies several minutes later about the oysters.

She could be having multiple simultaneous conversations. I'm one voice in a blur of voices, messages appearing on her water-smooth screen, like air bubbles from fishy mouths below. *Bloop.*

Bloop.   *Bloop.*   *Bloop.*

                              Bloop.   *Bloop.*

            Bloop.   *Bloop.*

But here on the sofa, I feel weighed down. More like a clam buried in sand than any fish tucked momentarily between slippery rocks. I still find Rita's hair around the house, still cut it from the vacuum brush with nail scissors. If I tell Callie who I am, will she retreat? Dart away for some other dark shelter?

❧

Rita got it in her head once that she needed to catch a geoduck. As a kid, her sister pointed out the larger holes in the sand as evidence of the world's largest bivalve mollusk below. "World's largest," she impressed on me.

"Yes, a giant among clams."

Her sister, she said, dug one up once, miraculously retrieving the creature near the surface. "Then it wasn't a geoduck," I'd said. We were at the beach that day. I stomped near a large hole, provoking its underground inhabitant into geysering saltwater.

"I'll show you," Rita said, and scanned the intertidal zone for the telltale holes.

When she began digging for the geoduck, I laughed. A futile task. "Why don't you make a sandcastle instead?"

She requested a shovel. Even funnier. I meant no harm with the laughter. I had a picture of her then as a child, in awe of her sister's catch—probably a dead clam—and I thought it must've been cute, these two chubby-cheeked siblings talking excitedly about their triumph. It's adorable when children celebrate their failures. It's just depressing when they continue with that into adulthood. But Rita didn't see herself the way I did. "I think I know what a geoduck is," she said.

"You think?"

Still, Rita had something to prove, and soon after, she came home with a giant piece of PVC piping and a pair of shovels.

Geoducks can dig deep, more than five feet, so you need the pipe to stop the hole from caving in. I was not attached to catching the thing, at first. I just liked seeing Rita so focused, and she looked cute in her jean shorts, her legs soon wet and sandy. She even snapped at me, frustrated when I stopped shovelling the sand on the outside of the pipe—she was trying to push it down deeper, madly scraping sand away from this tunnel to China. "Don't stop!" she said, incredulous.

"Yes ma'am." I think I laughed, but I still got to work. After twenty-five minutes of this, Rita's unwavering determination began to rub off on me. It's like the geoduck was doing this to us. How dare this unthinking tube of a creature be so hard to catch. "Fuck you!" Rita even shouted when she thought she almost had it. The hole was so deep now that Rita disappeared down to her waist, straining to feel for that shell full of flesh. I wondered how we were going to extract the PVC pipe when the chase was over. "Let me," I said, tapping her out.

With my head inside this sandy canal, I thought I heard the giant mollusk scratching downward, leading me on. It was markedly cooler inside the hole, the sound of my own breath held close. I closed my eyes as I pushed my hand deeper into the watery muck, and then I felt something.

Rita would later complain that I always tried to get her to do what I wanted her to do, instead of listening to her. But even if I listened, all I heard were half-truths and evasions. "Maybe..." I don't know what kept her from speaking up, but I wonder how she remembers the day of our geoduck hunt now. Because when I felt something at the bottom of that hole, I retreated immediately. "Go, get in there!" I said. I yanked her arm and pushed her. She didn't pay any attention to that at the time and neither did I—we were both so caught up in it. But I knew the clam was hers. I wanted to see her catch it. That's something you can never tell a person. "I could've had it, but I let you catch it." Gee, thanks. Because seeing her jump to her feet to display this grotesque creature held triumphantly like a torch was glorious. Glorious. A four-pound mollusk, its siphon as hideously phallic as promised, Rita's hair full of sand and that ratty sports bra visible through her wet tank. "Victory!" she shouted.

I hugged her and kissed her. She tossed the geoduck onto the sand and I felt her cool, salty-wet hands on my back, squeezing my flesh until it pinched. The mollusk didn't withdraw its siphon like other clams might. I don't think the shell can even close—it's bursting with flesh and I can't imagine where that phallus would hide. And then the geoduck moved. "Oh my god, look," I told Rita. Out the opposite end of the shell comes more flesh, not wrinkled and jaundice like the siphon, but smooth and pearly. It tongues at the sand, then pushes down farther, as if trying to lick up a sample. I learned later this limb is called the foot, but only because so few can imagine the power a tongue has to move a body. And the geoduck's tongue goes deeper, providing the leverage to upend itself, the siphon pointing up at the sky like an accusing finger, and the geoduck begins to struggle downward.

"It's getting away!" Rita said. But the geoduck is slow. It hardly looks worth the forty minutes of digging. "You really want to eat that thing?" I said, squeezing her tighter. "It's kind of sexy."

Rita went limp. "I am going to eat it," she deadpanned. "Whether you like it or not."

"Just checking," I said, and released her.

I was surprised how crunchy the geoduck was, sweet and briny, elegant to see it in thin slices laid out on the sushi plate. It's not surprising that I ate much more than Rita—she was never in it for the taste. And if I asked her about the geoduck now, would she remember why I pushed her?

↷

I've often wondered about how others feel pain. I read about nociception—the reflexive response to "adverse stimuli." Most animals have nociception. If you put your finger on something too hot, your body tells you to remove it before you even register pain. It's a reflex. So a reflexive response to things that can hurt you does not necessarily mean you are experiencing that hurt. Moments after touching the red element, your finger feels on fire, and you rush to the tap for cold-water relief. This pain teaches you to be cautious around things that burn.

If the geoduck could anticipate Rita's kitchen knife, would it have moved faster? She left the bulbous guts attached to the shell. She blanched the rest for ten seconds. She skinned it. She butterflied it. She flayed it. I wondered at what point it died. Whatever it was feeling, it showed no signs of struggle.

↷

Rita returns my text with a link to an article entitled, "10 Signs You Are in an Emotionally Abusive Relationship." The article begins with a fictional wife "building up courage" to tell her husband, Jerry, that she plans to return to school. Jerry replies, "Why would you do that? You failed the last courses you took, so you're not going to make it this time. Why would we waste our money on that?"

From there, the article breaks down the evidence of abuse into bite-sized morsels, scenarios without context. Some of the fictional husbands are undeniably cruel, but I keep returning to Jerry. How his wife has announced her plan without consultation—they likely share finances, as evidenced by Jerry's concern about tossing good money after bad. And what is she returning to school to study? This seems important to me. What if she does this, signs up for expensive private programs, impulsively trying to throw together a career—interior design but she's a luddite and couldn't manage the software, creative writing with some justification that this could lead to a career in marketing, but she's too precious about her poetry and blames the teacher for failing to inspire. And here is Jerry, at the end of his rope. Perhaps he has supported her unfailingly in the past, but now, with kids in university and retirement on the horizon with little in the bank to show for his own material sacrifices, his wife is announcing another project in personal development. And what about Jerry? Is he just a bank? Here's the hammer, darling, crack me open. But later he's a jerry can, his wife fingering the perpetrator, *You, Jerry*, the fuel of marital incineration.

What is Rita thinking? Does she identify with this woman?

A quote in the article from a Women's and Gender Studies professor named Pauline Jewett defines emotional abuse: "Any behaviour that does not affirm or nurture another's unique sense of self. Rather, it engages intentional and purposeful action to diminish a person's identity and personal power."

If Rita ever felt diminished by something I said, that was never my intention or purpose. But I'm confused to learn that my every behaviour must affirm or nurture someone's unique sense of self, lest I be deemed emotionally abusive.

On the dating app, women attempt to define their unique sense of self through tags and sparse description.

#Single #DrinkSocially #Nonsmoker #IEatEverything #PreferNottoSay

Noor, 37, Queer, She/Her, 37.5 kilometres away
I'm an introvert by nature, but confident and warm-hearted once I get to know someone. I love music, animals, good food and being in nature. It's been a few years since I had someone special in my life and I'd love to meet someone again some day to share in life's adventures.

She's a good match for most lesbians.

Alexis, 43, 51 kilometres away
   Single.

Doesn't know who she is.

Jennifer, 37, Lesbian, She/Her, 32.8 kilometres away
   I enjoy discovery, laughing and adventure but if I can find a calm moment with the right person, well, that would be awesome.

Red flag: Why pivot on "but"—is calmness in opposition to discovery and adventure? Is her high-energy search for laughter more a frantic attempt to suppress her addiction to chaos and misery?

What notion of these selfhoods must be affirmed and nurtured here, forever unchallenged? Maybe this is what I need to know, a question I've never thought to ask first. "Pathologically ambivalent," Callie had told me. And did I crumble from such an accusation? No, because we must see ourselves reflected in the way others respond to us, too. Isn't that what Rita told me? That if I think she cries a lot, it's because I make her cry? If I believe myself to be considerate—and I did look out for Rita, I wanted her to be safe and strong—doesn't her comment also diminish my unique sense of self?

I did reflect on Callie's accusation, and I opened myself up to entanglement. So when I met Marina, black eyes and enigmatic smile, I decided to surrender—

Callie messages me again: *So you hate oysters and you love red hair. Is that all I get to see?*

She's fishing for a photo. *I'm still debating what to include in my description.*

Callie: *Typing...*

           That you're funny? Thoughtful?

Am I already those things? *Maybe you should write it for me.*

I'll need to know more about you first...

You might have to interview my exes for the complete picture.

Typing...
    Typing...
        Typing...
            Then, finally, simply: *Lol*
I wonder what she chose not to say.

ꙮ

I met Marina when she laughed at some crack I made to Yang, my beauty-clay distributor. She just hovered nearby, her trade-show programme in hand. She laughed like she was embarrassed or shy, but I'd learn she was never either of those things, but perpetually amused. Like we are all just saying lines in a play and the predictability of this human tragedy is satisfying and hilarious. This is what I fell for.

We were staying at a beach-front suite on a secluded and sandy strip up the Coast one fall, floatplane-access only. Yes, please. There was no end to Marina's sexual appetite and all it would take for me was some faint whimper from that mouth, an expression of "Please."

I've tracked my physical and emotional needs over the years and discovered a pattern. Days before my period, I have thoughts of inadequacy and people seem more stupid than usual. During ovulation, I feel sad and horny, an urgent need to fuck away the emptiness. Because these thoughts and feelings correspond so predictably to my menstrual cycle, I learned they were simply the result of hormonal fluctuations, so I could ignore them until they washed away like a tide going out.

I shared this insight with Marina. "Exhibit A," she said. "Internalized misogyny—but the witness is not even ovulating!"

It may have been the first time I'd ever felt like the neurotic one. To my surprise, I appreciated this deft dismissal of what I'd said, the way she'd disempowered menstruation. I hadn't realized until that moment how oppressive my cycle had become, with its power to veto every thought or emotion.

By the time we took our trip to this secluded beach, I had been giving in to my feelings about Marina more and more. It's not significant that we'd both said, "I love you." I've never been in a relationship where we did not profess that quickly won sentiment after four weeks at most. Romantic love is almost a fetish. So it doesn't matter that Marina and I said "I love you." These were not the feelings I was giving in to.

At dinner, Marina plucked the eye of our coho salmon with a crab fork. I knew she had an adventurous appetite—sea urchin, duck-blood cake. She popped the eye into her mouth. I pretended to be unimpressed as I lifted the spine from the coho's baked flesh, but she knew I admired her for these trivial conquests.

"It's chewy," she said after several seconds, and spat a hard bead onto her plate like ejecting a grape seed. "You can have the other one," she teased, so I had to eat it. Revulsion is irrational—how can I consume the salmon's body but not its head? But more importantly, I needed to match her. I needed her to see that.

I adored Marina, her daring, her unknowable thoughts and private amusement. I had the feeling she could be content without me—or anyone, and this made her company a kind of rare privilege, like a bond shared with a wild animal: I was special enough to live with this solitary creature. At that beach with Marina, the cresting waves an erotic, fecund froth, I imagined us returning to this spot in five years, ten years, twenty. There are stories of human-animal bonds spanning decades—a chimp who remembers her former friend and teacher when, on her deathbed, he comes to visit. She palms his face and pulls him closer to push her forehead into his. I imagined love with Marina this way, a gradual, irreversible tenderness. I'd never wanted a baby before, but with Marina I even dreamed of such a thing—how her body would change, her flesh soften to nurse an infant, the vulnerability I would be graced to witness. How she would need me. And I was not ambivalent.

We found a handheld fish net in the hall closet of the vacation suite and decided to catch a couple Dungeness crabs at low tide. Clouds had taken over and turned everything monochrome, the dark grey sand, grey ocean, pale grey clouds. Gulls floated on the quiet water, white and grey, even their yellow bills muted now, and clumps of seaweed punctuated the smooth beach like splats of black paint. Marina's black hair whipped her cheeks in the wind so she looked wilder than ever and I pulled her close to me to kiss her neck. She carried the white bin from our bathroom, which we had designated our bucket. It was too cold now for rolled-up jeans and our bare feet pinked as we neared the salty water.

I touched Marina's arm gently, to stop her. "There you go—at your feet." A puck-sized portion of a crab's shell peeked out of the sand. I dug my middle finger into the sand on one side without thinking—I just knew which end was the rear by the ridges of the shell, the way we might know where the eyes are if shown a picture of someone's forehead. Its eight legs moved like treading water, claws weakly reaching for nothing, and I turned it over to show Marina the tell-tale male flap. Big enough, too. And I put it in the bucket.

But the next crab was female, and not only that but its abdominal flap extended outward, cupping a wad of bright orange eggs that reminded me of a lobster mushroom, a strangely solid fungal chunk of tissue. I tossed it farther out in the water because the gulls were around and I knew if they found it, they'd pick at it like some Promethean torture.

We waded in, the waves flapping gently but ice-cold at our ankles and found another crab fleeing for deeper water. I scooped it up with the net, but she was female, and the next one, too, all of them full of roe, the only colour in this landscape.

"I've never seen a pregnant crab in my life," I said. "This is weird."
Marina laughed.

"She's got eggs and I'm assuming they're fertilized," I explained.

"*Pregnant* can't be right."

I realized then that I knew nothing about the life cycle of crabs. I knew they ate dead things, and I knew which ones were male and female, that we call the guts "butter." It was after this trip with Marina that I learned more—that the crabs with roe are said to be "berried up." That mating is an embrace that lasts up to two weeks, insemination only possible when she is at her most vulnerable, recently molted and still soft. But at the time, I didn't think about that. When I tossed the crabs into deeper water to protect them from the gulls, I was thinking about population, yields.

"At least we know there'll be more crabs for next time," I said. I suddenly lost interest in catching another crab and felt instead our purpose was to rescue these females from their precarious hiding places in the sand, to ensure future abundance.

Marina plunged her arm into the water and picked one up herself, shrieking from the cold, perhaps, as much as the pointy legs clicking in her hand. "Monster!" Another female, its bulge of roe. "Maybe the eggs are good."

"Come on, toss it back," I said.

"It's just caviar," she shrugged.

An oystercatcher peeped across the water and several gulls joined the other one that floated nearby, eyeing us with too much interest. "It's illegal." I said this as if to a child, hoping to close the subject, as in, *I said no.* But I think what Marina heard was, *We'll get in trouble...*

"I don't think it'll kill her."

It wasn't the flavour of the coho's eye that had troubled me. It had tasted like salmon. The texture wasn't unpleasant, either, a chewiness that reminded me of wine gums. But while it was in my mouth, I could not forget what it was I was chewing, this organ that had looked out at the sea—the fish, the eel grasses, seals and orcas, protecting the coho from a moment such as this. I felt all these images chewed up in my mouth and my face must have given me away. Watching Marina with this clicking crustacean, I wondered if she knew my feelings for her, if she'd only eaten the eye to see me do it, too. And suddenly there was nothing adventurous about her appetite at all—adventure requires risk, and a raccoon receives no praise for its broad palate.

I strode toward her and knocked the crab out of her hand with the net.

"Fuck!" She held her wrist. "You just fucking hit me!"

"I said it was illegal."

"I was just joking!" She reached for the net, but I turned to walk up the shore. My legs were freezing anyway and my feet were turning red. "I'm not done," she said. "Give me the net."

"Forget about it. They're all females."

"Give it to me—I want another crab."

"You can't eat the eggs."

Marina laughed then, a laugh I'd heard only a few times before, never directed toward me. Not her laugh of charmed amusement but of her own kind of disgust, something she reserved for stupidity and need. "Is that what you're worried about?" she said.

I tossed the net toward her and she caught it.

"Thank you," she said, still smiling. "I promise I won't eat your eggs."

The gulls lifted off the water and joined several others on the sand, their insistent shrieks and wings out as they took turns hopping inward, a gently bubbling chaos. I knew what they were doing and I felt sick.

I didn't like who I was with Marina after that.

❧

Callie, 42, Lesbian/Queer, She/Her, 31 kilometres away

Hello lovelies! I love August campfires, watching the Perseids and exploring out-of-the-way places by motorcycle, but I love a night on the town, too! Let's go dancing or let's stay in and cuddle up with a movie. Hoping to find a beautiful love and make some friends along the way. :)

I message Callie, *How long have you had a motorcycle?* She was reluctant even to hitchhike on the island, so I'm surprised to learn she's taken up the most dangerous form of transportation legally available.

She doesn't reply right away. My comment about consulting ex-girl-friends for my description would be considered a red flag by anyone, so I wonder if she's decided to cut her losses. It's easy to abandon conversations here. With hundreds of lonely women to sort through, quick judgment is the only efficient filter. But she replies.

Since my twenties! I just craved that sense of freedom. I'm on my bike eight months of the year. My baby!

A photo appears. Callie straddles her baby, with its pearl-white fuel tank and matching cargo boxes. *I didn't realize you were a mother,* I write.

She's more of a romantic baby, actually.

So you're polyamorous? I don't know what I want from Callie right now.

Ha ha! No. She's all mine.

Typing...

But you can watch. ;)

I imagine Callie soaring past me on the highway, hair flaming out the base of her helmet. I would watch her. I would think, "Look at that woman's red hair. She reminds me of Callie, how she looked when she flew down that sandy trail to Duck Bay, then called up to me to join her on the barnacled beach below." And then she is Rita, heading up the trail, her curls full of sand. She stops. "I hate how you make me feel," I imagine her saying. Waits.

꙳

One year, my dad invited his friend Jonathan and his kids, Lauren and Roddy, to join us on the island. Jonathan was recently divorced, too, and his daughter Lauren was my age, but we didn't yet play together at that time. She whined about sand in her sneakers and her hat being too big, the sunscreen being too warm as it oozed quickly out of the hot bottle, about how her dad used too much. "Now sand is going to stick to me!"

Out in the skiff, my dad and I pulled up the trap and a dozen Dungeness crabs scuttled over each other. Nothing was left of the cod-head bait except a bit of slimy flesh knotted into the twine that hung them.

My dad invited the couple from the neighbouring cabin to join us for a seafood barbecue. Roddy and I collected butter clams and, once we'd filled our ice-cream buckets, I suggested we take the bikes to North Beach for oysters. I knew this would please my father. I learned later this was illegal, but we didn't think about that as kids, and the only thing my dad said about our oysters was, "We're in for some fine dining tonight!"

The butter clams sizzled on the barbecue until they popped open and Roddy and I drenched them in butter and lemon and served them to the adults sitting at the picnic table drinking beer and wine coolers. We made the oysters, too, which I would dutifully eat but never enjoy due to the bit of mysterious dark muck inside. But we boiled the crabs.

Everyone cooked crab this way. First the shock of fresh water poisons them, but not fast enough to avoid a death by boiling water. I thought I heard them screaming, but my dad laughed, said it was the sound of pressure changing inside the shell. They seemed to try to escape, bobbing up the sides of the pot, but this was explained by the boiling water. "It's like a Jacuzzi," my dad said. "Remember how you hold onto the side and let the jets float your legs up?"

When they're done, they have turned bright red. We served them on one large platter. "Dig in," my dad said. Crab and mollusks clattered as he piled them on his plate.

"My fork shrunk!" Roddy held up a two-pronged crab fork, then turned to Lauren. "*En garde!*"

"Don't..." Lauren sounded more like an exhausted mother than a sister just two years older. She examined a clam, poked it with a finger, as if to test for doneness, and looked as though she'd found a pulse instead. "Dad, I don't want this." Jonathan didn't seem to hear her, engaged in what was probably drunken conversation, but at the time to us kids was just adults talking. "Dad..." she nudged his side with her elbow. "Dad!"

"What? What is it Lauren? Can't you see we're in the middle of a conversation?"

"I don't want to eat this thing."

"It's a clam, Lauren."

"I don't want to eat this clam, then."

"So eat something else."

My dad gestured to the platters like a magician revealing his assistant still intact. "We've got a whole feast here!"

But this did not comfort Lauren. She eyed the plate of ashen oyster flesh, the dead crabs and endless servings of butter clams, and began to tear up. "There's nothing to eat!"

"There's lots to eat, Lauren," Jonathan said. "Do you realize how much this would cost in a restaurant?"

Lauren's desperation turned to anger. "I wouldn't eat this if you gave me a million dollars!" She pushed her plate away. "I want macaroni and cheese!"

I realize now that Lauren's discontent had been simmering all week and her protest of sea life dead on the butter-stained gingham was simply the moment the pot boiled over. Perhaps, too, she'd had too much sun that day, moping at the driftwood fort after complaining the water was too cold at low tide. But, despite his congenial toasts and praise for the chefs, which was funny because that was Roddy and me, Jonathan's blood had been heating up, too.

"Damnit, Lauren!" He slammed his drink down. "Don't be such a little bitch."

"I want my mom!" she screamed, then ran into the cottage. The couple from next door sat silently for a moment until the young woman said, "It must be difficult, being a single dad." And they consoled Jonathan, who said, "I give up. I just give up."

Later, my dad patted me on the back. "I sure am glad *you're* not a picky eater," he said. Lauren was up in the loft where we shared the bed. She'd exhausted herself from crying hours earlier, but I wasn't sure if she was asleep now or just lying up there, hearing everything my dad said in the kitchen directly below, still humid and perfumed with crab seasoning.

It's never as much meat as it seems on a crab. The thorax is discarded—even my dad never ate the buttery guts—the limbs are cracked, and crab forks tediously hook and tug the flesh. The only satisfying bites comes from claws. My stomach growled with hunger as I lay next to Lauren, sun-burned and frowning even as she dreamed.

꜅

There is a biologist in Northern Ireland named Robert Elwood who studies crustacea. In a YouTube video, he tells a story about his research. One day, a chef asked him if lobsters feel pain. "It's a possibility," was all Robert could say. So he designed experiments to find out. He expected to discover what most already believed, that a crustacean has only nociception—a reflex to withdraw from harmful stimuli; this is all it needs to survive. But pain is practical, too. Amid the miasmic odour of predators, Robert's hermit crabs remained in their electrocuted shells. Only when the odour dissipated did they flee for safer harbours. This motivational trade-off, they say, is the most compelling evidence of a crab's experience of something we might call pain—a memory of things that hurt us. Remember this shell is electric, this rock has a mouth, this smell means trouble.

But then there is pain without stimuli. The burning of a finger though it was amputated weeks ago, or the aches of an aging body. I think of the crab at the pier, the final segment of each limb snapped off before it was dropped into the empty bucket. Nociception can't save you now, and what can be learned from these phantom limbs?

I am certain now that if Lauren's mother had been there, she would have put something more together—rice with butter and soy sauce for Roddy, macaroni and cheese for Lauren. A vegetable. Even a few slices of cucumber would do, peeled. Sandwiches saved from tomato sogginess by a protective layer of lettuce. Occasionally nachos for dinner because the kids think it's fun to eat nachos. Apples that are crisp and sliced, not bruised Red Delicious because it all looks the same in your mouth. Those wedges of cheese that come individually wrapped. Grapes are not a waste of money. Nutella is okay on toast once in a while. Would you girls like some juice? Would you girls like some carrots and dip? We are going to make our own pizzas for dinner—doesn't that sound like fun?

What is the cost of such ordinary kindness?

I would not have felt the financial pinch of pesto for long. And Callie, a mouth full of doughy gnocchi, would not have cracked a molar. After that, her pain was a problem to solve. Take this pill, swallow your food whole. But there is a tool now that electrocutes a crustacean; it is unconscious in 0.3 seconds, dead in under 10. I thought the solution was not to do no harm, but to inflict it quickly.

When Rita left the café, I knew she would contact me again, returning and returning to test these electric waters. She's a glutton for punishment, I might say, except I know she is not a glutton for anything. There is some other reason to return. Perhaps there is something she keeps forgetting to say.

But I wonder how long Rita will feel me, like a missing limb still burning for relief, and to whom this pain belongs.

I want to ghost Callie. Where could such a conversation end up, anyway? But there is also nothing at risk in revealing myself—my deception may only confirm I am the petty monster she believed me to be.

Naomi, 44, Lesbian, She/Her
   Single.

What can I write that's true?
We know each other already, I tell Callie. *It's Naomi.*
Naomi who?
Not a picky eater. Smarter than that. Hates oysters. Loves red hair. Curly hair. Black hair. Funny. Thoughtful. Will boil you alive.
Naomi Mann.
Fisher. Harvester. Motherfucker. Tears the legs off daddy-long-legger.
Typing...
Never listens. Knows better.
Typing...
Now I think of eel grass, salmon, needs like weeds, and crab-trap netting tangled on my fingers. I hate that I think of muffins when I picture Rita with her curly hair full of sand. *I hate how you make me feel.* But she is coming toward me. Come, then, Rita. I'll toss you back or toss you aside like an empty shell. Please don't leave.
Of all the gin joints...wild, Callie writes at last. *But I guess the queer world is pretty small. It's weird you didn't say that right away, but I think I get it. Twenty years is a long time.*
She adds, *We were really young.*
"Emotionally abusive" are borrowed words, but how can I not infer some pain? In the way Rita left, in the way she returns. *That is generous of you,* I tell Callie.
Well, I'm no cheapskate...
I wonder who Rita is hoping to find when we next meet for coffee. I'll watch her pick the berries from her muffin, muster some new courage. I am a person who requires courage to address. I could say, "I'm sorry," and I know she would yearn hopefully toward me. I could say,

then, "You're safe with me," and it would begin to feel true. But I am full of irritation, spheres of damage.

To Callie: *I know I was a jerk.* "Pathologically ambivalent."

Ha ha!

Typing...

I thought I had you all figured out.

I type my response, then delete, type and delete, what I say next appearing and disappearing like dorsal fins off the port bow. More time passes.

ꜜ

There is a young woman in China who calls herself Wild Hui. She posts videos on YouTube in which she harvests pearls from freshwater mussels. In jeans and bright blue rubber boots, she wades into shallow rivers and picks up giant mussels from the sandy bed. She squats or sits on the rocks on shore to shuck them, stabbing a knife into the side and then ripping them apart, splayed like butterfly wings. The flesh inside in labial layers. The first time I ate mussels, they floated up in my soup, these tiny orange and black vulvas. I imagine Rita eating them now, using her fingers to gingerly pinch the flesh. Callie tweezing them loose with chopsticks and Marina popping the whole thing into her mouth to suck the meat and spit the shell onto her table-top midden.

After she's shucked the mussels, Wild Hui slides her tiny fingers all around the flesh, gathering up one iridescent pearl after another and dropping them in her jar or an emptied shell. They clink like glass. Her fingers are small and the way she moves them is practised and delicate. *Clink, clink. Clink.* But the more pearls she finds, the more devastated the flesh, and as she gathers several pearls in her hand, there is a soupy mess the colour of putty. She slices into its sack of organs and fingers for more pearls, and there are more. There are always more until she squeezes what remains with her small fists, knifes its tendons from the shell and tosses it aside.

Sometimes there are so many pearls it's like roe. And the overwhelming femaleness of this scene—Wild Hui's delicate fingers, the labial flesh, the pearls, even the jewellery they are destined to become—is erotic and violent and grotesque and beautiful. I can't look away. Sometimes, I feel my own vagina ache, like I want her fingers to destroy me, too, to find some beauty in that.

This Unlikely Soil

1

The Next Whole Earth Catalog contained more than six hundred pages of information, covering topics from livestock to cybernetics to sewing to electronic music. "We are as gods," it says on the opening page, "and might as well get good at it." A DIY manifesto for a different future.

It was the 1980s the first time Elana had seen this book, as she recalled, thumbing through the yellowed pages all these years later. She'd scanned the pages: aerial landscapes, galaxies, space colonies, books reviewed, "Africans," "Native Indians," a whole section on insects and spiders, drainage diagrams, permaculture, beekeeping, solar homes... Then, about halfway through, two women, topless, touching each other. A hand on a breast.

An article entitled "Amateur Insemination" explained how to impregnate yourself using a turkey baster or a needle-less syringe, how long the sperm can survive in a glass jar, how to know when you're ovulating, how lesbians are doing it. *Lesbians.* And then there was a picture of an actual lesbian named Lynn with her baby she got by following these instructions. The caption explained who she was, and that "the other woman in the house," the one with whom the mother and child resided, "cavorted around behind the camera to help with the first published portrait of a family made by amateur artificial insemination." Was this other woman also a lesbian, like Lynn? Lesbians living together and raising this baby named Brook?

The following two pages were a how-to on "Community Childbirth." A photo of a naked woman, but this one reclining into a man's arms, eyes closed, a giant head stretching her vagina into a football-shaped porthole. Nothing to worry about, the accompanying text tells her, childbirth is natural—only one in a thousand women dies from it and only one in four hundred babies. It's usually uncomplicated. And if not, there is a book available for $4.95 called *Emergency Childbirth.*

After considering it in the biological sense, Elana concluded she wasn't ready to turkey-baste herself into motherhood. The pain frightened her, and she couldn't imagine herself with pendulous milk-filled breasts—would she ever be grown up enough for such a task? But she wanted to be a part of this community that would grow their own food, install solar panels and help Lynn raise little Brook. Maybe she could even be the woman behind the camera.

At fifty-four, Elana has long since relinquished the notion of ever being anyone's mother. Not only are her peers having grandchildren, but she had a uterectomy twelve years ago to remove a fibroid the size of a watermelon. She'd been feeling slightly uncomfortable when she finally visited the doctor about it. Amazing how like herself she'd continued to appear—imagine the corners her organs must have been stuffed into to accommodate the growth.

Only minutes before receiving anesthetic did it dawn on her that this is it: without a uterus, she most definitely would not ever have a child. Has so much of life already come to an end?

The nurse, noting her distress, reassured her. "Just think—you never have to deal with a period again."

Meanwhile in Toronto, her younger brother has just had a child with his much younger wife, his fourth child in three marriages spanning thirty years. While visiting her mother, Elana helps set up Skype for almost two hours ("I can't tell you my password." "Just type it in then." "You're telling me too much at once!") She then endures a tedious slideshow presentation about the new baby. "Look at your brother: Fifty-three years old—he's like a Hollywood actor."

In one photo, David cradles a pale infant, as uninteresting to behold as anyone's infant, but he has some stupid smile that is unrecognizable to Elana. His wife drapes one arm around his shoulder, resting her chin on the other so their heads are side by side, her face smooth as an Asian pear, his, a dumpy potato. It looks like he's holding his granddaughter. "I agree—he looks ridiculous."

Elana's mother gives her a look. Disappointed again.

"I thought that's what you meant," Elana says. "You weren't specific."

Her mother points at nothing in particular. "Steve Martin just had a baby, you should know."

"What's more impressive is you know who Steve Martin is." She never asks Elana about a partner. Usually Elana doesn't have one, but it might be nice to be asked. Once she'd told her that, in one of those rare confrontations when they said what they think. "I'm tired, Elana, I'm old, I'm a widow," her mother had said. "If one lasts more than a few months, then you can tell me about it."

Her mother adjusts a clip in her hair, which is cut into a bob and seems to get yellower every year, no longer the dark hair of Elana's childhood, aerosol-sprayed into an immoveable dome. "This keeps falling out," her mother complains, tapping the clip. "It's too long now. I need to see my girl."

Elana takes the air taxi home. Expensive, but the visits are on her mother's dime.

❧

Elana's house is on her mother's dime, too. It wasn't supposed to be like that—Elana had asked for a loan for the down payment, one that she even believed she'd pay back. She'd eyed the property for two months, accessible from the highway yet tucked in amongst the firs and cedars down the slope. Then one day, a red banner across the realtor's sign: *Reduced.*

Her mother thought it was a good idea. "I worry about you," she said matter-of-factly.

Elana had been managing the Pet-Mart for three years, steady, reliable employment, but she dreamed of being her own boss, operating her own full-service kennel from her own property and now is the time to do it. An ex made a decent living this way—she even drove a Prius, and Elana worked for her later, first walking dogs, then learning grooming techniques. Why shouldn't Elana drive a Prius, too? Yes, the time is now, while she's got these three years of steady, reliable employment that proves she's a safe bet.

But the whole thing shifted from a loan to co-signing to her mother simply buying the property. Elana would live there, pay the mortgage and look after its upkeep. "This way you won't be in debt, and you can get a better sense of what's involved."

"At least you have a place to live," one partner said to Elana. "I wish my mother would buy *me* a house, for chrissake." Elana had quit her job—she'd saved enough money to devote herself full-time to building the business, for a while. When Elana couldn't get permission to operate a doggy daycare (neighbours objected to the potential noise of barking, although a full-service kennel offered the best possibility for financial success), she cried to her partner about being a loser, how she was going to be broke forever. "You're such a brat," her partner said. Things really fizzled after that.

Still, Elana takes pride in the property and her ability to care for it. Its purchase coincided with the sale of her mother's house and subsequent downsizing to an apartment suite. Hard to believe Elana still had a box of things left in the family home: high school mementos, her clarinet that conjured up an inarticulate kind of sadness. But beneath those items, a copy of *The Next Whole Earth Catalog*. Memories of unlived dreams attached themselves to this item, too.

But it wasn't too late, was it? Here she is on this property bordered by forest, and the potential to create something amazing is still there— she'll grow this business, grow food, turn scraps into soil, and sun into power for the little house, this intelligently modest dwelling. The tools are there—"she might as well get good at it."

It had taken all summer, but she dug up the Himalayan blackberry roots with a pickaxe and left them to die in the sun. She tore out the old fence and created an enclosure with chain link for dogs (maximum three at a time), converted the solarium into a grooming room and hung a sign at the highway for Dog Star Pet Services. She'll grow carrots, potatoes, beets, build a chicken coop and get some egg-laying chickens. So far, she's only constructed the frames for the raised beds and made a few tulip beds along the path from the driveway with the help of Jill and, less enthusiastically, her son, Tom. But that's okay, it's a start, that's okay. She started the compost heap. She's still figuring out the right ratio of greens to browns, so her food scraps turn to a soupy mess, but she'll figure it out, she will. She had also planted a weeping willow. One day, she'll lean against its trunk and sink into sleep as the breeze touches the willow's long, leafy hair.

꙳

Elana met Jill when she brought over her drooling Pomeranian (Tikka) and a teenaged boy in tow. The dog had belonged to Jill's late mother. The boy was Jill's son, Tom. He stared down at his phone. With a mustard-yellow tee that washed out an already pale complexion, and a constellation of pimples on his forehead, he offered an ugly contrast to his mother, whose messy up-do looked somehow artfully landscaped, locks coming loose in all the right places.

Clearly not a dog person, Jill thought rancid breath was a trait of the breed, and that a grooming and a toothbrush could resolve the issue. Elana was just finishing up with a standard black poodle. "He looks pretty content," Jill observed.

"These dogs are actually bred to be styled." Then, in an effort to engage Tom, "How do you like that for a life's purpose?"

He stared at the dog and the poodle tensed. "It looks mean."

"She likes her neck rubbed." Elana demonstrated, but the dog seemed indifferent this time.

The boy looked back to his phone until the Pomeranian, propped in his mother's arms, turned and panted in his direction. "That breath is rank!"

Jill fished a key fob out of her pocket. "I think you'd be more comfortable in the car."

After he left, Jill apologized. "We're both still getting used to the dog."

Elana suggested the dog may have a dental issue, such as an infection, and when this turned out to be the case (the drooling problem subsided with a regimen of antibiotics), Jill returned with a scented candle and a card. "Just something small."

It was not the first time a married woman had taken an interest in her.

Over the years, Elana had settled on a kind of uniform for herself, masculine enough to be identified as a lesbian, but feminine enough to still be considered "attractive" in the hetero world: a tank top and an unbuttoned men's shirt in place of a cardigan, but hair that hung loose to her shoulders, and all of this draped over a lean frame, one that came unnaturally to Elana, the result of disciplined deprivation. Jill, on the other hand, looked dressed for a night out even in jeans and a T-shirt, her hair streaked blonde and large hoops that some might have considered too young for her.

Elana opened the envelope. Inside, an art card depicted a nude woman kneeling beside a pond, holding two pitchers. She poured water from one into the pond and from the other onto the ground. Behind her, gold lamé stars and glitter. Written in calligraphy at the bottom, "The Star."

"It's a tarot card," Jill said. "I make them."

"It's beautiful."

"I just thought because you're Dog Star, you might like this one. It signifies a time of transformation and that you're entering a loving phase. This is just meant to be art though, not a reading."

Elana had learned it was best to ignore women like Jill. They don't know what they want; it's excruciating to wait for them to figure it out and it always ends in disappointment. Elana was not the desperate young woman she used to be, who whimpered after someone like some pug locked outside the bathroom while its master takes a shower. But whether she acted on it or not, there was no solution to attraction: a thread inside her snapped.

"This is really nice, thank you, Jill." Elana placed the card on the countertop and sniffed the candle. "Fruity."

"Mango."

"I'm glad Tikka is doing better." She gestured to the rubber boots below the pair of leashes. "I better go walk the dogs."

Then Jill asked her if she'd like to get a coffee some time.

❧

Over the next several months, Jill oscillated between wanting a casual fling ("I need to be free") and demanding Elana articulate "where all this is going." You would think a fortune teller would be a little more comfortable with the future, Elana had teased, which Jill did not like. Jill had never imagined orgasms like this, that sex would be so different (those rare times her soon-to-be ex-husband went down on her lasted only a few minutes, perfunctory lubrication for penetration). Sex was less ground-breaking for Elana, as Jill had yet to reciprocate. Jill was "a bit enthusiastic in your vocalizations," so Elana worried about the neighbours, who had played Beethoven rather loudly one evening. "Let them hear!" Jill replied. "I want everyone to know what an amazing lover I have."

But she didn't really want everyone to know—her husband, for example, didn't know, and of course neither did her son, Tom. The reason was complicated, she said. "When you've been married as long as we have..." she trailed off. "And when you have a child..." trailed off. "It's hard to explain."

Elana could never understand attachments or responsibilities, right? Her longest relationship lasted five years and ended when her partner moved to the city for work just as casually as if she were headed off to Mexico for a week in the sun. Elana didn't expect a lot from relationships, she thought, so she tried to be in the present with it— for the good parts, anyway. She enjoyed the sunny afternoons when Jill brought Tom over, and to see the tulips growing in the flower beds along the path. Tom, after learning the boundary of the property extended into the forest, suggested he should build a tiny home here, like his own escape pod, somewhere he can work on his shit. "You mean a fort?" Elana asked. No, he said. A tiny home. It's a thing.

Then Jill did it: after nearly a year of seeing each other, she told her husband she'd met someone and that she was leaving him. Elana was upgraded from "friend" to "the woman I'm seeing."

But she stopped bringing Tom over. "He's almost fifteen," Jill said, as if this explained everything.

When her husband called her a slut, she retorted that sex with a woman was better than she'd ever had with him in twenty years, and then you should've seen the look on his face. She reported all this conflict to Elana—slammed doors, group counselling sessions, her husband's sexual hang-ups. Things Tom had said, too, that Elana was a fucking dyke and his mother was just doing this to make his dad angry and she was a selfish cunt. "He says he thinks we're disgusting."

"I don't really need to know all this."

"I just don't know what to do."

If Elana had ever spoken to her own mother like that, she was certain she would have been cut out of the will, if that isn't already the case. "Take away his phone."

"I'm not going to do that—it's for safety."

"You don't need a phone plan to call 9-1-1."

"Elana," Jill held a hand up like directing traffic. Elana stop. Jill proceed. "Please don't tell me how to raise my child." She was only venting. She needed to get it off her chest. Tom is a good kid. This is really hard on him. He's just upset about the divorce.

"He slammed the door right in my face," Jill continued, leaning against the counter. Elana focused on slicing carrots for the soup. These carrots are from California. She should plant carrots this year for sure. "I had to stand there like an idiot, shouting through the door. I told him he's only punishing himself—he's the one who's gonna miss karate. He just wants to play shoot-em-up video games now anyway."

"Do we want tomatoes in this?"

"He probably pretends he's shooting at us."

Soon after, Jill found some temporary sublet to move into. Despite being "totally depleted," she seemed to have more energy than ever and started taking swimming lessons and a weekly "movement" class that involved a djembe and silk scarves.

She had so much energy, in fact, that it wasn't long before Jill had acquired an additional amazing lover, a man named Farzin whose ailing father lived on the Coast, who took Jill sailing in the old man's boat, just short trips around one of the little islands with private docks that rimmed the shore like thorns.

No longer interested in monogamy, Jill juggled them both and a part-time job. "I was married for almost twenty-five years," she said, closing the discussion. She leaned over, adjusting her breasts in the bra cups as Elana searched for her underwear at the bottom of the bed.

She'd spent the night, but Jill was apparently meeting Farzin at eleven in the morning for a sail. When Farzin arrived at the house to pick her up, Jill, without closing the bedroom door, trotted to the foyer and let him in. Before Elana could react, Farzin was in the house with a view into the bedroom, trapping a naked Elana under the blankets. "It's not like I packed a nightie," she said to Jill later, who responded, "I'm not ashamed. Why should you be?"

Then Tikka's drooling problem returned. Before Jill could sink another pile of cash into the dog, he died. The grief surprised her. It was her mother she was finally mourning, and Jill lost interest in sailing and groped at Elana for support, texting her to come over. *Please hold me.* Love, for Jill, meant drama, perhaps because a loveless marriage had meant so much routine. But Elana was done with all of it. *You need to stop texting me.*

Why are you doing this to us?

We're no longer together, if we ever were. I don't want to communicate by text message.

So call me. Talk to me.

Sorry, that was confusing—I don't want to communicate at all. Good night.

Jill found other ways to reach her, though. Diane, a friend through "Gertrude's Place," the monthly lesbian social group that met for hikes or potlucks or themed discussions, reported that some of the women wondered why Elana was being so harsh, that she was alienating Jill from the community, but it was Elana who now avoided the gatherings, not that she had gone much before.

If Jill simply left her alone, Elana could get back to work. Everything just stopped with Jill in the picture—why did all her relationships feel like eddies? Pleasurable rest-stops, disorienting traps. Only the willow continued to grow. But Jill kept texting, snail-mailed an embarrassing missive on how she fell for Elana. "It's not about gender—it's the soul," she wrote, which possibly explained the lack of reciprocity in bed. Where, exactly, is the soul located? Elana wanted to ask. And could you please put your tongue on it? Jill then moved on to sending art cards. The last one a tarot card, but instead of a medievally styled heterosexual couple, Jill had illustrated two nude women embracing, one with Elana's hair, the other with Jill's, but both with bodies that looked twenty years too young, buttocks sitting higher and rounder and breasts that were so large and firm the two could not squish naturally into a hug. They each held a goblet in one hand, and what appeared to be a planet rose behind them, smooth and purple, casting a kind of otherworldly glow on the nondescript horizon. On the back, an interpretation of the "Two of Cups," how Jill had lain this card when she put her intention to Elana, and that it meant they should be together.

Elana might have just recycled the card along with the other ones, but when she stopped by the thrift store later that day in search of a spiffy white shirt (her white shirts having all yellowed along the collar), the window display included two large wine glasses, spray-painted gold, plastic pearls and fake roses placed between them. "Congratulations Grads!" a sign read. But to Elana, the two cups were a sign for her. She sent a letter to Jill's post office box, sharing her interpretation of the sign, that their relationship had been as phony as those painted glasses, and enclosed Jill's art card.

2

Elana's mother Skypes with the baby. "They hold the iPad for her, so she gets to see her grandma. She's a beautiful baby, you know. Not every baby is beautiful, it's not a given."

Elana's Internet connection is unreliable so in conversations with her mother, the image kept freezing, her mother's open mouth looking like a creepy call for help. Is this what the baby sees?

"I'm sure the baby is great," Elana says over the phone.

"You don't have to take my word for it, you know. You could just Skype them—oh, but I guess you won't be able to see them if you don't have proper Internet. So that's not good. What's wrong with your Internet?"

"I don't know, Mother."

"I'm only trying to help."

"I didn't say anything."

"And now you're getting defensive again." She sighs into the phone.

"I only want you and your brother to be closer. You always do this, Elana. You cut yourself off from the family."

After Elana's father died, her mother started calling Elana regularly, to check in. "I'm only calling so you don't worry. I don't want anyone to worry about me." Elana upgraded to a phone with call display, and when she saw her mother's name, she told herself she couldn't afford the time. At first her mother asked why Elana was never home. "Don't you work from home? You're going to lose business and you can hardly afford that, I should know." Later, after her mother discovered call-display, she asked why Elana doesn't pick up. "It's not easy for me to call you, knowing how much you hate it when I do, but someone has to keep this family together." It was easier, Elana reasoned, to endure the phone calls than to justify the evasion later. When the requests for visits started coming, Elana applied the same philosophy. But she could only do one day per month—with the dog sitting, she had to come home the same day, so she needed to fly. The thirty-minute flight on the Cessna was expensive, but money wasn't an issue for her mother, Elana knew. "Can't you find some neighbourhood kid to cover for you sometimes?" her mother asked. "It would be cheaper than spending my money on flights. Wouldn't it? I'm just asking."

"I'm not cutting anyone off," Elana continues. "He has my number, too, you know."

"Your brother is busy."

"*I'm* busy." If you include the dog-sitting, Elana works seven days a week. She hasn't told her mother, but she took a job at the Pet-Mart again, this time as a clerk since they'd long since filled the manager position. Dog Star seems to have stopped growing, and she thought Pet-Mart may provide an opportunity to network with dog owners, except she isn't allowed to hand out her own business cards and the young manager asked her not to mention her business at all. ("We have our own products to sell.")

"Oh," her mother sounds surprised. "Are there more dogs than there used to be?"

"Why do you assume I could only be busy with dog grooming?"

"I don't want to argue, Elana." Another tired sigh.

Outside, the willow looks shaggy in the rain. Without the sun to bounce off the leaves, all she sees are the ropy branches like yellow bullwhips. Puddles seem to be forming near the dog yard. Beatnik, the Labradoodle, hides in the little house. Elana should towel him off and bring him in. Later. "I didn't tell you this before because you've made it pretty clear you don't really care, but I have a partner now. We've been together almost a year and she's got a teenaged son and he practically lives here half the time, and he actually depends on me a lot. He's going through a really difficult time—bullied at school, his dad's kind of abusive, all of that. So, actually, I'm not just sitting around here putting bows on Shih Tzus and thinking about David's latest child. The baby, I mean, not his wife."

"I didn't know," her mother says finally. "How could I when you never tell me anything?"

꙳

The white thrift-store shirt looks brand new, the plastic arrows both still inserted into the tips of the collar. She'd found a pair of green suede Hush Puppies her size, too. She tries the clothes on again now at home, buttoning the shirt over a greying sports bra, sliding a black belt through the loops on the slim-cut slacks. Pot lights cast ugly shadows on her face and all she sees in the mirror are creases, fabric tugging at hips, breasts.

She feels like a kid again, the horror of puberty upon her. As Elana began to resemble a woman, with oily skin and hair wild in the summer heat, it became clear she wasn't going to be a very good one. A second helping at dinner is evidence of her "determination not to fit into the blouse" her mother bought for school photos, while her brother is ladled another heap of potatoes. When she arrives shortly past curfew one evening, her mother suspects premarital sex, not with any boy Elana's own age, but with the band teacher ("A man doesn't stay late just so you can practise clarinet"), a man that would only require Elana be young and not beautiful, while her brother's tardiness is congratulated with a wink from his father—"You're home late tonight." Was it simply that he was a boy and she was a girl? That their parents' love for David was an investment, while for Elana, only a sunk cost? Or perhaps she really was the stupid, stubborn child her mother believed her to be. Perhaps her mother saw through even the lies Elana told herself.

She really believed that, for a while. She doesn't anymore. In another light, this shirt looks great. It did in the store. But this house is small and there is no good place for a mirror.

❧

To get to Dog Star Services from town, you must drive fifteen minutes up the highway. The road snakes, yet drivers cut corners, grazing the other lane or what little shoulder there is. Instead of billboards, small signs of corrugated plastic nailed to cedars punctuate the drive. Some look to the stars for signs, but here, they are literally in the trees. The messages are simple: "Excavator," with a phone number. "Prawns," with an arrow to take the next right. "Luxury Fashion Lingerie," and another number and an arrow for Bay Road. Elana reads them all when she drives, as if they may change. She's contemplated making her own: "Dog Grooming." Her friend Diane warned her this could dilute her brand. Elana thinks of the lingerie sign and laughs. It's true, and who cares?

Just before the turnoff to Bay Road, Tom thumbs a ride in the opposite direction. Jill would be frantic if she knew he hitchhiked. Elana considers turning around to offer him a ride into town, but she hasn't spoken to him in months, and he thinks she's disgusting and possibly still wants to shoot her. But that isn't his fault—look at what's modelled for him. All those misogynistic things his father says. Tom has never learned how to express himself effectively. He probably has outbursts at school, too. Maybe he's bullied. I bet he could really use that tiny home now, Elana thinks.

❧

Elana thrusts the pitchfork into the compost heap, but there is an odd lack of resistance. Rats have tunnelled through the rotting buffet. Do they eat it from the inside out or are they living in here, snuggling in their little house made of food? Either way, rats are bad, right? It's time she figures this out. *The Next Whole Earth Catalog* is full of reviews for books on composting, including one called *Harnessing the Earthworm*. The article explains that earthworms inhabit the surface layers of soil, swallowing up the soil and then extracting nutrition from the organic content, but they burrow deep, too, "riddling and honeycombing the earth to a depth of several feet." They wiggle up, depositing castings on top, essentially mixing the soil below with that on the surface, while its body chemically transforms the mineral subsoil into something fertile in which plants will grow.

This is what Elana wants, but her carbon to nitrogen ratio is way off. Compost bloggers seem always to have access to hay or sawdust, so Elana heads to Quality Garden to see what they suggest.

It's not unusual to see familiar faces around town, but Jill seems to be everywhere. At the garden store, she arrives at the cashier shortly after Elana with a tray of succulents. "I'm drawn to things that flourish in drought," she says. At the mall, Jill purchases wooden letters from the Dollar Store while Elana browses for storage containers. "I'm making a mosaic," Jill tells the disinterested store owner. "You know? Mosaic? But I'm using other objects as well as pieces of ceramic."

One day, Jill wanders into the Pet-Mart. Elana walks straight up to her. "We both know you don't have pets."

Jill adjusts her purse strap. "Excuse me?"

"Why are you here?"

Jill spins her hoop earring. She looks caught and Elana knows what will happen next. Jill will get shaky and then tears will well up in her eyes, she'll apologize for being unable to cope with the accusations. Wait for comfort.

"I know we've been running into each other a lot lately," Jill says.

"You've been running into me."

"And you've been ignoring me like I don't even exist. I don't know why you're still so angry, but at least you're talking to me. It's just that—"

Tears.

Jill retreats to the cat tower, out of the way of the entrance. She wipes her cheek and crosses her arms, waits for Elana to follow her over there. A cardboard cat peers out of the top compartment. "I don't understand why we can't still be friends," Jill says.

"You don't want to be friends."

"I don't want to be *nothing*."

She looks up at Elana, and there is something genuine in her face. Maybe it's the way her mascara has smeared. Grey roots reveal themselves and the white circles around her eyes give away time logged at the tanning bed. Suddenly Elana is overcome with pathos for this woman who so desperately tries to retrieve some idea of the youth she missed out on. A woman-lover, sailing trips, blonde highlights, whimsical stupid art cards. For a moment, she almost wants to embrace her. Plus, she's still friends with her on Facebook, so she's seen Jill's posts about looking for a place again and vague missives on what it means to be alone. "I know it's been difficult," Elana offers.

"You have no idea what I'm going through at home."

Sympathy evaporates.

"Tom is supposed to spend every other weekend with me, but he doesn't even show up and then I'm just worried sick that something's happened to him. He doesn't respond to my texts and then finally wanders in the next day like he's just been out to pick up the milk. And when I do see him, he barely speaks to me! So I laid into him, but then he told me that I 'have no accountability for my actions.'" She uses her fingers to indicate the quotation. "That I'm 'childish' and have 'no clue what it means to be an adult.' Tom is saying this! I mean, who *is* this kid?" Jill puts out her arms for a hug. "I'm lost at sea!"

It seems easier to go with the flow. Elana gives her a hug. Jill feels like an anchor.

꙳

The yard is pock-marked with puddles now, and Elana wonders if this is the result of the unusual amount of rain recently. Maybe the trees the neighbour took out have changed the hydrology? She starts to feel bogged down by the problem, too, but then considers putting a pond in the depression—if it's already prone to flooding, maybe this would be a good permaculture-style solution. Create habitat for amphibians and a place for little birds to cool down. She'd need a pump to avoid turning it into a mosquito nursery, although the bats might appreciate it. There is so much to think about.

⟩

Tom, surprisingly, had got himself a job at the IGA. Elana doesn't notice him at the till until she's already got two shoppers with their carts lined up behind her. The name tag pinned to his black golf-shirt reads "In Training. Thank-you for your patience." A large woman stands beside him, hands folded, and feeds him the code numbers for Roma tomatoes. That's gai lan. Those are shallots, not onions.

"Hello, Tom," Elana places the last bag of carrots on the conveyor belt.

Tom's face flushes like the Roma tomato. "Looks like you've got a bodyguard here, eh?" She turns to the supervisor. "Anyone giving him any trouble today?"

"Not on my watch," the woman laughs. "He's doing a great job, though," she says, as if Elana has a stake in the boy's performance.

"Good for you, Tom."

He picks up one of the oranges. "What ones are these?" he mutters to his supervisor.

"Navel," Elana says, rolling the remaining two toward the scale. One of the oranges veers strangely to the right and Elana picks it up. Two parallel ridges run down the side of the orange, a suggestive nub at the top, so that it looks like a vulva. She hands it to Tom. "Now that's obscene," she says. "Don't get any ideas, though, Tom—that fruit is mine."

No one says anything and the supervisor continues bagging. Elana feels her screw-up, feels it down to her toes, what now, what now...

"How are you paying for this?" Tom asks without looking up from the scale.

"With my job. No, just kidding. I've got a sugar-daddy. Just kidding."

"We could all use one of those!" the supervisor says.

Relieved, Elana waves her credit card.

Over the years, Elana's attendance at local lesbian get-togethers has dwindled, but she still subscribes to the email list because she remembers the days when she seemed to be alone in the universe. "Is anybody out there?" she wanted to shout from her porch. "Am I the only dyke on the entire planet?" It often felt that way.

The emails these days are comprised of calls for casual help in the garden, a free couch to give away, a carriage house for rent, a question about carpooling to Vancouver Pride, occasionally a tedious disagreement, some kind of controversy over the use of a banner in a Canada Day parade. Elana doesn't care. But she can't unsubscribe.

One day, an email to everyone from Jill.

The subject: fantastic gay photographer.

She's had professional headshots done (at forty-six, having acted in a number of amateur theatre productions, Jill decided to pursue work in film and television). But instead of professional headshots, Jill had attached three photos of herself breast-to-breast with a stout woman with spikey grey hair, amidst sword ferns and mossy evergreens, a blurry waterfall in the background, and both in jeans. Elana recalls that Jill's breasts, large despite her slight frame, pointed downward, with soft, pale nipples. But in the photos, mashed up against spikey-hair woman, they almost look pert. In another photo, Jill looks up and is turned toward the camera slightly (the woman kissing her neck), Jill's pale nipples miraculously pinkish-brown, while soft, granulated shadow painted artfully beneath her breasts creates an illusion of lift. The photos remind Elana of the Two of Cups, Jill's unnatural earth goddesses. Is it self-centered and paranoid to think this photo was meant for her?

She isn't jealous. Still, Elana is feeling something. It's repulsive to her—Jill is repulsive, and Elana feels guilty for that feeling. She was intensely attracted to the woman but finds herself mocking her body in an unfeminist sort of way. Angry. Suffocated. Yes. There is no getting away from her. She opens the photos on her computer to get a closer look at them, zooming in on Spikey-Hair's flabby stomach and trite rose tattoo. She probably thinks she looks like a real hot butch in this shot, not like Elana, whose hair is too curly ever to mould into anything hip. Who is this woman, anyway? Elana has never seen her. The photoshoot was probably Jill's idea. Stop looking at these photos. Delete the email. Then, minutes later, another.

Subject: Whoops!

Three of you have already emailed me—sorry! I attached the wrong photos! The files are just numbered so I got mixed up. I guess the cat's out of the bag—that is Beatriz. We had a blast doing an "erotic photoshoot" with that same photographer. Never thought I'd be brave enough for that, but it was fun! I got inspired after seeing the burlesque show at the legion. A celebration of all body types! Our society is so rigid with beauty ideals. I'd recommend a nude photoshoot to anyone—very liberating! Maybe we should do a calendar? lol

Okay, here are the CORRECT headshots.

Emails follow when another woman takes issue with burlesque, that those who call that feminism are "delusional," as it still promotes the value of women as sexual objects alone. "I don't care how fat someone is. That doesn't make it feminism." An argument ensues, not only around her criticism of burlesque ("It sounds like you've never even seen a burlesque performance"), but around the use of the word fat, a recent nude calendar of a women's hockey team, what it means and doesn't mean to be "sex positive."

Jill is probably hoping Elana will email her something horribly theatrical, like "I'm glad you're happy." Elana will not participate.

But she doesn't delete the photos. She looks at them again. Jill. It surprises her that Jill is with another woman, but she learns later (from Diane, who also attends the biweekly beer club religiously and learns everything) that the two met online, that Beatriz lives in Edmonton and they've only actually spent three weekends together. So she'd met Beatriz before that hug at the cat tower.

But Elana doesn't care. She doesn't fall into women like she used to—swiftly, recklessly. It had come to feel too much like drowning. No, not drowning—that danger is too clear. Like carbon monoxide poisoning. Sitting there, dreamy and dopey, too comfortable while she's poisoned. Those days are over.

Jill emails her.

Subject: Sorry

I'm sorry you had to see those photos. I didn't mean to hurt you.

Love always,

Jill

Oh, the drama of it! Elana could do nothing, but Jill will likely interpret this as hurt—too hurt even to respond. She could email her back and keep it light. "No worries!" But Jill would see that as false bravado. What Elana wants to do is flatten her. Your tits look awful. I don't care what you do, Jill.

What photos? Sorry, I've been having problems with my email account lately.

Jill texts her: *About the photographer.*

Did you send it to me?

This continues tediously for a few minutes and then concludes when Elana repeats the Internet-problem excuse.

Aren't you curious what the photos were?

I'm not asking, Elana thinks. I'm not interested in your meaningless relationships and attention-seeking fuck-ups. *How's Tom?*

A longer pause. *I'm worried about him. He won't talk to me.*

At all?

He doesn't tell me where he's going. I'm worried he's on drugs. I'm not sleeping properly and I just feel sick all the time.

Not too sick for photoshoots with Beatriz. *I'm sorry to hear that.*

Dramatic pause. *Thank you.*

꙳

She finally gets off the phone with her mother, another blackhole of a conversation. It had become clear that the rain had little to do with the network of puddles—the grass in that area was twice the height as anywhere else, and although the smell seemed to come and go, it frequently overpowered the property with a combination of skunk cabbage and ammonia. Instead of frogs and birds, mosquito larvae were surely incubating in the effluent. When a bit of sewage gurgled in the bathtub drain, Elana did the responsible thing and called a professional.

Since the house belongs to her mother and Elana is, effectively, the tenant ("That was *your* idea remember," Elana helpfully pointed out), it's her mother's responsibility to pay for the work. The old woman wasn't opposed to this. "I guess you'd have to walk a lot of dogs for a new septic system," she joked. Ha. But she required a play-by-play on the septic tank guy, Frank. Frank the Tank. "You can't trust a man with a name like that."

"Yes, you can. It's Frank."

Frank's first task was diagnosing the problem, which he attempted over the phone. You got a drain-field failure. When was the last time you had the tank pumped? Could be a pipe, though. He would have to come look in person.

Eventually, her mother relented. What else could she do?

Elana goes outside. A trough exposes the septic pipe. Frank had carefully excised blocks of sod, but as the problem revealed itself, he seemed not to care about salvaging the grass, and just shovelled it along with the upturned soil. No quick fix for this one, he'd said before explaining the cause of the damage. If you'd had the tank pumped regularly, we might have caught it sooner.

"Don't keep me in suspense," Elana had said. Was she supposed to know something about septic tanks? Her car came with a manual—why didn't the house?

Frank will return with the excavator. So that's where the pipes are, she thinks. So that's the drain field over there. So that's how a septic system works. She turns toward the driveway to contemplate the excavator's path along the side of the house or down the slope over the drain field—either way, the tulip beds are toast—and there is Jill, pointing at her, saying something Elana can't hear.

"Just a second," Elana calls as she heads toward her. She regrets the hug by the cat tower now. Or did her disinterest in Beatriz provoke an in-person visit? There is no middle ground with Jill.

"You made a sexual remark to my son while he was at work." Jill has had her roots done since they last saw each other. Her lipstick is the colour of putty, and it reminds Elana of earthworms. "Do you realize how inappropriate you are?"

"Tom's talking to you now?"

Jill shakes her head. "Unbelievable."

"You said he barely speaks to you."

Jill reddens. "I'm his mother, don't you get that? It doesn't matter what he says to me, it's my job to protect him. I love him with every cell of my body—" She covers her mouth as if she's just said something shocking. Then adds, "I don't have to explain myself to you—you have to explain yourself to me. What the hell were you thinking?"

The edges of a gold-coloured bra rise up from behind her black wrap top, reminding Elana of a solar eclipse. A gold chain disappears in the crevasse of cleavage. Lust is a strange thing. There are no rose-coloured glasses with lust. It's more like a star enters you, shines so hot and bright everything is over-exposed, ethereal and blinding. And the body needs water, reaches out for that breast, some unconscious memory of blind infancy.

"Okay, Jill." Elana holds up her hands in surrender. "I want to be mature about this. I'll talk to Tom—"

"Don't talk to Tom—"

"—to apologize. Isn't that what you want?"

"I don't want you to talk to Tom." She untucks the chain from between her breasts, revealing the tiny gold-star pendant, strokes it like a magic lamp. "Were you trying to hurt me?" she says hopefully.

❧

On the greeting card, a Weimaraner looks up, as if trying to see the foam bone tied to his head with a ribbon. Inside: "Sorry I was such a bonehead!" Elana writes a personal note, too:

Hi Tom!

I'm sorry for that off-colour joke the other day. I'm a compulsive jokester, as you probably remember. Sometimes they're funny, but most of the time they're pretty bad!

It was nice to see you. You're so tall! I guess that's what happens when we get older—but some of us are shrinking! (Not me, but my mother looks like a gnome.)

I've included my phone number here if you need it—if you ever need a ride or something.

Elana

She leaves it for him at the grocery store.

The willow is a relatively fast-growing tree, but that's not why Elana had selected it. She simply liked how the long leafy vines drape over ponds and swing drowsily in the wind. How nice. How restful. That it would reach its full height in just ten or fifteen years was a bonus. Elana would be retiring then, or at least at the age when her peers are retiring. Hopefully her mother would be dead, and Elana would inherit the property. Knock on wood. Before then, she could put a pond in. Koi. Maybe wire mesh over the top to protect the fish from hungry raccoons. Lots to manage. But she felt good managing things. She hadn't got to the vegetables or chickens or bat box yet, but one thing at a time. The compost heap was looking good now. Wood-chip kitty litter. That was her secret carbonaceous ingredient. Five bucks at Canadian Tire. That would make a great article in the next *The Next Whole Earth Catalog*, if there ever was one. When she turns the compost heap each week, she no longer jabs into slimy cucumber stumps and apple cores or an empty chasm or worse, a rat, curled up sleeping. The core of the pile is even black sometimes—charred? This is hot composting, she thinks—she'd read about that, too. This is an achievement.

Her mother wouldn't understand the significance. Or she'd ask too many questions. Are you sure it's not too hot? You don't want to start a fire—there are so many forest fires now and you're surrounded in forest, you realize. Yes, I realize. I won't start a fire. Don't be ridiculous.

Yes, on those sunny days with work gloves and grass-stained boots, Elana even dared to think of herself as downright capable.

Which is why it was particularly devastating that the roots of her water-loving willow had made a beeline for the septic pipe, squeezed until it cracked, then filled the pipe with its tangle of woody veins. Clogged pipes are wet pipes, the chemistry is off and anaerobic slime, an impermeable mucus, makes a mess of the drain field. "And that's the beast right there," Frank said, nodding to the tree. "Whoever did that wasn't thinking too far ahead."

Elana wonders if her compost ratio is dangerous.

4

"What roots?" her mother asks. Elana places a tea in front of her. The Americano is coming shortly.

"The roots of some plant someone planted. It doesn't matter." Elana had decided to tell her mother in person about the septic repairs. Their monthly visit was soon after Frank's diagnosis. She didn't want to tell her about the willow, didn't want her mother to assume Elana had screwed up. Why did she need to know the details, anyway? Elana was taking care of it. She selected the new white shirt, green Hush Puppies. Not a string of dog hair on the navy slacks, either. In the café's bathroom mirror, she looks hot. Monied. Smart. A new sports bra and a white tank smooths out all the creases.

"What plant? Must've been a big plant. Do you mean a tree? I want you to send me a picture." She leans forward to slurp her tea, yellow hair tucked securely behind her ear with a bobby pin.

"What will a picture tell you? And I thought your hair was too long. Are you growing it out now?"

"I want to see this tree, Elana, and I have a right to know. And I need to make sure you aren't being gouged by this Frank person."

"Americano?" the barista calls.

Elana retrieves her drink. "Thank you."

"I love your shoes, by the way," the young woman says. Maybe thirty-five? Could she be forty? It's hard to tell, but Elana looks young for her age, too.

"Thank you," Elana smiles, fortified for her return to the conversation with her mother. She takes her time at the cream and sugar, though. She doesn't want to admit she planted the willow tree.

"I'll send you the estimate," Elana says when she sits down again. End of discussion.

"I want a second opinion, too."

"There is no second opinion—Frank is it. It's a one-horse town, but he's lived there his whole life so he's not ripping anybody off, okay? Can't you just trust me?" She hears her voice becoming desperate, pleading.

Her mother lifts the tea bag from her mug. "Just what am I supposed to do with this now?"

Elana slides a napkin toward her.

"It'll leave a mark," her mother says.

Elana takes the tea bag to the garbage. When she returns, her mother points at the napkin. "This is why I need to see a picture of this tree."

They sip their drinks and the murmur in the café grows, punctuated by calls from the bar for lattes, Americanos and something called matcha. Elana notices some discoloration on her left shoe, a slightly yellow stain, like a fading bruise.

"Your niece is a year old now. I wish I could show you pictures from my visit, but Kim took the pictures—I forgot my iPad."

"Kim?"

"Oh, for godssake, Elana. Your brother's wife—you're sister-in-law."

Elana has never met Kim. She was invited to the wedding. "It's in Canada this time, so there's no excuse," her brother had written. But it wasn't just the travel expense. How could she possibly give a shit?

Her mother has moved on to talking about the seniors' nature club, walks in the city parks guided by biologists. "So, I know quite a lot about trees now, too," she says. "Did you know the inside of a tree is dead?"

"Maybe I can send you a picture of Tom."

Her mother folds the napkin in half and slides it over to Elana, as if it contains some message. "Tom? Will you throw this out for me."

"Yes, my partner's kid—my stepchild." Elana takes the napkin.

"Oh, yes. Why do they call them 'stepchildren,' anyway? Why 'step'?"

᷉

On her way to the beach with a couple of spaniels, Elana spots Tom thumbing a ride again.

Tom jogs hopefully up to the van as Elana pulls over, but when he discovers who's inside, he looks back up the empty highway. It's early—before eight—and a Saturday. She expects him to roll his eyes or maybe give her the finger and walk away, but he just stands there. He looks toward his feet, adjusts his backpack, which is slung over one shoulder, then straightens up.

"I'd very much appreciate a ride if you're willing to offer one. If it's not inconvenient."

Tom even manages a polite smile.

"Hop in." The van fills with the sickly scent of men's body spray, and the dogs nose at Tom's elbow. "Am I taking you to the IGA?"

"I need to go home first—to my dad's, but you can just drop me anywhere and I'll walk."

Still about ten minutes to go. Elana turns on the CBC. Some unremarkable indie rock. She turns it off. Tom unzips his backpack and Elana is hit with a second wave of toxic perfume. Tom takes out a small pillow of potpourri and places it on the dashboard. A gift from Jill to remedy a backpack basted with teenaged body odour? "Here," Tom says. "I don't really want this."

Elana lowers her window an inch. "Did your mom make that?"

Tom looks at the potpourri, as if considering the question. "I'd like to address the big animal in the room," he says.

"The dogs?"

"No, it's an expression."

"You mean elephant?"

"Whatever—just big animal. So just—when I was younger, I blamed you for my parents' divorce. But I want you to know that I realize now that it wasn't your fault, specifically."

"Not specifically."

"Exactly. I got that card you left me, but I didn't even remember you making a joke at all, so I guess that proves you're right, your jokes aren't funny." Tom lowers his window and holds his hand out to the breeze as the van flies down the highway.

Elana had scrolled Jill's Facebook, searching for a decent photo of Tom, but most of the photos were too old, taken before he shot up into the bony testosterone-filled monster. This absence of photos corresponding, perhaps, with the duration of Elana's relationship with his mother. In the photo Elana does have, Tom sits cross-legged under the willow, looking down at his phone. She remembers that day. "Tom!" she'd called from behind the camera. He did look up, she's pretty sure, but looked down again quickly, in the middle of a game, maybe, not the shoot-em-up kind, that was later. It would be difficult for Elana's mother even to see his face, let alone imagine the close relationship Elana claims to have with him. He could be some kid in a park. And then there is the issue of the willow. Where is this photo taken, her mother will want to know. Or maybe she won't. Maybe she won't ask anything about it, which is worse.

"Before I drop you, can I ask a favour?"

Tom's face seems to shrivel. "Depends."

"I want to get a picture of these dogs, but I can't let them off their leashes. They're a bit wild. It's for the website I'm making," she lies. "People like to see that their dogs actually go for walks and aren't just cooped up in a yard."

"So you want me to take your picture?"

"Oh. I thought we could both be in the picture." Elana hadn't thought about this most obvious solution Tom had proposed. "You know, so they see all the special attention the dogs are getting."

"A selfie you mean. That would be kinda weird, being on your website. Yeah, I don't want to be on your website."

❧

The pet store is now selling "doggy wellies," little dog rainboots in your choice of red or pink. When Elana was the manager, she never would have ordered crap like this. It truly is getting out of control, with ruffled dresses, dog socks with rubber "safety tread"—had the soles of dog's paws become softer in recent years? She reasons it could be useful for a dog with a foot injury, could assist in preventing infection, but these were mass-produced, popular items. She's sold two pairs of wellies already. The second buyer asked, "Will these fit a West Highland terrier?" Elana imagined the pathetic creature with its coarse white hair and short legs, the red wellies up to its armpits. "I think they may be a bit tall."

The man turned the boots over, inspecting the quality. "These are made in Canada," he said, nodding in approval. At the till, he explained how he'd discovered a nature series just for dogs that he streams for her while he's out. "She loves the beach scenes. You know, kids playing, sea gulls and crabs. And lots of close-ups like a dog's point of view."

The wellies are twenty-two bucks and still a horrible waste of money. "Dogs see more frames per second than people," Elana said. "Video is actually just a strobe light to them—they can't really watch TV."

The man handed her a credit card. "I don't need a bag."

"You'll want to keep the receipt."

Elana loves dogs, but she hates dog owners more and more every year. A Rottie running up to her in an on-leash park, the owner calling after it, "No, no, no!" Then, once establishing she has zero control over the animal, calling out, "He's friendly!"

A couple whose Jack Russell snaps a leash taut as he strains to bark at every passerby until the couple reels him in, pets him, cooing, "It's okay, it's okay," in effect rewarding the dog for its aggression.

Another woman who claps from her front door as her menacing shepherd follows a child up the street.

Another whose two children crawl on all fours to the baked-good display case, place their imaginary dog paws on the glass and whine, before one pretends to bite and the other gets up and shrieks across the room, clearing the café of its customers in the process.

A mother who agrees to ten more minutes after the girl screams from the top of the slide, "I said I'm not ready!"

A mother who intimidates her child with vague threats of anger when he refuses to abandon the stick he's named.

A mother more interested in learning how to use the slo-mo setting on her iPad video recordings than in knowing anything about Elana's life.

Elana sometimes feels forever a child, undisciplined, flailing, uncertain whether it's good or bad behaviour that will result in any attention at all. She's so tired of self-pity. She could love a child better than that, couldn't she?

5

A few weeks pass without a word from Jill, which confuses Elana. *Are you trying to hurt me?* Elana had hugged her again, unprompted, in the driveway that day. "Thank you," Jill whispered in her ear. Maybe it was just the proximity of another person's mouth to her ear and nothing to do with Jill, specifically, but desire leaked through her body. She wanted to be inside her, to slide her hand into those jeans, tunnel into the dark and wet. Not that she wants Jill back. That didn't come up in the conversation, either. Jill probably just wants someone chasing her around to keep her running to fitness classes. But what if she and Elana really had something, and Elana just didn't see that at the time because it was just a bad time, with all the changes in Jill's life—leaving her husband, discovering her sexuality, maybe, if that's what this is about. Maybe this hurricane of conflict isn't normal for Jill either, but really is just a crazy time in her life that they could look back on together one day. Could it be like that? It had felt grown up to end it. Boundaries. Don't take anymore of this shit. But what if this shit is what relationships are and Elana is just failing at them?

In *The Next Whole Earth Catalog*, a quote from Rita Mae Brown's foreword in *Our Right to Love (A Lesbian Resource Book)*, by Ginny Vida, describes different kinds of lesbians:

Lesbians as a group can be very confusing. There are lesbians whose politics are to the right of Genghis Khan. There are lesbians who make Maoists look moderate. There are lesbians who can only be described as dowdy dykes. There are lesbians who can't be described, they simply knock you out with their beauty... There are poor lesbians and rich lesbians. There are dumb lesbians (yes, I hate to admit it but there are) and there are smart lesbians. We come in all colors, too. Lesbians are everywhere, even in the morgue. We die like anyone else.

What kind of lesbian is Elana? A poor lesbian who comes from money, a knock-out if you're lonely or restless enough? Does that explain something? And what resources does this book offer to support her right to love? Loving was never Elana's problem—she fell into so many women or maybe they tangled around her, squeezed her until she cracked, but it was better than the wasteland, the empty planet, *Helloooo? Is anybody out there?* Either way, she loved. It was everything else she never understood. Maybe that's all Rita meant, that's it's all just as confusing as anything. It's all confusing and then we die, like everyone else. We die, so love me. Please will you love me now?

The backyard looks like an archaeological dig, and Elana has dismantled the raised beds, too, which were in the way of the excavator and too close to a septic drain field to grow anything appetizing, anyway.

Her mother calls to ask for an update on how the work is proceeding. "Don't let him postpone things."

"It's happening. It looks like Armageddon here."

"That concerns me, Elana."

"I'm joking."

"Yes, that concerns me also."

Since their visit, Elana's mother has spoken to Frank over the phone. She wanted him to walk her through the process. She learned the willow tree was largely to blame, though she didn't remember a willow tree on the property. You've been here twice, Elana pointed out, you just don't remember. It was always there.

"Then why didn't you have it removed sooner?" her mother asked. It didn't matter who planted the tree. Elana had allowed it to grow.

She emailed her mother the photo of Tom sitting under the willow: *This was one of Tom's favourite spots,* she lied. *After he was jumped by three homophobic kids at school, he sat under that tree for hours. He said he always felt safe there. So it certainly never occurred to me to take the tree away from him.*

"You never replied to my email," Elana says over the phone. "The one with the picture of Tom."

There is a pause before her mother replies. "Is that a question?" Her voice sounds different today. It doesn't have the easy tone of gruff proclamations, but instead a kind of pinched hesitation.

"Okay. I'll rephrase: Why didn't you reply to my email?"

Her mother exhales through her nose into the phone. Elana knows that exhale, like a bored dog making its point as it finally gives up, settles into its bed. "I'm not sure what you want me to say. Did you send me that as some justification for not removing the tree before it became a problem?"

"No, it's a picture of my stepson. I thought you'd want to know something about the people in my life—in my family."

"Alright. I'm a little concerned then, Elana. You said he was attacked by some homophobic boys? Is he gay, too?"

"No, his mother is—we are."

"That's troubling."

"Yes, I agree."

"But he has a father?"

"Yes, but he lives here basically half the time."

"I'm only asking a question."

"I'm only answering."

"I can't do this today, Elana. Something I ate is not agreeing with me."

Even her food argues with her. Is Elana so impossible? What do her conversations with David sound like? My darling son, your daughter is beautiful. Thanks, Mom, not as beautiful as you. My favourite child. You are so perfect—I wish I was still breastfeeding.

"Oh, Elana, one more thing," her mother says. "You'll find this interesting. I used Google to look up the origin of *step* in *stepson*. It comes from a Germanic word that means orphan. The idea was if a child's father died, he was an orphan. Since Tom's father is still alive, you could say *stepson* is inaccurate."

"Really. What should I call him, then."

"Oh." It seemed she hadn't thought this far. "I guess there isn't a word for it."

᠀

Not long after, Jill emails the mailing list about the "modern-day predator" she's dealing with and asks if anyone can offer her legal advice or knows a good person at "social services" she should contact. Her son has been "taken advantage of" by an older woman. Another lesbian on the mailing list urges her to drop the euphemisms. What are we really talking about here? *She's brainwashed him into thinking he's in a relationship—with a woman with two kids! He's only sixteen so I think I'm talking about statutory rape.*

Statutory rape is rape, writes Sahar with the soap business.

Sixteen is the legal age of consent, writes Jonesy who always wears a red bandana around her neck like a dog. *How old is this woman, anyway? You're undermining the impact of male exploitation of girls if you compare it directly to this. It's not the same thing and we all know it.*

The conversation circles from there, Jill's tone becoming more and more defensive, citing trouble at home, how it was only two years ago that Tom went to a coding camp at the library. How could he be ready for this? Boys are just as vulnerable as girls—we just don't talk about it. The term "catastrophizing" gets thrown around, followed by "gas-lighting." Finally, Jill texts Elana. *Why aren't you saying anything? Why doesn't anybody care about Tom?*

I care about Tom, Elana says. She does care. She cares about Tom. There is trouble at home. He is an immature, stupid kid, and not especially good looking, either. Maybe this woman is a predator—what else could she be getting from Tom besides power? *Have you talked to Beatriz about this?*

She doesn't know Tom. It's not the same.

Jill asks Elana if they could meet for a walk or something. The beachside drive is quiet, overcast and muggy. Mosquitoes are getting to Elana. Jill reviews the arguments on the mailing list, prompting Elana to refute them. But Elana was never political, so she doesn't know how. *The personal is political*, she'd heard many times. She folded brochures a couple of times at the lesbian centre in the city, but that world, with its wimmen's library and consensus decision-making and labrys pins, felt so far away from hers—she was renting a room from a straight couple who lived upstairs and having a relationship with the wife. She'd never even been in a room with so many lesbians. She should've felt at home, but their customs were foreign, and she didn't even speak the language. "I think it's pointless to argue," Elana offers.

"His father is useless. He just says it could be worse, that I should be happy he's not doing drugs. 'At least he's still coming home,' he said to me."

"Is Tom staying with you?"

"God no." Jill continues shaking her head.

Elana waves a mosquito away from her face. "Who is this woman, anyway?" The mosquitoes don't seem to bother Jill. Elana just has the kind of blood they're drawn to, and she never thinks to use repellent.

"She's just no one."

They approach a swath of wild roses and the breeze from the ocean mingles with the scent of the flowers. Jill tears a petal off as they walk by. "She sells the underwear I like, out of her home studio," she says finally. "Tom wanted to earn some money babysitting. She was still breastfeeding when they met!"

Elana slaps her cheek. On her palm, a tiny splatter of blood and a mosquito smashed into it like a bit of tar. It's the females that bite. And it seemed an odd coincidence that Tom should find another mother, literally. If there was one thing Elana understood, it was neglect. He went looking for that comfort somewhere else, Elana suggests.

"What in the hell do you know about neglect? Your mom gives you whatever you want—you never have to worry about anything."

"Your husband pays for your apartment." Elana wipes her palm on her shorts. She wants to pick up the pace, to outrun the mosquitoes, but Jill has stopped walking.

"That is not the same thing at all. Please tell me you know that."

꙳

The next phone call Elana receives is from her brother. He is her mother's emergency contact, although he lives on the other side of the country. Elana flies to Victoria to meet her mother at the hospital. She was lucky her "girl" was scheduled to come in to clean. The housekeeper had a key, so Elana's mother didn't have to "plan her life" around her schedule, and she'd discovered the old woman lying on her side in the bathroom, feverish and sick, vomit crusted all over the toilet bowl.

After her eighty-three-year-old colon honeycombed with pockets of infection, she'd developed peritonitis—infection of the abdominal tissue, threatening sepsis. There would have been symptoms—abdominal pain, fever, chills, nausea. All of them rationalized into a jar of mayonnaise left out on the counter too long. Despite the IV of antibiotics, her skin papery and grey, and the surprising smallness of her body, as if all the water had evaporated from her flesh, Elana felt little more than dreamy curiosity. Was this death?

Elana never thought of her mother as old. She was too powerful for decrepitude. Death was a certainty in every possible future, but the future always only a possibility.

Her mother lifts one finger, and Elana approaches. She pulls the chair closer to the hospital bed. Her mother turns her palm up. "Elana."

Elana waits for some instruction, but instead her mother nods once, silently. Elana curls her fingers around the empty palm. It's smaller than she expects, limp and cool. She turns it over, even this slight physical interaction oddly intimate, and examines her mother's skin, stretched taut over white knuckles, papery over blue veins. If she squeezes those veins, will she plug up circulation? Will blood pool and bulge below until the pipe bursts? It's hard to imagine this hand grating enough potatoes for forty latke-eating friends and neighbours or making horseradish from scratch for the Seder. Is it odd she never had help with those things? But Elana supposes it was a kind of ancestral duty or burden to show off, and always provided a reason for Elana to feel guilty for sucking the life out of her mother, literally working her hands until they bled, inevitably scraped by the grater when the root in her hand became too small. When did this hand last hold hers? She rests her forehead on the bed and begins to cry. Her mother misunderstands, touches Elana's head with her other hand. "I'll be okay."

Elana wants her to disappear.

6

On dying, *The Next Whole Earth Catalog* offers book recommendations: *The Wheel of Death; Common-Sense Suicide; The Manual of Simple Burial*; more. Of the latter, someone named Gurney Norman writes, "People choose their horrors. We choose war. We choose pollution. And, by default, we choose to make the rituals surrounding death grotesque. But what is chosen can be unchosen, once an alternative is clear." At the bottom of the third and final page on death, Stewart Brand describes "A Better Bathtub." But first, he explains the non sequitur, that this article "got squeezed off the cockroach and cheap living spread by lack of space, and nothing else really wanted to be on the suicide page, so I volunteered." He then offers one alternative to our grotesque death rites and endorsement of this innovative bathtub: "If I was going to die on purpose, I'd like to do it in my tub. (Afterward my friends could drain out the water, replace the plug, and float it and my carcass aflame into the Bay, chanting Viking sea burial hymns the while.)"

Elana flips to an article on space colonies instead. By the year 2000, the author claims, these colonies are a likely possibility. How to sort wisdom from novel theory.

But it's the article about space that made the most sense to her now. Driving home from the Pet-Mart, she is floating, weightless. The sun through the trees a strobe light—green-yellow-green-yellow-green-yellow. She thinks of the description of space, how it will really feel to live on a colony with the sky at your feet: "It's more like a Buddhist chant," *The Next Whole Earth Catalog* writer says, "'No-air-no-gravity-no-night-no-day-no-up-no-down-no-motion-no-past-no-standing-still-no-life-also-no-death-no-thing-only-waves-of-star-star-star-star-star.'"

The stoplight shakes her out of it. Tires once again on pavement. Then the signs: Excavator. Turns out that was also Frank. The prawns were gone. But one tree still proclaims, "Luxury fashion lingerie!"

᠌᠌᠌ꙮ

The young woman unlocks her "boutique," a shed disguised with a mural of ferns, trees and an unlikely profusion of roses.

Inside, wall to wall shelving of colourful bins full of bras and underwear make the already tiny room feel like a closet. Lacey pillows of potpourri overpower even the towering old piano next to the curtained corner that serves as a changeroom. Colleen is an odd name for a woman her age—she couldn't have been more than what, twenty-five?—yet there is something about the name that suits her. The French braid that hangs halfway down her back reminds Elana of *Little Women* or a polygamous cult, but the tight white tank top stretched over the black bra, Disney-length lashes and pink sweats suggest Sunday morning with an escort. "I just got these in." Colleen holds up a pair of underwear, black with a metallic sheen. Her putty-coloured acrylic nails look like crab legs against the fabric. "Seamless." She hands them to Elana.

Elana examines the space-age material, the garment oddly cold, and so slippery that it almost feels wet. She recognizes it as the same slippery skin she'd peeled from Jill's hips numerous times.

Colleen removes a stack of children's books from the top of the "check-out counter," an upcycled Singer table. She retrieves a four-wheeled plastic truck from the changeroom and tosses it outside. "I already told him this is not a storage unit." Elana isn't sure if she's referring to the child or perhaps a husband. The young woman clears a pile of clothing from a chair, tucking a black golf-shirt into a nearby drawer, then plugs in a string of white Christmas lights, which intertwine with plastic ivy along the top of the walls. "This is my space," she says, and sits in the chair. "Sorry it's such a mess. It's been a crazy summer. Usually I get busy in the fall, so I was kinda surprised you called, but a girl could always use some sexy lingerie, right? You want me to show you the matching bras for that? I like to mix and match, so I don't put them together. It's good to be creative, I think."

Elana squeezes the bra cups, which are heavy.

"Silicone," Colleen says.

She imagines how this bra would transform her, how the images screened onto her T-shirts would change—the slogans at the top distorted by strangely alert breasts, the remaining image obscured in the baggy, shadowed cotton hanging below. How the buttons of her good shirts would tug at the holes, how the creases would be even worse, how like a failed woman she would appear. Not like Colleen who, except for a slight tummy, is round in all the right places.

"Wow, silicone," Elana says. "Just don't know what's real anymore, eh?"

Colleen laughs in a way that makes Elana feel like an old man, the wrinkled baby who's said something surprisingly on topic. "Right? I carry Spanx, too, for full body contouring."

Is this where Tom has been spending his time? On the opposite end of the shed is a sagging loveseat, probably comfortable, probably filthy. Does this woman climb on top of Tom, her engorged breasts pressing into his adoring face? But that's disgusting. *He thinks we're disgusting.* It makes Elana feel sad.

Outside, the sound of tires on gravel. "Can you just lock the door there behind you?" Colleen points. "I don't want any interruptions."

Tom's floating now, but when Colleen gets bored, she'll cut the string and he'll be lost in the wind, won't he? Until someone else plucks him from the sky. She thinks of a balloon, how she can rub it on her hair, make it stay, briefly.

꙳

The forest is a kind of haven for Elana. She prefers to walk slowly along trails, take note of the things that surround her. Not that she knows the names of the plants and mycelium in her path. Only the broader categories: lichen, moss, mushroom. What does it really matter, anyway? She can see mushrooms popping up from the deadfall—what should it matter if she knows something about their genus? Her favourite trees are the big leaf maples, or "maples" as she knows them. The long trunks wend toward the upper canopy, delicate ferns growing from the thick pillows of moss, always waving gently in even the most imperceptible breeze, a magical staircase for fairies trying to reach the sunlight just behind those broad leaves above. Other days, the forest is ugly. Stumps with eyes gouged into them where loggers a hundred years ago shoved their planks to stand on and saw. Snags pock-marked where woodpeckers have tunnelled into them, extracting the insects that eat away at the carbonaceous carcass. Skunk cabbage in black muck. Something itchy. The tree trunks green, pale lichen growing all over, dry and flaky and persistent as eczema. At the start of its life, a conifer seedling grows from deadfall, the decaying tree providing nutrients, like a mother or a host to a child or a parasite. The mother rots away, and now the roots of the living conifer grow down over nothing at all, so that it looks like some woody octopus or a monster's many-fingered hand.

꙳

At the cemetery, the small crowd treads carefully toward the grave, queuing up for a "final act of kindness" to the departed, when they will each toss some soil onto the coffin below. Sandy, brown soil—good drainage? Could potatoes do well in this? Elana doesn't know. And who knows how long it's going to take Frank to put the yard back together. It's too soon for a funeral, isn't it? Last week, none of this was going to happen. Instead of using the shovel, Elana scoops up the soil with both hands. The septic system repair is not yet paid for. She hopes David won't make that difficult. She doesn't want to run into Frank around town, making guesses about how much longer until she finally pays the bill. He'd probably go easy for a while, since her mother just died, but how much time does that get you? Then her brother's young wife touches Elana's shoulders. "It's okay," she says gently. Kim. Her name is Kim. Elana still holds the soil in her hands. She's not sure where to put it—which end of the coffin? She tosses it and the soil drums the coffin like a faraway woodpecker. It doesn't feel like the final act of anything.

~

Elana had dug up the tulip bulbs and put them in a paper bag to store in a "cool, dry place," but she got distracted by something, the phone maybe, she can't remember. After Frank started work, she couldn't find that paper bag anywhere. She thinks of the photo of Tom under the willow. It wasn't such a nice place to sit. Ropey branches grew out of the lower trunk, then curled upward like quills so you couldn't lie back, couldn't lace your hands behind a sleepy head. "Tom!" she'd called, ready with camera. Jill had come over with a bucket of yellow plums ("We have so many at home," she said) to show Elana how to preserve them. That was the premise for the visit, anyway. Tom sat on the couch, playing a game on his phone, so Jill told him if you're just going to look at your phone, at least do it outside so you're getting fresh air. Why am I even here? Tom asked. He was being punished, Elana remembers now, for getting drunk with his friend, tied all summer to Jill, who didn't want him there, either. When he finally went outside, Jill took a bite out of a plum, asked Elana if she'd like to eat something as sweet and wet as this. It sounded so pornographic to Elana, so self-conscious, but the plum juice leaked down her neck and that was enough, and she kissed her until Jill gently pushed her away and said they'd have to wait until all the fruit was jarred, and she turned back to the sink, cinched the apron strings and began to fill the big pot with water, the vessel she'd put the jars in to seal them, and Elana felt for a moment that she could never be enough for Jill because she is a lesbian and that could never be what Jill really wants, could it? But in the next moment, Jill squeezed her hand as if she heard her thinking and wanted her to know that's not true, you are enough, this moment right now is enough, and Elana wondered if this is what it's like to have a family—some chores to do, a kiss, sweet and fecund, even the gloomy teenager outside forming a perfect triad because that's family life, imperfect but full of love, maybe this was love, and soon they would have a whole winter of yellow plums. She took Jill's picture at the stove, then stepped outside for one of Tom. "Tom!" Look up, smile for the woman behind the camera. One day, he'll thank his mom for caring enough to ground him. Yes, that's right, love means caring enough to spool him in.

Next time she's at the IGA, she asks the supervisor when Tom is working. "I'm sorry I can't give out that information," she says, which sounds like a lie.

Then one day, Tom is organizing the annuals on display shelves outside. "Fancy meeting you here," Elana says.

Tom inserts a tray of pansies, the petals splattered with soil, perhaps from a careless watering. "Pansies always looked too flimsy for me. I like a hardy flower. Tulips—there's a flower we can get behind, right?"

Tom shrugs. "I guess so." He moves to a shelf of succulents, rearranging them to make more space.

"How have you been? Everything okay at home?" One almost looks like a rose, pink tint and spiralling petals, except the petals are pointed and bloated. "Funny how these desert plants look so full of water, eh?"

"I'm kind of at work."

"You're *kind of* at work?"

"Yes." Tom looks toward the automatic doors, where a grey-haired woman greets customers from behind the Lotto desk.

Elana takes one of the bloated roses. "My yard's a mess. Just need something to put in the kitchen. I'm sorry to say the tulips have met their maker."

"Is that another joke?"

She wants to tell him the sad news, that the willow will be upended, the tulip bulbs somewhere in the excavated mess of soil. It'll be smoothed over one of these days but there's no telling where the bulbs will end up, if the flowers will pop out of the compost heap or simply rot in the dark six feet under. "Never mind."

༄

When Elana was a kid, next to the credit union a large weeping willow domed a grassy area. In the summer, cottonwood tufts drifted past and from beneath the willow's ribbons of leaves, they looked like fairies. Then a sign went up with an illustration of a multi-unit retail space. But they couldn't construct that building—the willow was already there. Her mother laughed. "Trees can be cut down." The first lesson in impermanence. But now she reads that the weeping willow is not a "long-term" tree, that its lifespan is only twenty to thirty years. One site recommends planting fast-growing willows for privacy alongside slower-growing oaks. When the oaks are large enough to take on the job, the willows can be removed. Place holders.

Elana places the succulent on the windowsill behind the kitchen sink. Outside, the willow's trunk has been segmented and left for Elana to take wheelbarrow loads to a burn pile or the dump or maybe sell on Craigslist. Was there any value in this wood? She searched for uses online and learned the tree would not even burn hot enough for a decent fire. Probably too full of septic wastewater. Frank dug out the stump with the excavator and turned the tangle of roots up to dry out in the sun.

The multi-unit retail space is worth a fortune now, gentrification turning the kitschy Trading Post shop into a craft brewery. She wonders what her mother would say to that.

7

On her way back from a grooming workshop in the city, Elana runs into Jill's ex-husband on the ferry. Brad joins the line for White Spot dinner. Elana grabs a tray but accidentally takes two, suctioned together by a veneer of water, so she turns to offer the extra one to the person behind her, and there is Brad. He doesn't seem to recognize her, mutters a thank-you and looks down at his smart phone. After slipping it into his pocket, he gives Elana a polite smile, but there is something sad and far away in his face. She almost feels sorry for him. Jill had described an irritable tyrant, impossible demands for quiet and neatly folded washcloths. Elana had asked Jill if he might have some kind of disease that made him sensitive to sound. And light. Mess. Talking. Questions. "Is he depressed?" But troubleshooting Brad's horribleness got old fast.

"Oh," he says finally.

"Yeah, oh."

"I almost didn't recognize you." He speaks as though they're old friends. "Trip into the city, eh? Costco run?"

"Partly." Cheaper even than the staff discount at Pet-Mart. She debates volunteering that information. Is there some peace to be made here? Is this maturity? "I was at a dog-grooming workshop."

"There are workshops on things like that?" he laughs.

"What about you?" Elana says, changing the subject.

He shrugs. "I go to counselling now. Didn't want to have to see my shrink around town, so I tie it in with a trip to Costco. She says I'm depressed. On meds now, so I just feel numb. I got no pride—I'm talking to you, aren't I? What do I care. Besides, she says you were just an escapegoat."

"I'll have the legendary burger," Elana says to the ferry worker. "No garden."

He follows her to a table, sits down, and continues talking about his problems, as though Elana would comfort him. The meds impact his sex drive, which is probably a good thing since he's got no one, anyway, and Jill is in and out, rubbing her new lifestyle in his face. "She thinks she's hot shit now, I tell ya. Worse than when you were in the picture even. But I'm not supposed to focus on that stuff. Supposed to focus on myself, so I am, you know? Even planted some potatoes. Never been my thing, really, but I had to come up with a hobby and the yard had kind of gone to shit since Jill left."

"How is Tom?" Elana cuts in.

"Tom? He's fine—got a girlfriend, so you know, over the moon about that I'm sure. He's no longer acting like a little shit, so that's something."

❧

A contributor to *The Next Whole Earth Catalog* writes that inhabiting a moon of Jupiter is a reasonable dream—after a trip to the moon, anything is possible. Elana thinks of the black slugs she tossed from the tulip bed so many times. What does flying mean to them?

❧

At home, a voicemail from her brother. He says to call him.

The excavator is gone now, the pipes laid, trough filled, new drain field. ("You still need to get the tank pumped regularly. Call me in three years.") The total cost for the repairs: more than she has. She emails David instead: "I'll try and call you on the weekend. Sorry. Been busy and just trying to stay above water." She shouldn't write that. She sounds incompetent. Rewrites: "Been busy catching up with things. Say hi to the family for me." There. She's someone who cares.

And maybe she does care. She cares about Tom, doesn't she? She even went to meet the statutory rapist, the breastfeeding mother with porno nails and a round ass. But she was just a girl, too, a woman less than half Elana's age. She should be worried about her. Where does Colleen think this is going? Elana presumes it's an affair, that the husband will inevitably find out and Colleen will have to make a choice and she certainly won't choose the kid who stacks flowers at the IGA. But what if it's one of those open relationships and Colleen can have her cake and eat it, too? Poor Tom. She's modelling seamless undies for him in that shed she calls a studio and it all feels good and it feels like love and they're making plans or maybe just being in the moment, but it feels like that could keep going, couldn't it? But at the other end of the shed, there are toys in the changeroom, toys the husband keeps putting there, maybe, to remind his wife that she is a mother, and mothers don't take teenagers to bed with them.

I didn't like how we left things last time, she writes to Jill. She could tell her she ran into Brad. Jill would want to know all about it, surely. But she doesn't want this conversation to be about other people. "Just leave it alone," her friend Diane had said. "She's seeing someone else now, anyway." But it wasn't about that, Elana insisted. Lesbians are friends with their exes, right? Why couldn't they be like that? Diane shrugged. "Sometimes it's good to just move on." Elana wasn't satisfied with that idea, and Diane has been with the same woman for eight years, so what does she know about it.

"You don't need to bite my head off," Diane said. "I think she's seeing some new guy, is what I was thinking about."

I don't want to be nothing, either, Elana texts Jill.

After a few minutes, a response: *I think I just need my space now.*

✎

Elana knocks on the shed door.

"You're early," Colleen says behind her. She's still in her pyjama shorts and housecoat and carries a mug of coffee. "You found out what size you need?"

Elana had made up the excuse last time, that she's looking for a gift, but now that she's here, she realizes she doesn't know what size. "Yes, all figured out," she lies.

She follows Colleen into the shed, which is much tidier this time but uncomfortably muggy. The fake ivy and Christmas lights are gone, as is the child's push car and the Singer table. "It's buy two, get two. So you might as well get something for yourself, too—some of these styles are really hard to find. Look at this—" Colleen retrieves a black-lace bra and splays it over her knee. "Wood grain—see it? I hate flowery things and there's nothing sexy about pink underwear."

Elana finds the matching wood-grain underwear in the same bin. It doesn't look very durable. One wrong move with a zipper and it's toast.

"Is this for like a bachelorette party or for a girlfriend, maybe?"

It was hard to tell what she meant by "girlfriend." Elana still heard so many straight women refer to their platonic friends this way. "It's for a friend who says she's low on underwear."

"Huh." Colleen slurps her coffee. "So what size is she? I should help you look because everything's pretty mixed up at this point." Colleen kneels and pulls a bin out from the lower shelf and takes out a pair of high-waisted electric blue underwear with two stripes of sheer fabric down the front. "This one has tummy control." She demonstrates the strength of the weave by stretching it a couple of times.

Elana still holds the wood-grain underwear. "I'm not sure," she says.

Colleen tosses the blue undies back into the bin. She looks at the carpet, which Elana sees now is covered in stubby orange fir needles. "I usually do parties," Colleen says. "Like Tupperware parties? This shopping-by-appointment thing isn't easy when you have kids, you know."

It hadn't been three minutes since Elana arrived. "I think I just need a few minutes to browse."

"Okay, I'm gonna wait outside. It's like a steam room in here anyway." Colleen takes her mug and leaves.

Not much of a saleswoman. Did Tom think of her as successful and independent? A collection of boxes blocks the loveseat now, some plunked on top, perhaps inventory or personal belongings. Is she readying herself for a midnight move? She's probably the sort of woman who'd leave the kids with their dad. What option would she have, anyway? If Elana had something to say to this poor girl, she should get to the point. For all her faults, she was still just a baby herself.

Outside, Colleen sits on a metal lawn chair, her housecoat draped behind her. She rests her feet on the edge of a pair of tires, so that Elana can see up her pink shorts, her private parts in shadow.

"I'll buy these." Elana holds up the black-lace set.

"It's buy two, get two."

"I only want these."

Colleen leans forward to take the fifty-dollar bill. "You should go pick two more things, honestly. I have the inventory." She puts the cash in her housecoat pocket. "Need a receipt?"

"I'm a friend of Tom's."

"Oh." She looks back to the house a little way up the driveway. "What was your name again?"

"Elana. Not so much a friend, exactly—more like an aunt. I'm a friend of the family. Well, his mother. And I'm here because I'm worried about Tom."

"Oh, wait," she smiles. "I know you. Jill told me about you."

Before Elana called to make the lingerie-shopping appointment, she drafted a speech. The speech was going to be delivered over the phone, a firm message, a disembodied voice, like "This is your conscience speaking," wise-woman archetype and all that. Something simple to snap Colleen back to reality (reality meaning teenagers are off-limits), like a bolt of lightning. "Consider me your bolt of lightning," Elana had written, but never said. Instead, she made an appointment to buy lingerie, deciding the in-person visit would be more impactful.

I'm here for Tom, she'd say in person. *Think of me as his fairy godmother.* She'd thought a little mystery would shake her up—a stranger who knows too much, a butch who means business. *I know you're looking for a way out of your marriage. You want to feel strong. You want to be admired. Maybe you even want to retrieve some of your own youth that's slipping away under the burden of children and an ignorant husband.* She assumes he's ignorant. *But this isn't the way. You're an adult and Tom is a kid from a broken home. He's searching for a mother, not a lover, and you're taking advantage of that, whether you realize it or not.* This would be the first time in a long time that someone had really, truly *seen* Colleen, that inside she was still just an angry kid, inarticulate and powerless. She might even cry, might even collapse and Elana could hold her and rock her like a baby. "You're right," she might blubber. And then set Tom free.

"She did, did she," Elana bites. "What did Jill tell you, not that this is relevant at all to our conversation."

Colleen tosses the last of her coffee, splattering the dusty driveway. Her toenails sparkle with yellow glitter paint. "Wouldn't you like to know." She knocks her knees together like a fidgeting kid or maybe she saw *Basic Instinct* and thinks this is some Sharon Stone-inspired sexual taunt. Legs apart, together, apart. A puff of blonde pubic hair. It only makes Elana feel gross. She waits for Colleen to continue, but she just keeps smirking, and in this moment of strained silence, Elana actually considers Colleen's statement: Wouldn't you like to know.

Would she? Elana stuffs the lacy contraptions into her coat pocket. Something about the best orgasms of her life probably. Jill would tell anyone about that, but the real stuff, the stuff where Jill doesn't come out looking so good, where Elana decided not to be her midlife crisis, not to allow Jill to dictate the terms of their agreement—the relationship, which should have been a safe haven, a place to call home, but where Jill had instead rendered Elana nothing more than a tenant. Who can live with a mother like that? Poor Tom. Tom is why she's here.

"Actually, I don't care. I'm here for Tom's sake."

"She said you gave good head."

"Is that what she called it?" Disgusting.

"That's what *I* call it. But it's kind of hard to believe, now that I've met you."

"I'm not discussing this with you. You're a child."

"You've got nothing else to discuss. 'Like an aunt'? Tom's never even mentioned you. Actually, you know what?" Colleen stands. "Get the fuck off my property." She heads toward the main house. On her pink shorts, *BABYGIRL* in bold black letters printed across the buttocks.

⟩

On the drive home, Elana gives a new speech. Put your fucking legs together, you disgusting cow. You think I wanna see your sweaty vagina? I don't care, nobody cares. Tom cares because he's a sixteen-year-old boy who'd be just as thrilled with a lubed-up water wing. That's what you are—a flotation device to cling to, a tiny home to play house in. A toy. Something to suck on. Don't you see how stupid you are?

Colleen would crumple then—the unbearable truth! Wouldn't she?

But even in Elana's fantasy, Colleen only smirks. Nothing hurts. Tom never even mentioned you.

Then Elana cries. She thinks about the ridiculous ruse she concocted just to talk to this woman about a kid who doesn't even like her, and cries about that. She thinks of her yard, razed by the excavator and her own stupidity, the willow desiccating, and cries about that. She thinks of how she can't pay for the septic work and has no idea if she's inherited anything or if her brother is her new landlord and if she's going to have to ask him for money, and she cries some more. The road is practically a blur with all her stupid tears. She turns into her driveway, her stupid Dog Star Pet Services business, how ridiculous, and cries about that. She works at the Pet-Mart, she thinks, and not as the manager, and cries about that. She takes inventory of all the ways in which she is totally pathetic, not wanting to stop this crying, wanting to just pound it all out right now, her whole pathetic, chewed up, stupid empty life. But suddenly something occurs to her.

"Tom never even mentioned you."

He never even mentioned the woman he blamed for his parents' divorce?

And then the omission becomes something else entirely. Because Elana's mother died—she died, and Elana hasn't told a soul.

＞

David sounds older, not that she's seen him much these last few years or ten. "Of course I sound older, Elana." There are no surprises. Mom hated being in debt, so she'd paid off most of Elana's mortgage from the sale of the big house. The property goes to Elana, and the bulk of the assets go to David and his children. Elana can remortgage if she needs to, if the remaining payments are too much for her to handle. "I could always handle it," she says. "It was never a question of whether I could handle it."

"Do we have to continue like this? It's just the two of us." He sounds so young then, like the little brother who made cracker-and-cheese towers for Elana, who drew up membership cards for their book club of two. Could he be her brother again?

"It wasn't easy with Mom," Elana begins.

Suddenly, he's gulping for air, crying like a baby. "I can't believe she's gone, I can't believe we're orphans. Who's gonna be proud of us now?"

"How can you say that, David? You're fifty-three fucking years old, and you're always gonna have some woman looking after you."

＞

The roots of the willow tree don't look like much, just worn-out rope caked in mud, something that would snap even if used in a tug-of-war between children. How could these old ropes have choked a PVC pipe? Even more amazing is the fact they had held up the top-heavy willow. Elana sits on the amputated trunk. She'd heard once that our hair and nails continue growing even after we're dead. Had anyone trimmed her mother's hair?

In *The Next Whole Earth Catalog*, in an excerpt from *Care of the Dying*, Richard Lamerton writes that on our death beds, a wonderous maturation takes place: "Priorities fall into place, tolerance and courage may grow in the most unlikely soil and more amazing still is the serenity which so often comes to one from the dying." It is the role of those around the dying to prevent anything that may hinder this growth. An excess of pain or painkiller, too much knowledge or ignorance of what is happening in the body, the mechanism of its demise. "When a man's responsibilities drop away... there remains a great beauty which has been covered by the busy-ness—or laziness—for many a year. Death removes the covers: this unmasking can be a thrilling revelation."

"I'll be okay," her mother had said.

What could she unmask now? The pipes are buried again, and she'll have to wait until spring for the tulips. Will anything grow in this unlikely soil?

She looked it up and learned it's not true that our hair continues to grow—the increasing length is only an illusion created by the receding flesh. Still, she imagines her mother's yellow bob loosening from flimsy clips, how long until it starts to curl at her ear lobes, then unfurl down her neck, gently touch her shoulders.

For a moment, she wonders if she will want her roots touched up. Then her mother is gone once more. And it's like that: here, gone, growing, decaying, remaining, ever-present. "My mother died," she tells the tree, curling her fingers around a root. "I don't know how to feel."

༉

She'll have to rebuild the raised beds, reseed the lawn. She's so tired of starting over again and again and again. Only the compost heap is undisturbed. She jabs the pitchfork into the pile and turns the soil. Something has changed—the chemistry has shifted, and dozens and dozens of worms have somehow found their way here, tunnelling in the darkness, consuming the walls, revelling in the decay.

That's a good sign, Elana thinks. Something will grow in this.

Acknowledgments

I wish to thank, first and foremost, Laurie Lesk, who has not only been my first reader and editor over these years of writing but indulged many hours of conversation about the characters and ideas explored in these pages. I am certain this book would be a shadow of its current self without the privilege of this time together, her generosity and imagination.

Thank you to Daniel Heath Justice, Kent Dunn, Kara Crabb and Madeline Sonik, who provided valuable feedback on earlier iterations of these stories, and to Anne Fleming for her work in the final stages of editing this collection. The stories are better because of your thoughtful readings.

Thank you to the Canada Council for the Arts, which funded the completion of this project. This grant—the first I had ever received for one of my own writing projects—was so validating, I don't think it's an exaggeration to say the consequent boost to my self-esteem improved my writing. Thank you also to the BC Arts Council for funding my writing retreat at the Banff Centre, which was truncated by the declaration of a global pandemic, but during which time I began writing "Midden."

Thank you to Stewart Brand and Ginny Vida for their permission to use quotes from their books and to all the contributors to *The Next Whole Earth Catalog,* that wild and wonderful publication that helped inspire "This Unlikely Soil." I hope that story engages with your reviews and articles in a way that delights on some level.

Thank you to the team at Caitlin Press—Malaika Aleba, Sarah Corsie and Vici Johnstone—for your hard work and care in publishing this book.

I wrote these stories while living and working on the unceded and ancestral territories of the shíshálh and Squamish Nations (in what is currently known as the lower Sunshine Coast, BC), who have cared for this Land since time immemorial, and whose fight for justice continues—as I write this, the shíshálh Nation, using ground-penetrating sonar radar, has begun the heartbreaking search for children's graves at the St. Augustine Residential School.

About the Author

KARA CRABB PHOTO

Andrea Routley is a writer and editor. Her work has appeared in literary magazines, such as *Geist* and *The Fiddlehead Review*. In 2020, her novella, "This Unlikely Soil," was shortlisted for the Malahat Review Novella Prize. Her debut collection, *Jane and the Whales* (Caitlin Press, 2013), was a finalist for the Lambda Literary Award. She is an MFA candidate at UBC (Okanagan) where she is at work on her third book. Though a small-town queer at heart, she currently resides in Vancouver, BC.